SCORCH

HJ WELCH

D1500851

For Nick, Brian, Kevin, A.J. and Howie D.
No I'm not kidding.

SNEAK PEEK

Elion

ELION COULDN'T BELIEVE THIS WAS HAPPENING.

He placed open mouthed kisses down Blake's throat, listening to him moan. There wasn't a camera for miles. This wasn't for show. This was real.

Blake Jackson wanted him. Celebrity heartthrob to girls across the world. And here he was, cradling Elion to him as he kissed his way along his perfect, sculpted abs.

Elion could feel Blake's cock thickening underneath him as they lay in the grass under the sunshine. They were all alone for the very first time, and Elion didn't want to waste the opportunity he'd been given.

If Blake wanted to try playing boyfriends for real, Elion was going to make the most of it. He reached down and palmed Blake's erection through his jeans, making him buckle.

"Too much?" Elion paused in concern.

He didn't want to push Blake too far, too fast. He was certain Blake wasn't as straight as he and everyone else thought he was. But Elion didn't want to scare him by asking for more than Blake could give.

Blake shook his head. "Just a long time since anyone but me has done that," he said with a shaky laugh. He pushed into Elion's hand, demanding more.

Elion was only too happy to oblige.

"Oh yeah?" Elion asked, leaning down to kiss him on the lips again. "Do we need to check it still works? I think we need to check."

Blake laughed into his mouth. Elion loved how good it felt to be the one who'd cracked Blake's hardened exterior. Seeing him relax and open up to him was a gift.

Elion didn't know how long this might last, or what it even meant to Blake. Blake had only gone along with the relationship for the sake of the show. Sure, they got along like they'd been friends for years. Better than friends at times. But Blake had asked him not to overthink this.

Blake was almost certainly not looking for a boyfriend. But that didn't mean Elion couldn't show him how good it could be if he was.

He cut his laughter off by latching his lips around Blake's nipple. He groaned and arched his back at Elion's touch. His warm, hard body promising Elion all kinds of delights.

"Christ, you're so sensitive, aren't you?" Elion said, utterly delighted.

Blake whined. "Don't tease."

"Teasing's the best part," said Elion wickedly.

He was naturally playful during sex. But with Blake he felt he needed to keep it even more lighthearted. He didn't want him thinking too much. This might be the only time they had together, and he wanted to enjoy it.

He wanted Blake to enjoy it.

Elion moved to the other nipple, sucking it into a nub and grazing his teeth against the tender skin. He reveled in the way Blake was moaning his name. He was painfully hard in his pants and needed to do something more for them both, soon.

Reaching down, he looked at Blake as he cupped his long, hard cock, thumbing the fly of his jeans. "Can I?" he asked.

Blake's blond hair was mussed and his usually pale cheeks flushed. He looked divine.

A nod was all it took. A signal that Blake wanted this, needed it as much as Elion did.

Even if this was their only chance, it was real for now. Elion was going to make this the best it could be for Blake. There was no sense in worrying what was to come.

It was time to live for the moment.

BLAKE

BLAKE DIDN'T KNOW IT, BUT EVERYTHING WAS ALREADY SET IN motion before his plane even touched the ground.

He rested his head on the small glass window and watched the Cincinnati airport circle into view. One step closer to home. One step closer back to a normal life.

With a sigh he shifted his weight and tried not to disturb the sleeping woman in the seat next to him. The flight from L.A. was only four hours, but she had been unconscious the entire way. Blake was grateful. He didn't feel like making small talk.

Several people had recognized him as he'd made his way through check-in and security earlier. He hadn't minded signing a few autographs for the kids, but some older fans had asked if the rumors were true.

Had Below Zero really broken up?

He scoffed and arched his back, making his back pop. He needed to stretch.

It really depended on your definition of 'broken up.' If it was 'dumped unceremoniously without so much as a thank you from their record label,' then, yes. The band had broken up. 'Creative differences,' the press conference had said.

That was horseshit. But of course their contract stopped Blake and the four other guys from badmouthing Sun City Records anywhere. Even after getting let go, they still had to toe the line. Unless they wanted to get sued.

For the past few years, Blake hadn't gone a day without being told where to go, what to wear, when to work out, and how much he could eat. All of it with Joey, Raiden, TJ and Reyse by his side. Now he was traveling alone, set adrift, with no idea what he was going to do with his life.

A voice came over the intercom announcing that they were beginning their decent and to make sure passengers had their seats and tray tables upright. Blake bit his thumbnail and continued looking out the window.

It was hard not to feel like he'd let down his parents, who'd thrown everything into his success. But when it came down to it, Below Zero's last record had been produced too fast, not marketed well enough, and sales had suffered. There'd been nothing he could do.

It wasn't the end of the world, he knew. But at the same time, this had been his whole life for five years. Now he was just Blake Jackson of Perryville, Ohio again. A twenty-something who used to be famous.

Not that he'd miss the celebrity. He'd never gotten used to the constant attention or strangers knowing his name. It had been bearable with the other guys by his side. However, the prospect of going back to his small home town was actually appealing when coupled with the hope that he wouldn't be bothered nearly as much as when he was traveling.

As the plane bumped down onto the tarmac he nodded to himself. Things weren't so bad. If he could find a way to nurture his love of dance and stay in touch with the guys, maybe everything would be okay.

It wouldn't be a struggle to keep talking with Joey. They had shared an apartment back in L.A. and been best buddies, pretty much inseparable. Sure enough, when Blake switched his phone off of airplane mode he had a couple of messages already waiting from him.

Joey sure as hell wasn't going home. He was sticking it out in L.A. and already had a new agent getting him auditions. Blake truly wished him the best of luck. But he would miss him.

Raiden, like Blake, had cut his losses and was already back in Kentucky with his folks considering what to do now. TJ's entire plan seemed to be to party so hard his Instagram was in danger of overloading and his liver failing. At least he was having fun. Allegedly.

Then there was Reyse. Blake sighed and waited for the seatbelt light to turn off. He didn't begrudge Reyse Hickson anything. He was his friend and he wished him all the best. But there had never been any doubt as to who the most talented member of the five of them was.

It was easy to guess the real reason behind the label's decision to drop the band. They'd already hitched their wagon to what promised to be a far more successful solo artist.

The woman beside Blake finally woke with a snort and looked around as if she had no idea where she was. "We've landed," said Blake when she looked at him.

"Oh, right," she mumbled, rubbing her eyes. "Thanks. Hey, aren't you from that band? The one with the *'Oh oh oohh'* song?"

She sang the 'Ohs' badly, but enough for Blake to recognize it as Hearts Bound, their most successful track. "Um, yeah. That's us."

He did his best to be patient with the woman as she started grilling him on the music video for that song.

Apparently, their live performance at the MTV Awards was much better, and they should have made a video like that. He smiled politely and did his best to sound sympathetic.

But he was trapped until their row was allowed to slide out and disembark. He didn't really feel like defending things the band and their management had done when he still felt like everything was too raw.

He was able to distract her by getting her carryon down from the overhead bin. Then he let a family ahead of him, so the woman was swept away in the tide of people.

A pretty air stewardess standing by the door gave him a blush and bright smile as he went past, but he didn't mind that so much. "Thank you for traveling with us Mr. Jackson!" she blurted as he went past. He gave her a smile back and felt like he'd made her day.

That side of fame was nice. It was when people felt you owed them something despite never having even met them that grated on his nerves. Still, he was grateful for all the success he'd had, and refused to resent it.

Blake sighed as he made his way off of the plane. With his sunglasses and baseball cap to cover his golden hair it helped to avoid people recognizing him. But he still hurried through baggage claim and through the terminal to Arrivals.

It was sort of pathetic that his life fit pretty much into two huge cases and a carryon bag. Admittedly, he'd left a fair number of things with Joey. Mostly silly knick-knacks. He didn't expect to ever see them again. Just maybe this way, Joey wouldn't feel so alone.

He stopped before he and his bags rolled out into the waiting area. There had been a few times when fans had been waiting to great him on the other side of the barriers. Hopefully this wouldn't be one of those occasions.

He had other messages, but he fired off a quick few words to Joey first, telling him he'd landed and asking how his audition that morning had gone. Blake worried about him keeping up with the rent even though Blake had paid his half up until next month. Joey was as stubborn as he was gentle though, so with any luck he'd be okay.

That wasn't Blake's concern right then though. He'd done what he could for his buddy. Now, he needed to think about himself.

Typically, his parents hadn't come themselves. According to one of his many texts, they'd sent him a car instead. A driver in a well-cut black suit and tie was waiting for him with a placard that simply read *'Blake Jackson'* on it. He walked towards him, keeping his head down.

He'd like to think his mother hadn't added *'Below Zero'* to the sign out of respect for his privacy. But deep down he knew it was because she was so mad at the label she was already set on putting it behind them. Omitting the band name was simply an act of spite Sun City would never know about.

The driver was nice enough. Pleasant, but painfully formal, insisting on taking Blake's bags across the concourse, then not uttering another word.

Blake couldn't help but look at other families being reunited. Little kids waiting on tiptoes with bunches of flowers. Couples embracing tearfully. When they reached the curb outside one guy in military gear dropped unashamedly to the ground to scoop up his frenzied German Shepherd.

That wasn't the kind of greeting Blake had ever expected here today. So he swallowed down the ridiculous lump in his throat and rubbed his eyes under his glasses. No one particularly gave him a second glance, and for that he was grateful.

He dozed throughout the drive, despite it only being mid-afternoon. Cincinnati International was also the Northern

Kentucky Airport. So technically, they started out of state then drove around the city to reach Perryville.

"Home sweet home," Blake murmured heavily as they got off the interstate.

He pressed his temple against the cool window glass and watched all the neatly trimmed lawns go past. Everything was so *low* here. Cincinnati had its fair share of tall buildings to make the skyline vaguely interesting. And Perryville, like most of Ohio, had plenty of hills. But it was like the buildings barely dared climb above a second story.

The grass and trees were a lush green, thriving in the spring weather. Sadly, the buildings were an overwhelming wash of grays and whites, all blending into one.

Blake knew these streets, and yet he didn't. He wouldn't get lost if he had to find his way home. But what did this town really hold for him? Who lived behind these doors now?

When fame had come calling, he had been more than happy to leave it all behind without a second thought. Now, this was all he had, and he had no clue what 'this' was.

It was still early days, he told himself sternly. And he was definitely still young enough. He could do anything. He just had to put his heart into it.

His family home was on a quieter road. It was set further back from the sidewalk after a long stretch of lawn. Oak trees bordered the property. They were taller than both the dark slate roof and telephone poles running down the street.

Unlike most of the other homes in the town, the Jackson residence was a rich brown with large stones set into the walls. The darker tones gave it grandeur and Blake tried not to gulp as the car swung into the driveway.

He'd last visited a few months ago at Christmas. His parents were generally more interested in flying out to see him in L.A. or on tour. Jodi got dragged along whether she liked it or not.

He smiled. At least he was genuinely stoked to see his kid sister.

The driver helped him with his bags again, but nipped back into the car before Blake could offer a tip. His parents probably took care of that on their account. It still made him feel kind of cheap.

Great. Just what he needed as he walked up to their four-story mansion.

It didn't feel right to use his key. It felt even dumber to ring the bell, but that was what he did before he got caught loitering.

Footsteps and voices filtered through the mahogany door. They were then punctuated by scrabbling claws and the tell-tale piercing howl of a certain naughty girl.

"Watson!"

As soon as the door opened Blake dropped to his knees. He knew he should probably greet his family first, but none of them would be half as pleased to see him as the three-year-old beagle that launched into his arms.

"Who's a good girl? Did you miss me? Did you?"

Eventually, he couldn't delay looking up any longer. In one motion he lifted his gaze to meet his parents' eyes and stood. His shoulders ached a little where he pulled them back. His dad's face was a mask, but his mom's crumbled as he soon as he gave her a weak smile.

"Oh sweetheart," she cried. She was several inches shorter than him, yet somehow still managed to throw her arms around his neck. "Don't worry. We've got it all figured out." She sniffed and hugged him tighter.

Blake gingerly patted her on the back. He didn't trust himself to say anything, but dread welled up in his gut. What was 'all sorted out' supposed to mean?

Without his mom, he probably would have been content to dance in local shows and compete for state titles and the like. She'd always been the one with the big dreams, so the band's demise was probably taking a greater toll on her than it was him.

When she let him go his father clasped his shoulder with a large hand, squeezing tightly. There was no mistaking where Blake had inherited his stature from. Richard Jackson had the height and shoulders of a linebacker and the jaw and steely eyes of a huntsman. It was part of what made him so intimidating in court.

Blake was no stranger to have his photo taken. He was glad he always saw a warmth in himself that he'd never once seen in his father. Not even in times like these, where, presumably, he was offering comfort.

"Welcome home, son."

Blake dragged his bags over the threshold into the foyer, Watson skipping around underfoot. Then, finally, he felt a familiar solid punch to his arm.

"Took you long enough, jerk."

"Jodi!" their mother admonished, appalled. But Blake just grinned.

"Hey sis," he said, pulling her slim but wiry frame into his arms. As usual, she was dressed in athletic gear with her long hair up in a ponytail. "You got big."

"Can you believe our baby's going to college in the fall?" their mom cooed.

Jodi rolled her eyes as their mom placed her hands on her shoulders from behind and shook her.

"Don't jinx it," Jodi said tiredly.

"We're waiting to hear back from the NKU scouts," their dad said gravely.

Blake's eyebrows shot up. "Northern Kentucky? They want you to play softball?" Jodi shrugged, like it didn't mean the world to her. "Dude, that's incredible!" It was his turn to thump her. "Why didn't you tell me?"

"Because we don't *know* anything yet," Jodi told him.

She called Watson to heel from where she was still winding between their legs, her tail whacking into everyone's shins. For a small dog, she certainly managed to make her presence well known. Jodi then turned and the two of them marched purposefully across the entrance hall, past the stairs and down the corridor towards the kitchen.

Blake swallowed the lump in his throat. This one felt an awful lot like guilt. He'd missed a lot by being away.

His mom wrapped her hands around his thick bicep and tugged. "Come on sweetie, we've got a lot to talk about."

2

BLAKE

The guilt morphed back to nerves as Blake let his parents steer him to the kitchen after his sister and their dog. As much as he wasn't sure what he was going to do now, he had nurtured the vague hope he'd be allowed two seconds to catch his breath before the subject of his uncertain future cropped up.

The kitchen was about the size of his and Joey's entire flat back in L.A. The center was dominated by a large marble island with tall, white stools planted around at regular intervals. Jodi was already sitting with a carton of juice. Watson was dutifully by her feet, waiting for the drama to begin.

Blake nervously ran his thumb up and down the glass of iced tea he was handed. "Thanks," he said automatically.

"Oh honey, don't look so blue."

His mom hopped up onto one of the stools. Like Jodi, she was kitted out in work out gear, although Blake suspected this was the kind of outfit she wore traveling *to* yoga or pilates or step class. It was too expensive actually be sweated in.

14

"Winners don't wear frowns, they wear…"

Blake was sorely tempted to snap that he wasn't thirteen any more. But his dad was there, standing by the fridge with his arms crossed.

"Crowns," Blake supplied wearily.

His mom gave a little clap. "Now, look at both my babies here, together. Jodi is on the up and up and so! Are! You!" She punctuated the last three words with a wag of her manicured finger towards Blake's face across the island table. "I told you your Momma had your back."

Blake swallowed. "Mom…" he began.

I just need a break. I haven't even been up to my room. I want to sleep.

She waved her hand then grinned like a cat with a canary. "How would you like to dance?"

"Right now?"

She tutted patiently. "All the time. For a career."

Hope fluttered tentatively through Blake's chest. All he'd *ever* wanted to do was dance. Singing had come a distant, awkward second to that feeling of his body moving perfectly in time to the music.

"I'd love to," he managed to stammer.

His mom clapped again. However Jodi bit her lip and focused on stroking Watson's big, floppy ears. There was something he was missing.

"Well," said his mom. She laid her hands flat on the counter top and fixed him with her bright, blue eyes, the lashes spiky with black mascara. "You remember that old community center over near the international market? The strip with the discount tire store and pizzeria?"

Blake blinked at the non-sequitur. "Uh, yeah?"

She waved her hand at his confusion. "They did it up. Or, they *are* doing it up. And thanks to a generous donation from your dad's firm, it'll be completed in no time."

15

Blake still wasn't getting it. But he raised an eyebrow at his dad, who simply nodded once back him. "That's good."

His mom was getting agitated that he wasn't connecting the dots she was giving him quicker. "We got first dibs on the space. It's yours, every week day three thirty until six, and every Saturday nine until seven!"

Heat prickled cross Blake's skin. He was supposed to have guessed by now, but he couldn't see what she was saying. He didn't need all the time and space to dance. Sure, the mirrors, if they had them, would be nice. But he could totally just use one of the rooms here for a studio.

He felt a hand slip over his fingers. He didn't realize he'd clenched into fists and he tried to relax.

Jodi gave him a small smile and squeezed her long fingers against his knuckles. "To open a dance school," she said softly. "To teach."

For a moment Blake couldn't breathe. Then it was like all the air rushed into his lungs at once and he gasped embarrassingly loudly. "Are you *serious?*" he cried. He tried to stop the tears welling in his eyes. Men didn't cry, after all. But of all the ways he thought this God-awful week could end, he never thought this would be it.

"That depends," his mom replied, clutching her hands to her chest. "Are you happy?"

Blake stumbled off his chair and threw his arms around her small frame, making her squeal in delight. "This is the *best...* I can't... How did you?"

She laughed and he felt his dad pat his back. "You've worked hard, son," he said. Blake pulled away to look at him. "You deserve this."

"We already have some potential other teachers for you to meet," his mom gushed excitedly. "And thanks to some quick old-fashioned flyering by my girlfriends we've already got so much interest for auditions. That is, if this is what you want?"

Blake shook his head, the grin on his lips threatening to split his head in two. "Want? Mom. Dad." He looked at each of them in turn and squeezed Jodi's hand. "This is a dream come true."

His mom slapped her own hand in a sort of self-high-five and jumped down from her stool.

"Great, this is just great. Baby, I knew you'd love it. See! Momma knows best! Okay." She started fiddling with the collar of her pink velour sweatshirt. "Did you get that?" she asked cheerfully. Blake wasn't sure who she was speaking to.

Without warning, a stranger walked into the kitchen from the hall. Blake jerked in surprise, quickly looking to his folks for an explanation.

"Yeah, that was great Jenna," said the petite, dark-haired guy. He was looking at a small video camera in one hand and adjusting the head-set he was wearing with the other. He paid no attention to Blake, despite his spluttering. "Let's set up the shot again for some medium close ups, and get the boom mic in to grab better audio off of Blake."

"What – Mom?" Blake's heart was hammering against his chest as he floundered. Jodi still wore the same scowl she'd had at the front door. His mom was all a-twitter and his dad simply continued to loom.

"Honey," said his mom. She placed her hand on the small of his back and steered him towards the guy who was still only paying attention to his technical gear. "This is Seth, our show runner. I'm sorry to spring that on you, but we all know acting isn't your strong suit. We had to get the *real* surprise on camera."

"Hey man," said Seth. He still didn't look up from the playback screen, instead walking over to a laptop a P.A. had appeared with from out of nowhere.

Blake's brain was whirring at an alarming rate. There was no room to consider anything beyond the fact there was a dude with a fucking *camera* in his home. And not just him. Now a chubby, dark-skinned guy had materialized from behind where Blake had been sitting. He was carrying a boom mic while three people with cameras positioned themselves around the island counter.

"Why is there a film crew?" Blake demanded. He didn't want to get too angry with his dad beside him. The last thing he wanted was a fight. But he was pretty fucking pissed. What the hell were these people doing? Was the dance school thing even real?

"Honey!" cried his mom as a tall woman with ear gauges moved Blake into place in front of one of the cameras. "What point is there opening a dance school if no one knows about it?" Well at least she hadn't been faking about that.

"By releasing the content directly ourselves online," his dad's low voice rumbled, "we control the output and take the lion's share of the advertising profits."

"It's perfect!" his mom cooed.

"Can I give you this mic pack, Mr. Jackson?" Ear Gauge Girl held up a small, black box with an antenna and a cylindrical microphone the size of his thumbnail. Experience told Blake the box was the battery pack and sure enough, the girl slipped it into his jeans' pocket leaving him to thread the mic wire up under his t-shirt.

But he just held the bullet shaped device between his finger and thumb. Counting to ten wasn't working. He kept getting to three or four then his temper flared again. The breaths he was taking weren't quite reaching his lungs. "You want me to make a TV show?"

His dad moved from by the fridge. Now Blake was looking for them, he could see that he, his mom and Jodi were all discreetly wearing the microphones too.

"After everything we've invested into you son, we couldn't let you down." He landed his heavy hand on Blake's shoulder. "This is your future."

"We have to strike while you're still hot," his mom told him, shaking her fist.

Somehow, Blake's feet were moving, and he found himself sat back on the same stool as before. It was his usual spot at the table. He'd eaten Lucky Charms here and done his Spanish homework. Now there was a camera lens in his face and a boom mic above his head.

Jodi hadn't moved. Neither had Watson by her feet. As the crew rearranged to set up the shot, a smile lit up Jodi's face again. Leaning over, she gave Blake's wrist a tight squeeze, digging her fingernails in. The sharp pain focused Blake, bringing his attention back into the room, clearing his head.

Still smiling, Jodi winked at him.

"Just go with it," she said between her teeth, barely moving her lips.

"Okay," said Seth loudly. "Reset for take. Jacksons as you were. This is a special. Blake." He looked up at the sound of his name and met Seth's gaze for the first time. "We won't ordinarily ask you to repeat a scene, but like your mom explained, the first shot was for authenticity." He looked back down at his camera screen. "We'll grab some pick-ups of you looking confused, happy, then re-do the hug. All set?"

There were several nods of consent, then Blake realized they seemed to be waiting on him. "Uh, yeah," he stammered. He'd done more than enough work in front of a camera. In the past though, he'd always known he was going to be filmed *before* it had begun.

What had happened? He'd walked through the door thinking he'd take a week or two off to re-evaluate his life. Of course, teaching dance had crossed his mind as an option many times. He wasn't sure how to set up something like that. But for thirty seconds he'd believed his parents had covered it and he was actually going to be able to do something that he truly loved, away from the spotlight.

Now there was a makeup girl powdering his face and two lights set up behind the camera with a reflector angled to give him the best coverage. His heart was still racing and cold sweat was running down his back. But he dug his thumbnail discreetly into his palm and took in a slow, steading breath.

"Alright," Seth cried. He settled himself into one of the seats, pointing his camera at Blake's mom. "And...rolling!"

There was nothing Blake could do but smile.

3

ELION

THERE WEREN'T MANY PLACES ELION WOULD CONSIDER TO BE even fractionally sophisticated in Perryville. But the Cool Beans coffee house certainly tried its best. The attempt to pull off Seattle-style chicness was adorable. At least the owners were trying for original.

Which was probably why it was the only place he'd stuck around long enough to hold down a job. Good vibes, little responsibility, easy routine. There were worse ways to earn a buck.

However, there were days like this where he felt like he'd rather be broke and living on the street than have to deal with a single customer again in his whole life.

"Yeah, I know!" chattered the young woman on her cell at the front of the queue. She wore a frilly blouse that, were Elion interested in such a sight, offered a great view of her firm breasts. *"No!"*

Being a Friday afternoon the place was pretty packed. She didn't seem to notice the tuts and eye rolls she was already getting.

"Can I help you, Ma'am?" Elion prompted her.

She held a finger up to him and flipped her wavy hair over her shoulder. "Uh huh," she said, nodding. "Uh huh. Yeah, that's what *I* said."

Elion sighed and looked around at the rest of the patrons. His colleague Devon was already serving the next guy in line, so all Elion could do was wait until this chick deigned to give him her order.

The lighting was dim on purpose to make the place seem cozy, even during the day. Naked brickwork walls and lightbulbs hanging above the counter gave it an industrial sort of feel. The bunting and mounted vintage bicycle on the wall meant the atmosphere leaned more towards hipster. All their menus were written by hand on chalkboards.

One of the owners, Lily, picked wildflowers herself every day. It was one of her favorite chores of a morning to arrange them in glass milk bottles to display on the counter and the dozen round, wooden tables.

Almost all the squishy armchairs around those tables were occupied, and the queue was getting longer. A tickling bell signaled to Elion than more patrons had just arrived.

"Ma'am?"

"Yeah, hang on babe," said the woman into the phone. She placed her hand over the receiver. "Sorry sweetie, I'll just take a Unicorn Frap." She took her hand away again and began twirling her hair. "So, like I said, he totally didn't care-"

Elion sighed and looked over at Devon. She gave him a sympathetic shrug and started serving a guy in cycling gear. Elion purposefully didn't make eye contact with anyone else in the line, especially as the next couple seemed to be having an in depth conversation. Although they weren't happy about something, they looked to be the only ones not pissed at *him*.

"Ma'am," Elion said again. He plastered his best shit-for-brains grin on. "They only serve those at Starbucks."

She raised her perfectly painted on eyebrow at him. "Huh?"

"It's trademarked," he said cheerfully. He folded his hands onto the counter in front of him, still grinning. "If I made you one, they'd sue the fuck out of us faster than you could drink it. How about you try ordering something else?"

The girl frowned into the phone, then looked back over at him. "I'm sorry, I didn't quite catch that. If there's no unicorns, I'll take a popcorn instead."

Elion hopped to the side and pointed helpfully up at the drinks menu. "No Frappuccinos. They are *aaaalll* very trademarked. By Starbucks. Which is two blocks over."

She blinked and looked around her, as if only noticing where she was in that moment. "Oh," she said sulkily. "Okay, well, there's no need to get rude about it."

Using all his will power, Elion clung on to his smile, despite his gritted teeth. "You have a great day now!" he called after her, giving a single wave over his head.

"Lily will kill you if she catches you cussing at patrons," said Devon. She raised a pierced eyebrow at him. *"Again."*

Elion blew a raspberry at her. "Like Ms OMG heard me through that fog of cheap hairspray. Anyway, who's next!"

The couple were still talking intently. The girl – and she was a girl – probably first year of college or still at high school – was tall and athletic looking. Her Perryville High Panthers t-shirt confirmed as much. The guy was older and oh *boy* was Elion pleased to get an extra second while they talked to drink him in.

Young Captain America brightened up the room with his golden hair, swept neatly to the side and falling just above his ears. His broad shoulders looked to hold a great weight, his woes emphasized by the frown on his pretty face. He had his big hands shoved in his designer jeans. He was nodding at something the girl was saying.

Their body language as they moved around the other guy's bike to Elion's side of the counter didn't say romantic couple. The angles of their torsos were all wrong. His heart picked up. Could this Abercrombie model potentially be single?

Whether he was interested in guys was purely optional and not something Elion needed to concern himself with to have a flight of fancy. He was the most gorgeous specimen to saunter into this joint in a long time. Elion was suddenly grateful to Unicorn Lady for holding up the line meaning he could be the one to serve him.

"It's just so un-fucking-believable," hissed Blondie. "She's lost her mind!"

Panthers Girl sighed with real sympathy. "But this way you at least get to dance."

"It's – it's a farce! I don't want to be some fake reality housewife…whatever!"

He looked so troubled it tugged on Elion's heart. Someone that gorgeous didn't deserve to be that unhappy. He decided these guys could maybe get free cookies, if he was stealthy enough. He dug out his most sincere smile.

"Good afternoon, how can I-oh holy *fuck!*" He slapped his hand over his mouth, clunking a ring against his teeth. "Sorry, but – Blake, is that you?"

The guy turned from the girl to fully face him. "Um?"

Shit, he looked uncomfortable. "Sorry, sorry," said Elion, waving his hands apologetically. "But you're Blake Jackson, right?" He pointed at himself. "Elion Rodriguez. You probably don't remember, but we took Miss Dixon's English Lit together for like three years running. And Biology with that dude with the yellow fingernails."

Realization dawned on Blake's face. Elion exhaled in relief. "Mr. Pritchard," he said.

"That's the one," said Elion excitedly. He clicked his

fingers. "Wow, how you been? Seriously, it must be what? Five years?"

Blake nodded. "About that," he said. He reached over and offered Elion his hand, so he leaned over the counter and shook it. "It's good to see you."

His eyes quickly raked over the pink tips of Elion's black hair and the tattoo on his wrist. Sure, he was on the skinny side compared to Blake, but he knew he looked okay. If you didn't mind a more alternative style. Which a lot of folks around here did.

Blake smiled though. "You too. You working here?"

"Yeah," said Elion, spreading his hands out as if to say 'this is me!'

"Allegedly," Devon coughed into her hand.

Elion gave her the finger. "Right, Blake. What can I get you? And…" He looked expectantly at the girl.

"Jodi," she said. She jabbed her hand towards him for a shake of her own. "Blake's sister. So, you guys went to high school together?"

"The boy needs a drinks order," an older lady griped from behind them. "Then you can flirt."

"I can do both, Ma'am," Elion assured her with a salute.

For all his bravado though, he glanced nervously at Blake and his sister. He hadn't forgotten how loaded the Jacksons were, and here he was, slumming it at a lowly coffee shop.

"We'll take two cappuccinos," said Blake, fishing out a leather wallet.

Elion spun and got the milk foaming. "So, like, how's that popstar thing going?" he asked casually over his shoulder. Like everyone knew someone who'd gone on release several top forty hits. "Guess that 'Most Likely to be Famous' award worked out pretty accurately, huh?"

He turned back around to get the espresso machine going. But Blake's face had fallen and his jaw was tight. Jodi sighed and placed a hand on her brother's firm bicep under the tight t-shirt he wore.

Shame washed over Elion like a cold bucket of water. He'd one hundred percent fucked up.

"Sorry," he blurted. He grabbed two cups and saucers so he could occupy his attention elsewhere. "You probably get people bugging you about that all the time. I'm just happy to see you."

Like that wasn't sycophantic. Blake didn't know who he was. He had no idea of all the hours Elion had spent staring dreamily at the back of his head in Trig. He was a million years out of his league, and straight as an arrow to boot. He needed to get a hold of himself.

Blake, though, handed over the cash for the coffees with a small but seemingly genuine smile. "It's not that," he said. "The band sort of broke up."

"Below Zero broke up?" a young woman from down the line blurted out.

Elion, Blake and Jodi turned to see most of the coffee house were looking at them. Had they all been listening in?

Blake shifted his shoulders and cracked a smile. The tension from before all but vanished. "Yeah. We're sad to let our fans down, but there were creative differences and we felt it best to part ways while we're all still friends."

That was the most rehearsed PR bullshit Elion had ever heard spoken in real life.

Jodi scowled and stepped protectively closer to her brother as people crowded around him, answering more questions and signing autographs.

"Are you still recording?"

"Does that mean you've moved back?"

"Oh honey, I'm so sorry!"

Jodi nudged the cups back towards Elion. "Can we get these to go?" she asked under her breath.

Elion didn't need telling twice.

"I didn't mean to throw him to the wolves like that." He hastily poured the hot liquid into two cardboard cups.

Jodi shook her head at him though, swishing her long ponytail from side to side. "He's just having a bad day."

"Still," said Elion, handing their drinks back to her. "Tell him I'm sorry." Then, because it was hard to make his mouth listen to his brain at the best of times… "If he comes back in, his next cappuccino's on me. And yours."

The serious expression she had worn until now lifted. "Thank you," she said and touched the back of his hand. It wasn't flirtatious at all, but warm. "I'm sure we will."

The Jacksons made their polite, but swift, exit not long after that. Elion was impressed that even though Jodi was younger, she was the one to steer them towards the door without offending a single patron.

Elion hadn't noticed Devon sidling up to his side. Everyone was too busy ogling the local celeb to focus on ordering coffees or muffins in that moment. She bumped her shoulder against his and smirked.

"So that was fun."

"That wasn't fun," said Elion. His voice didn't squeak, definitely not. "That was…like one of those dreams where you show up naked to an exam."

Devon licked her lips and smacked her hand firmly against his ass. "No one was naked here hun. Let's hope you get luckier next time."

He spluttered, but she'd already moved back to the counter to serve the first person that had grown bored of the drama.

Elion tended to the next few patrons in a daze. Of all the people that could have walked through the door that day, he would never have expected Blake Jackson to be one of them.

He was pretty sure he'd done okay. He replayed the

conversation over and over again in his mind. As far as he could tell, he'd not humiliated himself, even though he felt bad for drawing the attention of the crowd.

The chances of Blake coming back in were probably slim. Even if the band were no more, an Adonis like that was meant for bigger things than Perryville, Ohio. He still amused himself daydreaming about flirting the next time, giving Blake that free coffee.

Which reminded him, he'd already earmarked two cookies to give away. Seeing as they were wrapped now, it didn't seem right to put them back on the counter. So he gave them to an exhausted young mom with one kid wailing in a stroller and the other straining against his leash. The tearful thanks the mom gave him lifted his spirits further.

Even if Blake was only in town for a week, this was the best coffee place in town that wasn't a bland mega-chain. He was bound to come back.

Elion spent the rest of his shift singing along, poorly, with the radio, dodging the coffee beans Devon regularly threw his way, and smiling at every single customer he served.

4

BLAKE

ULTIMATELY, IT HAD BEEN BETTER TO DO WHAT JODI SAID AND go with the flow. Once Blake accepted that the TV show was happening, he could try and simply ignore the film crew and focus on what mattered.

His mom had named the school the ever-so-subtle Blake Jackson Academy, and the show the very-questionable Feet of Flames. Blake really wasn't convinced about either. It wasn't worth arguing though, so he'd thrown himself into preparing for the open auditions. Those had taken place that morning.

He'd been delighted at the turnout. It probably hadn't hurt that his face had been on the flyers his mom's friends had put into the entire town's mailboxes. So they'd had all sorts swarm through the doors of the new dance studio, the smell of fresh paint still lingering in the air.

Tiny toddlers who were more excited by their sparkly tutus than learning how to *plie.* Tweens anxiously checking to see what everyone else was doing before joining in. Fans from out of state with two left feet more interested in taking photos of him than any choreography. They did, however, have several genuinely talented kids and young adults that set Blake's imagination alight with possibilities. And then there were those who weren't in any way gifted, but had tried so hard Blake could practically see their determination radiating off them.

The Plan – with a big P – was to shoot twelve episodes and release them via YouTube. The episode length would, apparently, depend on what storylines they came up with.

"Sorry," said Blake. He shook his head in confusion. "Don't you mean the storylines that *develop?*"

They were back around the marble island in the kitchen. Dozens and dozens of applications attached to headshots littered the surface in front of them.

Seth didn't pause from shuffling the papers around. "No, we need to control the story from the get-go. Make sure the finale works. What about her?"

Blake's mom wrinkled her nose. "How many Asians do we have already?"

"In total? Three."

She plucked the application from his hand. "I don't see her in the star pile, but she was good for background."

Blake scowled at the both of them. "The only thing that should matter is their ability," he said.

His mom laughed. Seth didn't even acknowledge him. "Honey," said his mom. She tapped his hand and indicated the messy pile they were dealing with. "Why don't you fish out your ten absolute favorites? Then we'll try and get a good mix of them between the classes."

"What about her?" Seth asked.

He happened to pick out one of the ones that Blake was trying to find. "Yes, Karyn!" he said, pleased something was finally going his way. "She's incredible."

"She's a brat."

He turned and regarded the fourth person sat around the table.

Nessa Prince was the other teacher his mom (and presumably the production team) had found to take some of the classes. They had a range from babies to high school age and Blake couldn't teach them all, let alone choreograph every routine. But that was obviously not the only reason Nessa had been hired.

She was almost as tall as Blake with light brown skin that practically glowed with healthy nourishment. There was enough of it on display to make a fair assessment. Clad solely in bright, patterned leggings and a sports bra over her ample boobs, her long, lean stomach proved how much time she spent at the gym. From the mane of dark brown hair she'd casually thrown up in a half ponytail Blake would have bet money on there being extensions hidden away in there. Her teeth were perfectly straight and white, the kind of smile you saw on most people in L.A.

He'd seen her move too. Without a doubt she knew what she was doing. But her vitriol against the young Karyn surprised him.

"She was easily one of the best we saw today," he countered carefully.

He *almost* didn't notice when the camera operators repositioned themselves to angle at the two of them. Kala, the producer with the ear gauges, was watching him from behind the cameras. He refused to get into an argument, but he guessed that was what they probably wanted.

Nessa shook her head. "I didn't say she wasn't," she agreed. "But she has an attitude problem. I don't know if that's what the school needs."

Blake tried to recall what he'd seen of her away from the floor. All he could recall though were her perfect *fouette* turns and excellent posture. "I'm sure she was just nervous."

Nessa arched her eyebrow. "She's going to walk all over you with an attitude like that."

Blake sat back on the stool. What the hell had gotten into her? "You know what?" he snapped, slapping Karyn's application paper on the table. "This is my school. She's the best, and I say she's in."

There was a beat. Then his mom and Nessa and relaxed, smiled, and his mom even gave him a quick clap. Seth flicked an eyebrow, but otherwise didn't react.

"That was great, guys," said Kala approvingly, nodding at the cameras.

Blake's mom squeezed his knee. "You're getting it, hon!"

He looked around at them, then fixed on Nessa. "You were messing with me?"

"I was bringing the drama." She grinned and handed him back Karyn's application. "Of course we should take her. But," she arched an eyebrow at him, "I did mean it. She is going to be a handful."

"That's the point," drawled Seth. His eyes flicked between two more resumes.

"Right," said Blake slowly.

He really wasn't getting the hang of this play-acting bullshit. This was obviously another reason Nessa had been hired. She seemed to have the hang of it right away.

His eyes flicked discreetly over to her again. She was obviously gorgeous; any idiot could see that. But for some reason Blake didn't feel any flicker of attraction towards her. If the guys were here with him, he was sure that TJ would have been putting the moves on her by now. That boy used sex like a handshake.

But Blake remained unmoved. He was fussy though, he knew that. It took a special kind of girl to hold his interest outside the dance studio. Even then he took forever to put the moves on and get any. Not everyone was cut out to be a Casanova like TJ, he supposed.

He and Nessa were compatible on the dance floor, and that was all he cared about.

Seth looked up at the big guy on the crew, Marcus. He operated the boom, but that wasn't always needed. In the auditions he'd used it to get all the kids chattering. But here, they were all mic'd up, so Marcus was now first camera man while Seth was casting.

"I'd say another ten minutes on the applications, then we set up for talking heads?"

Marcus nodded silently.

"Oh," said Blake's mom, waving another candidate's profile around. A guy called Tyler. "How about you argue over this guy next? Nessa, you could point out how hot he is and Blake you could get offended and insecure!"

They had auditioned a few older dancers for an elite team of just half a dozen. Blake would be the center point, naturally. Then they would be the close of the big show they were steering the season climax towards.

Blake tried not to scowl as he took the guy's application off her. "I'm not insecure, Mom. He's good, but so am I."

"Yes." She glanced at the camera and gave him a thumbs up. "That's it, honey, good."

Blake rubbed his eyes. "I only want seven for the elite squad. He's talented, and, seeing as it seems to matter so much to you, he's also black."

"And smoking hot," said Nessa, taking his picture and fanning herself.

Blake's mom raised her eyebrows at him, but he refused to be goaded. "Tyler is in."

Tyler went on the Definitely pile.

They needed up to a dozen featured characters apparently,

of all ages and abilities to create a varied cast. They had an adorable four-year-old with blonde ringlets and big, doe eyes named Madison. Also a stocky, ginger boy with startling potential named Brady in his freshman year at Perryville High. Then of course there was Karyn. Thirteen and gangly with, as Nessa said, a potential attitude problem. But when she started to move there was no taking your eyes off of her.

They had their black and South-East-Asian quota for the main cast already, which Blake still wasn't comfortable with. But he didn't care so much who they wanted to put in the credits of the show. He only cared about the caliber of the dancers. All the dancers.

Unfortunately, Seth and his mom didn't necessarily see it that way.

"But she doesn't know the difference between third and fourth position," Blake argued. He was talking about Taffy, a girl with model good looks. However, she was an atrocious, awkward dancer who had been very slow to pick up choreo. "She cannot be in the senior class. That's advanced; she'll hold the other kids back."

"She's a childhood cancer survivor and her mom was Miss Ohio," said Seth. Blake waited for a follow up, but there wasn't one.

"So?"

"So, she's in," said his mom. "Moving on. We need a fatty."

Blake choked on his own saliva and glared at her. "What did you just say?"

She shrugged. "We need a fat kid. Question is; one that can dance? Or one that can't?"

"Can't," said Seth, fishing out another headshot. "People like someone to pity, poke fun at. He'll be a meme within a week."

That was so awful, but Blake's mom was already nodding.

He glanced at Nessa, who gave him a pained look, but only shrugged.

Rather than come out and disagree, Blake came at it from a different angle. It was a technique that had sometimes worked with his mom in the past. "Mercy is a big girl," he said. He showed them her photo. "She's not the best, but she's a trier, and a really sweet kid."

"We have enough minorities," said Seth. "You don't want viewers to mistake this for an inner-city ghetto."

"But-" spluttered Blake.

Seth carried on like he hadn't heard him. "She's not fantastic, but she's not terrible and she has no sob story. If you even have her in the background, she'll attract the eye in a negative way. Hard no."

Blake could feel his anger rising. "You're not going to let her in at all? Not even one of the beginner's classes?"

"Sweetie," his mom said, reaching out to take his hand. Her tone was firm though. "Seth knows best, he's done these shows before."

Blake pulled his hand out of reach. This was supposed to be *his* school. He wanted a safe space where kids could come and express themselves creatively. To flourish. *I never asked you to turn it into a circus,* he thought savagely.

But he could already hear his dad's voice: *'After everything your mother and I have done for you?'*

"I want her in the class," he tried one last time.

He didn't even get an answer. Seth ignored him entirely as he typed on his laptop. His mom just shrugged again and began talking to Nessa about branded school training wear. Kala was the only one who met his eye, but that was only to shrug apologetically.

This was such bullshit. He couldn't take any more.

Without bothering to ask permission, he rose from the table and stormed out the kitchen. His mom called out after him, but he tuned her out. No doubt he'd get his ear chewed off for that later, but right then he didn't care.

He thundered through the foyer and out into the street, slamming the door behind him. Fury propelled him onwards, until he realized he'd made it a few blocks over and had no idea of where he was heading.

He stopped at the end of one of the identical roads. He'd made it into one of the regular neighborhoods, not the million-dollar estates of his street. All the houses were one story with slanted roofs and simple, square front yards of closely trimmed grass. With no one else around that he could see, he dropped his head back and let out a frustrated roar.

Two weeks ago, he and Joey had been playing video games, having ditched some Hollywood party in favor of pizza and zombies. Now he was here, in the dreary, lonely town where even the smallest decisions had been taken away from him.

The only spark of life he'd seen so far had been from his dog Watson. That, and the bizarre encounter with his old classmate, Elion.

Blake took a deep breath, and began walking again, vaguely aware of heading towards the small strip of stores that the Cool Beans coffee house sat in. It was stupid, but thinking of Elion made him smile.

He had only dim memories of him from school, but they were there nonetheless. Normally, being recognized put Blake on edge. It was unnerving when a stranger knew so much about you and you knew absolutely nothing about them. But the way Elion's face had lit up spoke of camaraderie, not fan worship.

Blake hadn't kept in touch with anyone from his class, other than the usual 'friendship' on Facebook. But he wasn't actually close with anyone there. It might be nice to get to know Elion and swap some stories of the old days, good or not.

Plus, he was the only guy he'd seen in town with any kind of style. Blake felt the need to reach out to someone else creative, even if that artistic flare only stretched to colorful hair.

Jodi had said Elion had promised him a free coffee too, after the minor scene that had happened on his last visit. The gesture was unnecessary, but that made it nicer. So, it would be rude not to take him up on it, surely?

By the time the half a dozen establishments came into view, he had several good reasons to head into the coffee shop. The least of which was they actually did really great cappuccinos. He wasn't sure if he was looking to make a friend. It had been so long since he'd tried to connect with anyone new. Maybe he just wanted an excuse to get away from the casting and this was the most convenient.

Whatever his true motivation was, as he pushed the door into the coffee house, he hoped that Elion was working.

5

ELION

If he moaned louder, Elion thought maybe Devon might take pity on him. Instead, she threw a dishrag at his face.

"Dev-von," he whimpered, slumping against the back wall. "Be nice."

"It's your own fault you're hungover," she said. She was making a caramel latte and the customer was regarding Elion's display with somewhat wide eyes. He didn't mind. It passed the time to put on a show every now and again.

However, there were other people waiting, and Lily was lurking around somewhere. As much as Elion enjoyed playing the brat, he didn't want to lose his job.

In his defense, last night had been special. Worth drinking a bit too much even though he had to be at work today. A couple of his school buddies had come home for the weekend and they'd stayed up most of the night catching up.

Back in the day, they'd had a pretty sweet group from the LGBT alliance that hung out twenty-four-seven. But of course, everyone else had gone to college, all over the country, leaving Elion in little old Perryville. As fun as last night had been, it had also reminded him what he'd missed out on. He'd probably had a shot or three of tequila that he shouldn't have to chase the bitterness away.

So he could suffer the pain today as penance. He would never want to feel jealous or resentful of his friends and a big fat headache would remind him of that.

He made sure to chug down glasses of water and bounced from customer to customer. There were more important things in life than frat parties, after all. Also, the upside of not going to college was he wasn't saddled with student debt for the next two decades of his life. So, things could be worse.

The hot topic of conversation had of course been the re-emergence of Blake Jackson last week. Elion had tried to hold his tongue, but after a couple of beers the story had eventually slipped out. He'd done his best not to sound like some lust-struck fan.

At least he could say he'd never really listened to Below Zero's music. There might have been a little drool when he'd recounted how hot Blake had gotten since school, and damn, he'd been seriously fine back then as well.

But the truth was Elion was more intrigued by what had obviously been causing Blake so much grief. It was probably the band splitting up. That had to be tough. Elion couldn't really imagine what it was like to tour the world and make records and have screaming fans only to come back…here.

As he emptied the dishwasher Elion scowled and told himself, yet again, that there were a thousand worse places to be. He was only jaded because he'd never experienced anything else. Seeing his old buddies was just making him go all 'grass-is-greener.' Once he'd had a good night's sleep he'd grow up and remember all the things he had to be grateful for.

"Elion, are you free?"

"In mind," he sighed. He stood and placed his hand on his heart. "In body, I am shackled."

Devon stared at him through her eyelashes. "You are such a catch," she said, deadpan. "It's time for your break."

He blinked and frowned at her. Sometimes, when he was this hungover, he honest-to-God could forget what month they were in. So time-of-the-day was utterly hopeless. But he was still almost certain that he'd had both his breaks for the day. He was due to go home in an hour.

"No, I don't think so. But if you wanted to nip out for a quickie, all you had to do is ask."

Devon rolled her eyes. "Ew. Take your damn break."

She spun on her heels and immediately began making a couple of drinks. Elion frowned and wondered what he'd done to piss her off so much that she'd banish him from the counter.

That was when he looked over at the guy hovering by the order pickup station.

"Blake?" he blurted.

It was a good job he'd not been holding anything, because he would have absolutely dropped it, and a lot of things around here were breakable. Blake looked at him with a sheepish grin.

"So, how about that free cappuccino?"

Elion would be lying if he said he hadn't envisioned Blake Jackson sauntering back into the coffee house over the past few days. In his fantasies, Blake would be cool and commanding, and Elion would have been just telling his co-workers an absolutely *hilarious* story.

Instead, he was pretty sure he had cocoa powder smeared through his hair. And Blake had his hands shoved in his sweatshirt pockets and was looking at Elion with such trepidation he had to glance over his shoulder to double check there was nobody else he could possibly be talking to.

"Dude, hey!" he said. He rubbed his palms hastily on his

apron and skipped over to the counter. "Of course, coming right up."

He was mildly impressed he didn't blurt out how awesome it was that Blake had come back at all. Not even a little. He just started frothing up milk with a silly grin on his face. No words seemed to be happening, but that was better than embarrassing words, so he'd go with it.

"Um," Blake said. "Did...do you have a break?"

Damn Devon.

Except, hang on. Was this all-American-old-high-school-crush-legit-popstar asking if he wanted to hang out?

"Yes," Elion blurted. "Yes, yep, literally just going on a break now, isn't that weird? I mean-" he panicked. "Not that you were asking me to join you...were you?"

Blake cast his gaze downwards and bit his lip. "Only if you're free. I thought it might be nice to, you know, catch up. Or something."

Elion already had his apron untied. "That would be so nice, I mean great, I mean-"

He forced himself to breathe, then looked pointedly over at Devon.

She was already holding Blake's finished cappuccino and Elion's personal favorite, Jamaica iced tea.

"Have fun," she said forcefully.

If he questioned it, he might talk himself out of it. So Elion took the drinks and used his hip to bash his way through the swinging door and out into the coffee house floor. He smiled at Blake, then looked away and blinked rapidly, his heart pounding.

"So, um, I think there's a free table this way."

Elion led Blake towards the back. It was likely that people turned their heads to watch them passing. Everybody and their dog seemed to have heard about the local heartthrob's untimely return. But Elion didn't care about that. He cared, deeply, that as he dropped into the squidgy armchair by the jukebox, he and Blake were the only ones at their little, round table.

"I didn't think you'd come back." Yeah. Because that didn't sound needy at all.

Blake smiled though as he pulled his coffee cup towards him. "I'm not sure how being back in Perryville is crazier than L.A.," he said with a laugh. "But it is."

As he stirred sugar into his drink, Elion noticed a dimple in Blake's left cheek. He liked it.

Clearing his throat, he dragged his pathetic thoughts away from an idea where he made that dimple pop out as often as he could. "Really?" he managed.

Blake nodded. "There's...just all this shit flying around. Anyway." He took a sip of his coffee and leaned back. "I felt rude running out the other day and this place is cool, so... here I am."

Here you are. Elion gave himself a mental snap and grabbed his tea. It was sweetened just how he liked it, bless Devon. "It must be so surreal," he said.

Blake nodded. "It's been...fast," he said.

Elion stirred the ice cubes in his glass. He tried to think about something they had in common, something they could reminisce over from school. But there was nothing. Elion had never traveled, he knew almost nothing about music, and they didn't have any mutual friends. All he knew was how amazing it used to be to watch Blake dance.

"So, you're teaching now," he said, latching onto the thought. "Not singing."

Blake chuckled. He glanced around, then when he seemed confident no one was eavesdropping, he leant over. "I never really could sing," he said.

"You can't have been terrible," Elion said.

He licked a drop of dark pink tea that was running down

the glass. When he looked back up, he realized Blake was staring. Shit, he should probably tone down the flirty stuff around the straight guy.

"I mean," he said, clearing his throat. "You had to sing live and stuff?"

Blake's shoulders looked like they relaxed, just a fraction. He smiled, pulling his lower lip between his teeth. That did all sorts of things to Elion's body. He shifted, trying to ignore them.

"They'd turn my mic down," Blake said in a conspiratorial tone. "Or auto-tune on the fly. I could carry the melody, yeah, and they'd let me sign a verse here and there. But mostly I was there for the dance breaks."

Elion couldn't help but laugh. "Wow. So, I get to call you Milli Vanilli from now on, yeah?"

"Shut up!" Blake laughed properly, and smacked Elion's knee. Even through his jeans, the touch sent electricity across Elion's skin. "I wasn't lip syncing, I was actually singing. Just...a little flatly. The other guys really could sing!"

They were both grinning at each other. It felt good, natural. "You must miss them," said Elion. "Unless there's some juicy gossip about their hideous diva tantrums you'd like to share?" He leaned over and crossed his heart. "I promise me and my ninety-three Twitter followers won't tell a soul."

Blake smiled so much the dimple returned. Elion was definitely vulnerable to the giddy feelings that brought out in him.

If he wasn't careful, this could get dangerous. Fast.

6

ELION

"I DO REALLY MISS THE OTHER GUYS," SAID BLAKE AFTER a while.

He sighed and leant back in his chair. The coffee house was busy around them, however Elion was pleased that most people were keeping to themselves and not paying them much attention.

"Especially Joey," Blake carried on. "He's the youngest in the band, the one with the curly hair?"

Elion scoffed. "I know who Joey Sullivan is," he said, like he hadn't obsessively been Googling the band since he'd bumped into Blake last week.

That brought back a small smile. Blake nodded, sipping his coffee. "We were buddies. I bet you two would get on, actually."

He said it with a hint of wistfulness. But of course Elion had to spoil the moment. "Yeah," he said, unable to help the irony that slipped out. "Because we're both gay, right?"

Blake arched an eyebrow at him. "No," he said firmly. "Just because he's gay doesn't mean you're his type."

Elion pretended to prickle, brushing imaginary dust off his shoulder. "How do you know I'm not his type?"

Blake leaned in closer. There was a sparkle in his eye Elion hadn't seen before. "Because he likes adults. Grown men."

"Hey!" said Elion. "I'm an adult. I have a job, and a car. Sometimes there's even gas in it!"

Blake continued to laugh. It was a quiet rumble, but the more he did it, the more his body loosened up. It was addictive to watch.

"Okay, alright," he said. "Seriously though. He's really passionate, never does things by halves. Full of life."

He held Elion's gaze for a second, then looked down with a frown as he swirled what was left of his coffee.

In an attempt to gloss over the strange moment, Elion held his wrist out, showing Blake his tattoo. *Carpe Diem,*" he said. "Seize the day. I know it's cheesy, but, yeah. Life is for living. I think Joey and I can agree on that."

Blake put his coffee cup down and lightly touched Elion's wrist, turning it over to get a better look at the tattoo. His fingertips were warm from where he'd been holding the cup. Elion did his best not to shiver.

"Good philosophy," Blake murmured.

He let go of Elion, returning his hand to him, and Elion immediately felt the loss.

"I think I could learn to embrace the day a bit more." Blake scrubbed his face. "Be more grateful for the opportunities I've been given."

Elion wasn't sure what to say to that. The worry lines were back on Blake's forehead. "Yeah, but you've got to look after you too, right?"

Blake smiled. There was no dimple. "Thanks so much for the coffee. It was really nice to see you again."

That sounded an awful lot like he was leaving. Elion

panicked. "Oh, hey, any time. Seriously, if there's anyone who knows how it is to feel out of place around here, it's me. We should, you know, do it again sometime?"

Like that would actually happen. But Blake's face lit up. "Um, sure. If you're sure?"

Elion waved his hand around at the shop. "I think I can fit you in to my hectic schedule," he said dryly. "Here, let you give you my number."

Relieved, Blake went to reach for his phone. But before he could, Elion mirrored his action from earlier and grabbed his wrist. He pushed the sweatshirt sleeve up, then nabbed a pen from his pocket.

"Um, what are you doing?" Blake asked. At least he sounded amused.

Elion waggled his eyebrows at him as he started scrawling the cell number up his arm in black marker. "This way you won't forget," he said with a wink. "When you're cursing my name later, scrubbing this off, you'll remember to send me a selfie."

So much for not flirting. But for real, how many opportunities was he ever going to get to make friends with a popstar? And Blake didn't seem to mind. He was grinning and shaking his head as Elion finished up the last digit.

"Fine. But I'm getting you back for this." He held up his graffitied arm, then rolled the sleeve back down. "People are going to think I got attacked by a rabid fan."

Elion patted him on the knee. "You can assure them that I have *much* better taste in music than that."

Blake smacked him off with a laugh then rose to his feet. "Catch you later, man."

Elion tried not to stare after him as he walked out. The way his jeans clung to his toned thighs and ass, though, made it difficult. Especially when he stopped for a little girl who ran up to him to ask for an autograph. The way he smiled down at her and then crouched so she could clumsily take a selfie with him was downright adorable.

Once Blake was finally out the door and had vanished from sight, Elion lingered a moment and finished his tea. He wanted to tell himself that Blake wouldn't text. He was a boy, after all. But the way he'd lit up at the suggestion of taking Elion's number gave him a bit of hope.

Maybe he really did want to be friends with a small town nobody like him? Stranger things had happened. He'd come back for that coffee, after all.

"You owe me eleven bucks," said Devon as he returned to behind the counter.

"Jesus, this place is such a rip-off," Elion grumbled. He added it to Devon's running tally she kept on a notepad by the sugar, then looked up to find the owner Lily glaring at him. Some of her greying hair had escaped its bun and was hovering around her head like a static cloud. "I mean, check out all the quality, organic produce!" Elion tried to cover.

She narrowed her eyes at him, then shuffled away to rearrange the sandwich display counter.

"Hey there," said the next customer in line cheerfully.

He was a small guy in his early thirties with dark hair. He looked to be with the big black guy next to him. The taller dude was staring intently at the phone in front of his face as his thumbs twitched over the screen. The smaller guy's eyebrows were raised and he looked excited.

"Was that Blake from Below Zero?"

Elion shrugged. "Yeah, it was." He didn't particularly want to talk about Blake with a stranger. That felt like going behind his back, gossiping. But he couldn't really lie when the guy had obviously seen for himself.

"Wow, that's awesome," he said, rubbing his chin. "Oh, we'll take a couple of flat whites to go." Elion nodded and grabbed the cups. "So, do you guys like, know each other?"

Elion flicked his eyes over the small guy. It seemed a bit unusual that he'd be a Below Zero fan, but then, some people were just celebrity obsessed. Elion was one to talk though. He was only interested because he thought Blake was sweet and hotter than hell. Maybe this dude had his own crush?

That made Elion more sympathetic. "Yeah, kind of," he admitted. He didn't know anything incriminating enough to let anything slip anyway. "We went to high school together."

"Perryville High?" the guy asked. "That enormous place that looks like a prison?"

Elion chuckled. He must not be local. "Most schools in Ohio look like prisons. But, yeah. We were just catching up."

The guy leaned in. His friend was still totally wrapped up with his phone. Elion guessed he must have been playing Candy Crush or something. The level of concentration and the fact it was right in front of his face suggested he was defending a high score.

The smaller guy looked around, but there weren't any other patrons hovering at just that moment. "So, are you two, like, together?"

Elion couldn't help but laugh. At least the guy didn't sound totally disgusted at suggesting such a thing. It added to Elion's crush theory.

"Uh, no, he's not my boyfriend," he said quickly. He knew he was probably smiling a bit too much, still dizzy from his and Blake's chat before. He tried to tone it down. "He's just getting settled back in town, you know?"

The guy looked thoughtfully towards the door. "Is he cool in real life? Or is he one of those guys who turns into a jerk when the cameras are off?"

"Oh no," said Elion hastily. "Nothing like that."

He slammed the coffees down with a bit too much force. After causing Blake grief the last time he came in with fans,

Elion would hate to let this guy leave with a bad impression. Just in case he said unflattering things to other people.

"Yeah, he's a really great guy, totally genuine." He carefully mopped up the coffee he'd spilled. "I'm so glad we had a chance to reconnect."

The smaller guy nodded. "Good to hear. It sucks when people turn out to be douchebags, you know?"

"Oh, completely," Elion agreed. He pressed lids onto the coffee cups and eased them over to the other side of the counter. "There you go, sir. That'll be nine-fifty."

"Thank you," said the guy with a smile. He paid with his card and dropped some change in the tip jar. "You have a great day now."

"You too," Elion responded automatically.

The guy took the drinks off the counter and headed towards the door, the bigger guy following, still glued to his phone.

Elion shook his head. "It must be nuts being famous. Having people talk about you like that. Don't know how Blake copes with it." Devon smirked at him. "What?" he asked with a scowl.

"Nothing," she said. "I'm just sure you'll find out soon enough."

Elion huffed and went to go bus tables. That was nonsense. He'd be lucky if he ever spoke to Blake again. Sure, he was here for now. But he was made for bigger things in this world than Perryville. That was partly why Elion had felt confident enough to give him his number. It wasn't like it was going to lead to anything. But the thrill of being so bold still had his whole body tingling.

Exciting things very rarely happened to him. So he wasn't going to overthink it. He was just going to enjoy it while it lasted.

7

BLAKE

THE FIRST HINT BLAKE KNEW SOMETHING WAS WRONG – *REALLY* wrong – was the shriek that resounded through the house on Thursday evening.

His mom was having a screening party as the first episode of Feet of Flames went live. Several women in their forties had invaded the house a couple of hours ago and had been getting progressively tipsy since. Blake had had neither the desire to watch the car crash of a show, nor to be groped by unhappily married middle aged women. So he had kept, far, far away.

He honestly had no idea what the actual quality of the show would be. He knew it would be a disaster for him personally, because he'd never wanted it to be made in the first place. Also, he hated reality TV with a passion. Nothing about it was real.

Given that he knew that, he probably should have been more prepared.

"*BLAKE!*" his mom's hysterical cry resonated against the walls.

He knew better than to keep her waiting. "Coming!" he

bellowed back. He rolled off his bed and jogged down the stairs towards the den with an increasing sense of dread.

A rapid re-evaluation of everything they'd filmed that week gave him no clue as to what he should have be worried about. Episode one had been all about the auditions and who had made it through. He'd dutifully done his talking heads and basically said what Kala had told him to about each of the kids.

The only time he knew he'd messed up was storming off during the casting session. But even then, when he'd sheepishly returned after seeing Elion, he found out his tantrum had apparently given them a nice storyline.

Kala had met him on his return. She had calmly informed him that walking off set still wearing his microphone was technically invalidating the insurance. However, the footage of his mom's hissy fit about it afterwards had apparently been gold. So she didn't seem to really mind.

For a second Blake had panicked about being accidentally wired for sound while going to see Elion. That was *definitely* nobody's business except his. But there had to be a receiver in range for them to pick anything up, so he figured it was fine.

It had to be the hissy fit his mom was pissed at. She was most likely furious that he'd made her look ugly, or something. This was ridiculous though. He wasn't going to slink into his own living room like a scolded child. He was an adult. Resolutely, he gritted his teeth and straightened his spine.

"Mom, is everything okay?"

He walked into the spacious den. The room was dominated by the enormous custom-made couch that lined three sides of the square well in the center of the room. On the fourth side hung a TV on the wall so large it essentially turned the space into a movie theater. His face was paused awkwardly on the screen.

He cringed and turned his gaze away from it to focus on his mom. She was dressed in three-hundred-dollar skinny jeans and a bedazzled tank that read 'Princess' across her pushed-up boobs. In one hand, she sloshed a crystal goblet of rosé wine. In the other, she wielded the TV remote like a weapon.

The pink spots on her cheeks told him how much trouble he was in. If any blemishes could make it through the layers of foundation she wore, things were biblically bad.

Of course the film crew was there, led by Kala and the big guy Marcus. All of Blake's mom's friends were ridiculously attired for sitting around watching TV. Some of them were even in cocktails dresses. They were obviously all hoping to appear on next week's episode.

For some reason Seth was standing in front of the camera. For a guy with such small stature, he still managed to radiate an air of authority. It was something about the way he positioned himself with his arms folded and head high in the face of Blake's mom's undeniable wrath.

"*Somebody*," she seethed, flinging her hand with the remote towards the TV. "Needs to explain this. *Now!*"

She pressed play.

Unfortunately, Blake had to stand and watch the tail end of his part around the casting table. There was a small bit of him that was proud of the way he'd stood up to his mom and Seth. But they cut it to make it look like he'd stormed out over Tyler, the other dancer they'd accepted on the elite team. Not Mercy the average, overweight dancer. Sure enough, the show then cut to Nessa talking about how Blake needed to get over his insecurities.

He ground his teeth together. It was obvious by his mom's expression they hadn't got to what had upset her yet.

Even when they showed her shrieking about him up and leaving when he had a job to do.

The next shot threw Blake completely. Someone had evidently captured his exit from the house and even storming down the road. How had he not noticed that? How far could these camera lenses zoom?

But then it just kept getting worse.

"So, I was out in town with my girlfriends," a new talking head chirped.

That was Karyn. The protégé dancer who Nessa had marked out as trouble. The tween had come across as shy and reserved when Blake had watched her audition. Like she wouldn't say boo to a goose. But now she was doing her segment like a pro.

They interviewed everyone in different places for their talking heads. He recognized where she sat as one of the corners of the dance studio, although they'd moved a houseplant around. She was looking at whichever producer was to the right of the shot like they'd all been told to do. Her makeup was heaped on way more than any thirteen-year-old should have, and a smirk was on her lips that Blake found alarming.

Then the shot cut to the exterior of the Cool Beans Coffee House.

Icy coldness washed over Blake's entire body and he swore his heart stuttered its next beat. It wasn't like he had anything to *hide*, he quickly assured himself. But still, what the fuck were they doing there? He'd gone there specifically to see Elion and escape this shit!

"I wasn't that surprised to see Blake show up," Karyn carried on. The picture showed her and a couple of other Barbie-like tweens all perched on a squishy armchair together. They were slurping smoothies in a picture of teenage innocence. "He comes here *all* the time."

"That was the second time I'd been there," he couldn't help but protest out loud.

Several scandalized voices *shushed* him.

Then Elion's face appeared. Blake wanted to cry out *'What the fuck?'* but his throat clamped up.

There was a shot of Elion smiling from behind the counter, a reaction from Karyn and her pals, some cut-aways of coffee being made, then...

Then someone had filmed Blake and Elion sat together around the small table. Except the very first shot was of Elion's hand on Blake's knee. *"I didn't think you'd come back,"* he said while the image lingered on their touching. Blake shook his head in horror, that wasn't how it had happened, was it?

Elion hadn't been wearing a mic, obviously, but the sound had been captured via Blake's and they had subtitled his murmured words for the show. The picture cut back to Karyn and the girls craning their necks to 'look' at them, but they hadn't been there! Blake was absolutely certain. The crew must have gone back and filmed the girls another day.

But the way it was edited made it looked seamless. "It's so great to see them together again," said Karyn's talking head dreamily. She clutched her hands to her chest, then the shot went back to her 'watching' Blake and Elion.

There was a second of them smiling, then it cut to a wide shot of the coffee shop. It was just long enough to make it appear like they were gazing longingly at each other. Another shot of Karyn, then Blake and Elion laughing as Blake batted Elion's hand away from his knee.

They unmistakably looked like a couple.

Blake was stunned speechless. This was a total fabrication.

"Did you miss me?" Elion asked.

The words didn't sound natural, but maybe because that

was because Blake *knew* Elion hadn't said that. They were barely friends, for fuck's sake! The camera was focused on Blake smiling though, and the subtitles made it come across more like a real sentence. What had they done? Picked out words from the rest of the conversation and strung them together?

The Blake on screen nodded, Karyn and her buddies swooned, then the shot cut back to Elion writing his number up Blake's arm in the marker.

It had taken him twenty minutes to scrub that thing off. He'd sort of loved it in a strange way, laughing as he'd texted with Elion throughout the ordeal. That was the only time they had spoken since the coffee house, but it had been fun.

The actual number had been blurred out during editing, but Karyn's talking head was there to explain everything to the audience. "Elion wanted to make sure Blake didn't lose his number this time," she said with a big wink.

Just when Blake thought the nightmare might be over, the shot changed from the far away one that had captured him and Elion at their table. Now it showed Elion back behind the counter, making a couple of coffees.

"We went to high school together," said Elion, looking to the left of the camera.

This looked like it was shot in portrait mode on a phone. Again, Elion's sound was being caught by another mic. Presumably whoever was on the left of the shot.

"Yeah, he's my boyfriend. He's just getting settled back in town, you know? He's a really great guy, totally genuine. I'm so glad we had a chance to reconnect."

Between each sentence, the camera cut away to wide shots of the coffee house, or back to Karyn and her girlfriends still 'watching.' Maybe they weren't being shown in the right order. But all those words were unmistakably coming out of Elion's mouth.

Anger rose up inside Blake. Had Elion been in on this too? Why would he set him up like this? *Fuck.* He was probably just looking for his own fifteen minutes of fame like every other asshole out there.

Karyn's talking head in the studio popped back up again. "I just think it's incredible, you know?" She sighed and swept back her shoulder length, dark blonde hair. "They may not be together anymore, but Below Zero are such inspiration for the LGBT community. First Joey came out as gay, now Blake is being open about his bisexuality. Is it cheesy to say I'm proud of them?" She laughed. "I'm going to say it anyway."

The image froze on her beaming face.

"What the *hell* were you thinking?" Blake's mom rasped.

For once, Blake wasn't unsure of what to say. He was more than incensed himself. "That is completely and *totally* fake!" He turned to Seth. "I don't know how you stitched that together, but Elion and I are just friends. That's all!" A thought occurred to him. "Did you get permission from him to air this?"

Seth shrugged. "The laws are different for online content. None of you are getting paid, all the money comes from advertising. He could sue us, but," he smirked, "is a poor kid like that going to hire a lawyer?"

Blake was utterly appalled. "So you admit that you made that all up?"

"Of course," Seth replied. Like it was no big deal. The women sat around the sofa were flicking their wide eyes between them, sipping on their pink wine.

Blake's mom made a high-pitched noise. Watson, who had been napping on the fluffy rug on the floor, whined as well then scampered out of the room. Blake wished he could follow her.

"This wasn't in the version you showed me!" Blake's mom yelled at Seth.

Kala and Marcus had moved about the room, still filming. Blake wasn't sure if it was too meta to show them arguing about the contents of the previous episode. Maybe they were just stockpiling reaction shots. They obviously liked to film things then edit them where they didn't belong.

"You wouldn't have approved," Seth replied smoothly.

"Because it's a lie," Blake stuttered.

"Because Blake *isn't bisexual*," his mom screeched. "How dare you slander him in that way?"

Was that really what she was so mad about? Not the entirely fictional story, or that they hadn't asked Elion's permission. She was losing her mind at the suggestion that Blake could be in any way queer?

He wanted to say something, but there probably wasn't much point. Blake *wasn't* bi. Still, the idea that he could be really wasn't as horrific as she was making it out to be.

"The Elion kid is gay though," said Seth, cocking an eyebrow. "The tension there was delicious. I saw an opportunity and I took it." He shrugged. "Elion was more than happy to play along."

Was he now.

Blake ignored as Seth as his mom continued to have at it. The sickening realization that he'd been betrayed washed through him like acid. The only thing he felt had been truly real since he'd come back home, and that turned out to be all fake too.

He didn't pause as he fired off a simple message.

'I thought I could trust you.'

Blake hit send.

8

ELION

ELION STARED AT HIS PHONE SCREEN AS IF HOPING THE message would start making sense. Or that the growing sense of dread would dissipate. Neither happened.

'What the hell are you talking about?' he wrote back.

He bit his thumb and paced around his small bedroom. He made the bed as something to distract him. Then he stacked up some dirty dishes and took them down the hall to the kitchen where his mom was making something spicy with chicken.

"Dinner's in ten," she said. She stirred the pan with one hand and typed rapidly on her phone with the other.

Elion was normally always hungry. Now he just felt sick. The phone pinged with a message and he practically threw the dishes into the sink. Ignoring his mom's protests, he scurried back towards his room, opening the text.

'I saw your interview. I hope you enjoy your flicker of fame. Trust me, it's not all it's cracked up to be.'

"Well, that makes absolutely no sense," said Elion aloud to himself.

He sat heavily on the bed and tapped out a hasty reply. He

had been elated to see Blake's name on the text I.D. Now he was panicking that he'd done something to piss him off. He couldn't see how that was possible.

The only people he had talked to about him were his friends and co-workers, who he trusted, and that guy in the coffee house after Blake had left. He'd made sure not to say too much to any of them though. And anything he had mentioned had definitely been positive.

'I didn't do any interview. I honestly have no idea why you're mad at me.'

The response came in the form of a YouTube link.

He clicked on it, and after the ads played a TV show started. Blake's face was the first to come up on the opening credits. Oh, that was right, he wasn't just teaching dance. Someone said they were making a reality show out of it too. This must be it.

He was still none the wiser. He couldn't bring himself to sit and watch kids trying to dance or the pushy parents encouraging them. So he skipped ahead through the episode, moving his finger a fraction at a time, trying to see what Blake was talking about.

It became pretty obvious once Elion's face popped up on the small phone screen.

"Oh my God," he whispered.

He went a few minutes back on the footage, then watched in horror as the scene of him and Blake unfolded in all its grotesque glory.

There was no sense in texting back. He smacked the call button and jammed the phone against his ear. "This is *bullshit,*" he cried before Blake could even greet him. "I *never* said I was your boyfriend. I had *no* idea there was a camera crew there. And I sure as hell didn't give them permission to fucking *film* me at the counter!"

There was a pause. "Yeah?" said Blake from down the line. He sounded hopeful.

Elion rubbed his hand through his hair and began to pace his room again. "I swear to you. I didn't even know you were making a show until Devon mentioned it yesterday. They twisted what I said just like they twisted all the rest of it."

He heard Blake sigh. "Jesus, man, I'm sorry. I jumped to the wrong conclusions."

Elion laughed bitterly. "I bet. Can you take it down?"

"There's a contract with the production company that means we have to keep it up," Blake mumbled miserably. "We could still take it down and fight them on it. But then that looks suspicious. There's already a lot of views on it. So, the advertisers will want to keep it up too."

Elion stopped walking. "How many views?"

Blake didn't answer for a beat. "Over twenty-five-thousand."

"Fuck!" Elion yelped. "It only went up an hour ago!"

"I know," said Blake dejectedly. "Look, we're having a crisis production meeting here. Do you maybe want to come over? This involves you too now."

Elion's horror was momentarily put aside at the realization that Blake had just invited him to his home. But then he remembered why, and he couldn't hold onto even a glimmer of excitement.

Sure, everyone around here knew he was gay. But this was a small town and people just generally kept to their own business. What if some homophobic asshole saw this and decided to make the drive for a little faggot-bashing? Or what if the people on his doorstep who normally left him alone read the comments under the video and realized that actually, it would be kind of cool to mess with him.

Because the comments were starting to come in.

'Whos this prick tryna make Blake gay??????' read the top one. *'He better WACTH OUT!'*

There was no putting the cat back in the bag now. The best he could do was make sure he had a say in what these people were going to do with his life.

"Are you telling me you didn't have anything to do with putting me on the show?"

"I would never have let them film us," said Blake. "I'm fucking furious and I'm going to do everything I can to fix this." Elion believed him. They were both victims here.

"Okay. What's your address?"

THE JACKSONS' house was exactly the kind of mansion Elion would have expected. Its dark colors looked menacing in the dusk and it was so tall in loomed above the telephone poles and power lines running along the street.

He parked his rusty old car in the drive out front and rang the bell in trepidation. This whole situation had gone sideways so fast. There he'd been, just hoping he might get to see Blake one more time before he disappeared into the big wide world again. Now he stood on his doorstep, his heart in his throat.

He hoped he wasn't mad at him anymore. He said he wasn't. In fact, he'd apologized a couple of times over the phone. But Elion would feel better once he knew for sure. After all, he was the gay one in this situation. If he hadn't flirted so damn much, they wouldn't have had anything to make that ridiculous story up with.

Before Elion could worry himself into any more of a frenzy, the door opened. Blake's sister, Jodi, was on the other side. A tan, black and white beagle was circling around her feet.

She was no longer in sports gear. But even in denim shorts and a floral t-shirt she still had an athlete's look about her. It didn't appear that she was wearing any makeup and her hair was once again high up in a ponytail. It suited her though.

As she fully opened the door, her scowl transformed into a smile, then a look of pity.

"Uh oh," said Elion.

Jodi glanced behind her. "I can say you were a Jehovah's Witness if you still want to make a run for it?"

Elion laughed ruefully and rubbed the back of his neck. "Nah. I'm here now. Best to probably try and sort it out as best I can."

Jodi stood back to let him in. "Look, for what's it's worth, I told them this was completely outrageous."

The dog was head-butting his leg, so he stooped to stroke its back.

"Watson," Jodi admonished, but Elion shook his head.

"It's fine. Thanks," Elion said, stepping over the threshold. "This whole thing. It's, um, kind of insane. My biggest concern when I left work earlier was what I was going to have for dinner. Lucky my mom is awesome and agreed to save me a plate for later."

Jodi looked at him with sympathy again. "Come on," she said. "They're in the den." She closed the door and led the way.

The dog almost tripped him up sniffing at his sneakers. "Hello again," he chuckled, leaning down to scratch between its long, floppy ears.

"She likes you," commented Jodi with half a smile.

Elion sighed and stood up straight. "I'm glad somebody around here does."

The den looked like it was up ahead. Elion could hear raised voices and he winced. But Jodi turned to face him before they could walk any further. "This isn't your fault," she said, holding up her hand. "Or Blake's. Our mom brought this on herself by making this stupid show. You do whatever you have to to protect yourself."

Elion blinked. She may have looked younger than him, but she didn't sound it. "Um, okay," he said. She nodded and they carried on into the adjacent room.

Blake may have been the popstar. But it was time for Elion to face the music.

9

ELION

THERE WERE SEVERAL PEOPLE GROUPED AROUND THE SQUARE
sofa set inside the den. They all turned to look at Elion as he
came in, falling silent. He gulped.

Blake was easy to spot straight away. He looked gorgeous
as ever even though all he had on was an old pair of
sweatpants and a plain blue t-shirt. It really brought out the
color of his eyes. And clung to all those lovely muscles, of
course.

Elion didn't want to risk getting caught ogling though
when that was what had got them into this trouble in the
first place. So he turned to inspect the rest of the gathering.

There was a middle-aged white couple who he guessed
had to be Blake's parents. Mrs. Jackson was slim and fit,
dressed a little young for her age with her hair in a ponytail,
just like her daughter. Mr. Jackson had his hands in his suit
pants pockets and his angular jaw was set at a displeased
angle. He wasn't wearing a jacket, but he still sported a shirt
and tie.

Elion fidgeted in his beat-up sneakers, ripped jeans and

cartoon cat t-shirt. Christ, why hadn't he thought to change before racing over here?

Three people were dressed more casually at least. The girl with the ear gauges he didn't know. But the short guy and the chubby one he did.

"Oh, hey asshole," he said cheerfully with a wave. "Here to film me illegally again?"

The petite guy didn't flinch, but Mr. Jackson held his hands up. "Okay," he said. His voice was like gravel. "Nobody has done anything against the law here. But tempers are running high and we need to discuss how to proceed. So why don't we all just take a seat and talk this through, rationally."

Mr. Jackson had a commanding tone about him that made Elion wonder if he was a lawyer or something?

As the group shuffled Elion thought it would probably be best if he just stood. But Blake caught his eye and subtly jerked his head. He was inviting him to come join him.

Well, if he got nothing else out of this shitty situation at least he could rub shoulders with Blake. He jogged down the couple of steps into the well where the couch was nestled and dropped onto the cushion by him.

"Thanks for coming," Blake muttered into his ear. "I'm so sorry about all this."

It was hard to be mad looking into his baby blue eyes. "It's cool," Elion assured him. Even though it really wasn't.

Watson, the dog, came and threw herself over Elion's feet. She shuffled a bit, closed her eyes, and looked like she fell asleep immediately. Looks like he wasn't going anywhere soon.

"What I don't get," said Mrs. Jackson, like she was carrying on a conversation, "is why you made it look like Blake's gay."

"Bi," the shorter guy corrected. He wasn't half as charming as he'd been in the coffee house. Elion felt so stupid for being duped like that. "He's had girlfriends in the past, yes?"

"Whatever, Seth," Mrs. Jackson snapped. "What possible benefit could you have for making him look gay? Are you trying to sabotage the show?"

The guy, Seth, blinked slowly. "You wanted this to stand out from other shows on the market in the same genre. Did you know the main demographic we're targeting for our audience is between eleven and sixteen-years-old? Do you know how many people in that age group as well as those up to those in their mid-twenties, now identify as being LGBT plus?"

Mrs. Jackson looked like she was going to answer, but Seth obviously didn't need that.

"Fifty. Fifty percent. That's half of your potential viewers, Mrs. Jackson. Not to mention Hollywood is the queerest industry there is. They're finally being given a chance to represent different sexualities in a positive light and self-made content like ours is the best place to explore these new opportunities without studio interference."

"But you did it without asking us first," Mr. Jackson snapped.

"Blake isn't even gay!" shrieked Mrs. Jackson.

"Yeah," mumbled Elion. "Because that's such an awful thing."

He could feel his skin prickling but he refused to look away from Blake's mom. Surprisingly, he felt Blake himself shift a little closer to his side.

"Yeah, Mom," he said. "I know I'm not technically gay or bi or whatever. But Joey is. *Elion* is. It might not be the truth, but Nessa isn't that much of a bitch. You seem okay with the show lying about her."

Mrs. Jackson's mouth pursed in a hard line. "People love a bitch. They don't love the gays. Sorry, honey," she added towards Elion without really looking at him. "Not that there's anything wrong with it. But Blake, you're not like them."

"Well, now people think I am," Blake said. He was doing well at keeping it together. But as they were so close Elion could feel him trembling ever so slightly through the sofa cushion. "What do you want me to do? Come out and say it say it was all a joke? I may not be a part of the LGBT community, but I support it. I support my friends."

Mrs. Jackson laughed shrilly. Jodi rolled her eyes at her and began fiddling with her phone.

"Then what do you suggest?" Blake's mom asked. "We let people think you're gay? The ratings will never get off the ground."

"Actually," said Seth. He turned his laptop around and showed he some sort of graph. "Ratings are twice what I'd predict for a debut episode with this limited time and budget for advertising."

Mrs. Jackson immediately calmed down. "Twice?" she repeated.

"You're trending on Twitter, too," said Jodi. She waved her phone at the group. "The hashtag is #BisexualBlake and people have a lot to say."

"Good or bad?" Blake asked. His voice was strained.

His sister grimaced apologetically. "Both."

"Both is good," said Seth. He turned his laptop back around. "Get's people talking. I bet our ratings will double again if we keep this up."

"What do you mean, keep it up?" said Mrs. Jackson. "This is a dance show, not some vehicle to promote the gay agenda."

"Ahh, the gay agenda," said Elion with a smirk. He leaned back and crossed his arms. "Yes, next week we'll make all the kids dress up in drag and point out that Jesus doesn't *actually* hate fags."

"Young man," said Mr. Jackson. He felt Blake flinch beside him. "You are in my house and you will show some respect."

"Why should I?" Elion shot back. "Your stupid show has used me and all you've done since I arrived is insult me. Now people are posting death threats in the YouTube comments and probably on Twitter too."

"Actually," said Jodi, leaning forwards. Watson lifted her head, but she still didn't move from Elion's feet. Jodi was smiling. "There's loads of really amazing stuff on here too."

She stood up and came to sit by Blake. Elion spotted the girl with the ear gauges twitch, as if to pick up one of the cameras. But Seth surprisingly shook his head.

Jodi held up her phone. "Yeah, some people are saying you're doing it for attention since the band split up, and other horrid things, but look at all theses."

"You're an inspiration," Blake read aloud, scanning the tweets. "Good for you. We love you Blake. Below Zero love forever. #Proud. #ElionIsHot."

"Let me see that one," said Elion, leaning forwards.

"Here's what I propose," said Seth, seizing their attention. "We incorporate the love story into the series arc. If people respond well, we ham it up. If it dwindles, or starts doing more harm than good, we stage a breakup."

The big guy and girl with the ear gauges nodded at each other. "Could work really well," said the girl.

"Only *if* the view ratings are as good as you say," said Mrs. Jackson.

"I am not comfortable with this at all," said Mr. Jackson. He folded his hands on the table in front of him and glowered at Seth. "Making my son out to be a homosexual was not part of the agreement."

"No," said Seth. "The agreement was to make the show *work*. And so far, it is."

"Dad," said Blake. His fists were clenched by his sides. "You're making it sound like they made me look like something *bad*."

Mr. Jackson scoffed. "To a lot of people, it *is* bad. Highly un-Christian."

"And to a lot of people, it's an inspiration," said Elion. Un-Christian his gay-fucking-ass. Since he was feeling particularly reckless, he reached over and took Blake's hand. "If there's just one kid who watches this show and feels slightly less alone, then I'll do it. I'll be Blake's boyfriend for a couple of episodes."

He could feel everyone in the room looking at him. But he was only looking at Mr. Jackson.

He got a bad feeling from this guy. He didn't like the way big, tough Blake was flinching from him. It was almost imperceptible, but Elion could see it was there. He wanted to defy him just for Blake's sake alone.

And he meant it. If the ratings really were that high, and amidst the usual *'You're going to burn in hell!'* shit there really were as many positive comments as Jodi said, maybe they could make a difference. He would have given anything to see a happy gay couple on TV when he was a kid.

"Really?" said Blake. Elion turned to regard him. "You'd put yourself out there like that?"

Elion shrugged. "I'm already out there. Like you said, the other options are to admit it was all a lie, or have us break up in episode two. That would seriously upset all those LGBT kids that have written in to support you."

"And the LGBT allies," said Jodi firmly.

"I'd predict it would kill the show," Seth said, his eyes glued to his laptop screen.

Elion felt a small spark of pride from their support. "So, yeah, no problem."

Elion was tempted to add that it would scarcely be a hardship to pretend to date such a gorgeous guy. But with Blake's family all around them, not to mention the stone-faced crew, he held his tongue.

"Okay," said Blake slowly. He'd not let go of Elion's hand yet. In fact, he was clinging to it. It made Elion happy to think he might be offering him some comfort. "I feel bad pretending to be bi, but that ship has sort of sailed, hasn't it?"

Jodi snorted. "Just a little."

Blake nodded, then turned to Elion. "Well, this would be one way to hang out, right?" He laughed.

Elion had to school his reaction. Blake had been intending to hang out more? *Play it cool*, he commanded himself.

He winked. "You wait baby, I'll be the best fake boyfriend you ever had."

Yeah. *So* cool.

10

BLAKE

BLAKE FELT LIKE HE REALLY COULD HAVE DONE WITH WALKING to the studio the next day to help clear his head. But, of course, his mom wouldn't hear of it.

"What would people think?" she asked with a shrill laugh.

That I was out for a walk, Blake thought to himself. He didn't dare say it out loud though. So instead, he sat up front in his mom's SUV and listened to her chatter over the too-loud radio about her plans for filming that day. They had their first afternoon of lessons, and she was keen to gloss over yesterday's drama.

"Did Elion say he was coming?" she asked with an air of nonchalance.

Blake felt a flair of irritation, but he was able to keep it to himself. She was *much* more amenable to Elion now Seth had shown her the comparable ratings for other shows. The LGBT community had spread the word like wildfire online, and views had steadily been increasing overnight.

Blake was torn. On one hand, he was pleased with the amount of comments Jodi had shown him from people around the world saying how great it was to have someone 'like them' being represented in a show. There were already several blogs reviewing their pilot episode, praising the show for its fast pace, drama and diversity.

No matter how well he spun it to himself though, Blake always came back to the fact that it was all a *lie*. He wasn't bisexual and he wasn't with Elion. If anyone ever found out, he'd be so ashamed he wasn't sure he could live with himself.

The only silver lining was that if he had to pretend to date a guy, Elion seemed like the perfect option. He didn't know him all that well yet, but they already got along well. That was undeniable. And last night, when they'd made a start by holding hands, that didn't feel weird to him.

Being best friends with Joey had meant that, over the years, he had wondered from time to time if there was something more there. He and Joey had even tried to kiss once, but it was over before they started, with both of them cracking up and making puking noises.

But with Elion…well, it had been nice to hold hands. He felt comfortable around him, and he made Blake laugh too. He guessed that if they were going to pretend to be boyfriends, they would need to do more PDA. Maybe they would have to even kiss? Blake shifted in his seat and tried to work out how he felt about that. He'd kissed actresses in music videos. It would probably be the same sort of thing. That didn't explain why his stomach felt like it was flipping at the idea though, so he decided to worry about it if it happened.

"Yeah," he said with a tight smile. "He's coming after his shift. So, you know. Be nice to him."

Unexpectedly, his mom lurched forwards and slammed the radio off, plunging them into silence. Blake huffed and rolled his eyes.

"What's that supposed to mean?" she demanded.

"I just mean," he said carefully, trying to think how best to placate her. "You were pretty worried about people thinking I was gay. And I get that, I totally do. There have been some really nasty things said online. But, if we could just make sure that worry doesn't come across as *our* homophobia, I think Elion would really appreciate that."

His mom relaxed in the driver's seat. "Oh, of course. *We're* not homophobic, after all." She nodded and flicked on the indicator to make a turn. "That's very thoughtful, honey. You're so caring."

He breathed a sigh of relief but didn't say anything more in case it upset the balance again. They drove the rest of the way in silence. He loved his mom, but their relationship was better when they only spoke over the phone a couple of times a week. He was going to have to keep himself in check now he was back home. Otherwise, the fights would be daily.

She only wanted what was best for him, he knew that.

"So, I was thinking," she said as she parked the car. They hopped out into the heat of the parking lot. "You've got your first class with Karyn today. I think her and Nessa should go head to head, then she can cry, then you can defend her. Sound good?"

Blake managed to smile, though it probably didn't reach his eyes. "Sure."

As they traversed the lot towards the community center, Blake spotted a couple of people loitering by the entrance way. Unfortunately, so did his mom.

"Oh Christ," she said with a click of her tongue. "That's one of the rejects. Just ignore them honey. The crew know who to film and who not."

Do they? Blake didn't want to bring up Elion again, so he kept that to himself.

"It's fine, Mom," he assured her. "You go ahead and I'll be in in just a second."

She didn't reply, but she turned her nose up and marched

by the young girl and a woman Blake guessed to be her mom. It was like she didn't even see them there.

Luckily, they were more interested in talking to Blake. "Mr. Jackson?" the woman asked.

"Hi," he said. He stopped in front of them and readjusted his bag on his shoulder. "It's Mercy, right?"

The girl nodded. She was about ten-years-old, black and quite chubby. Her mom was much the same. This was one of the kids he'd been so desperate to accept. She definitely showed potential, but the production team had thought otherwise.

The woman had her head held high and a hand protectively on her daughter's back. Their clothes didn't suggest they came from much money, and neither did her purse. But their hair was meticulously braided, their shoes scuff-free and the mom's makeup was nicely done.

Blake had pinned Mercy as a hard worker. His observations now only added to that.

"Yes sir, that's me," said Mercy.

Mercy's mom squared her shoulders. "My daughter has a question for you. Go on, sweetie."

She rolled her hands and looked up at Blake with wide, watery eyes. "I just wondered what I did wrong, Mr. Jackson?"

Blake dropped his bag to the ground and knelt before the girl. He was angry she would even think that. "Oh no hon, you didn't do anything wrong. It's just a lot of kids auditioned, and they had more experience than you. But I tell you what." He pulled a notebook out of his backpack and a pen. "We're having auditions again in the fall, as well as some fun summer classes." He'd not told anybody that, but this was his damn school and he'd get his way on this or he'd quit. "That gives you a couple of months to work on your stretches and technique."

His hand flew over the paper, listing several websites and YouTube channels to subscribe to. Mercy leaned over and watched what he was writing. "What's that?" she asked, biting her lip.

"This is homework for you to do," he told her. "I know if you work really hard, you'll get better. And I'd love nothing more to have you in my class. Do you think you can do that?"

He ripped the page from the book and handed it to her. She accepted it with reverence. "Yes, Mr. Jackson. I can do that." She nodded and smiled at him. "I swear I'll work real hard."

"Good girl," he said.

He raised his hand for a high five, which she gave him with all the strength she had. It was barely more than a tap, but Blake shook his hand out.

"Wow, watch it there, missy. You're super strong." She giggled and he winked at her. "Now you look after your mom for me. And work on those kicks and turns, alright?"

"Yes, sir," she said with the kind of genuine sincerity that only children could manage. He waved them off then turned back to the community center.

Elion was leaning against the door frame, watching him with a smile.

Something unidentifiable swooped through Blake's insides. Guilt, like he'd been caught doing a bad thing. But also happiness at seeing Elion when he wasn't expecting him. It was strange, he hardly knew the guy. But compared to everyone else around him in his life right now, he was the one Blake felt most relaxed around.

Except maybe Jodi and Watson. But his sister was at softball training and the center didn't allow animals inside unless they were service dogs. But with Elion there, suddenly Blake didn't feel like he was quite so alone.

"Hey," he said.

Elion nodded at Mercy and her mom getting into their car. "That was nice. What you did."

Blake shrugged, unsure what to say. He just did what he thought was fair.

Instead of answering, he began slowly walking into the community center. Elion fell into step with him, his hands in his pockets.

"So, this is the first lesson, huh?"

Blake nodded. "I've never actually taught a whole room of kids before," he admitted. With all the upset over the stupid show, he'd forgotten how nervous he was about standing up in front of a class.

He'd choreographed a hell of a lot over the years. But it had always been for routines he himself was a part of. What if these guys hated his moves, thought he was dumb? He'd be crushed, for sure. But the show would fail as well. Then his parents would be pissed as anything. What if-

"Blake?"

He realized that Elion had his hand on his arm, a concerned look on his face. "Hmm?" It seemed especially warm where Elion's palm laid on his skin. Almost like it tingled.

"You zoned out," said Elion. "Are you okay? Do you need a minute?"

Blake's pulse was running a little fast. But he took a breath and shook his head. "Just first-time jitters," he said.

Elion waggled his eyebrows at him. "I can help with first-times," he said, his voice laden with innuendo.

Blake snorted with laughter and immediately felt better. "Shut up," he said. They continued walking down the hall.

The place still had a vague smell of new paint, but that would soon go with the competing odors of kids' shoes and sweat and spilled juice from their snack packs. For now though, the pale blue flooring and cream walls were unblemished, filled with potential.

"So," said Elion. "How, um, do you want to play this?" His hands were back in his jeans pockets and he licked his lips. He was nervous too.

That made Blake feel reassured.

"I only ever had one girlfriend," he admitted in a rush. "Which is pretty lame for a celebrity," he added with a chuckle. "But I never dated anyone in L.A. or on the road. Lola and I were together in high school, but then she went off to college on the East Coast, and, well, I didn't."

Lola had been sweet and smart with a great sense of humor. They'd tried to make it work for a couple of months. In the end, Blake had felt it wasn't fair on her. They'd remained friends and he wondered if one day they might reconnect. It still hurt sometimes to think of what they'd lost.

He shook himself out of his melancholy. That wasn't the point.

"I'm not sure how to be a boyfriend. Especially, um, with a guy."

Elion didn't seem fazed. "Just like with a girl. We can hug a bit and hold hands, and I'll watch you adoringly when you dance."

Blake rolled his eyes. "Please don't."

"Fine," Elion huffed. "I'll drool and pretend I can't contain my boner. Better?"

Blake laughed loudly. They were at the studio doors and he paused, not wanting to face the students or the cameras just yet.

Elion frowned at him and licked his lips. "That doesn't bother you, does it?"

"What?"

Elion rubbed his hand through his hair. The fuchsia tips really suited his dark complexion. Blake assumed he was

Latinx but he hadn't asked any more about it. Raiden had taught him it was rude to ask people where their families were from. Blake wanted to show Elion more respect than his parents had thus far.

"The flirting. I don't mean to do it half the time, but it's like a default setting." Elion laughed then bit his lip. "But it does make straight guys uncomfortable sometimes."

"Oh," said Blake. He'd not really thought about it. "Well, I mean, we're friends now, right? Or getting that way. And, well, you know..."

Elion looked at him blankly. Then he clicked his fingers. "Oh, you mean that thing where several thousand people think we're dating?"

"Yeah, that," said Blake with a smile. There was never any pressure from Elion. Hopefully he would be fun to hang around with. "I think a small amount of flirting is necessary to keep that up."

"Well then," said Elion. He leaned in to whisper in his ear. Blake could see people inside the studio turn their heads to watch. "I better do a good job then."

He winked and pushed the door open. Try as he might, Blake couldn't stop the shiver that ran down his spine.

Maybe there was a small part of him that enjoyed Elion's flirtations?

Would that be so bad?

He'd just have to find out.

11

ELION

THE MAIN STUDIO WAS IN A COMPLETE FRENZY. THERE WERE A dozen or so producers, camera operators, sound people and makeup artists. P.A.s were trying to corral parents (mostly moms) into the allocated seating area when all they wanted to do was fuss over their kid's hair or give last minute advice.

This was the senior class, so there were tweens and teenagers loitering along every wall, self-conscious of where to stand. Some were cocky and preening in the floor to ceiling mirrors that lined three out of the four walls fixing their lip gloss or stretching their legs way further than Elion thought nature could have possibly intended.

He had already sat through one of the baby classes. But that was full of adorable toddlers who mostly spun around while their parents 'oohed' and 'ahhed.' This was the premier lesson, the one everyone old enough had auditioned with the hopes of getting in.

Elion was already wired for sound, but one of the producers, the ear gauge girl Kala, was moving him around to a new position. "So," she said, pushing him into a new seat.

"You're not going to just sit there and watch this one, are you?"

Elion frowned. "Um, what else am I supposed to do in a dance class?"

She slowly blinked her eyes at him as a makeup artist gave him a touchup on powder. He wasn't used to wearing makeup, but he had to say he was quite enjoying being fussed over.

"You're here to do one thing," said Kala, narrowing her eyes. "Be the boyfriend. That means drama. If you don't bring it, Seth will cut you to create it. Is that what you want?"

Elion glanced towards Blake in his skin tight t-shirt and dazzling smile. This may have all been fake, but he was still enjoying it. If he and Blake 'broke up,' they wouldn't have an excuse to hang out a fraction of the time they were going to on the show.

"No," he replied. "That's not what I want."

Kala nodded at him. "Then find a way to bring some drama, before someone else does."

She purposefully nodded towards Nessa. She was sitting on the floor in sideways leg splits, her elbows leaning on the floor like it was nothing. This offered a spectacular display of her cleavage.

Unable to help himself, Elion automatically glanced towards Blake. But he was engrossed talking to a very excitable-looking mom. It would be stupid for Elion to be jealous if he was looking at her, except…that was what Kala wanted, wasn't it?

Sure enough, when he looked back at her, she winked. "Good boy." Then she stepped behind the camera in his face. It was like she disappeared once the thing was on.

That was okay though, it made it easier for him to pretend she wasn't there. Instead Elion scanned the room and tried to think how he'd make himself more interesting.

She was right. His sitting there silently watching was boring.

Blake finished talking to the mom and caught his eye. Without thinking, Elion leaned forward on his seat in the sidelines and crooked his finger. Blake's eyes went wide. He looked around him, as if to check if Elion was urging someone else to come over. Elion nodded encouragingly. Blake seemed to get the hint.

"Um, hi," he said as he stopped in front of him. There were three rows of free standing seats, and Elion was in the first.

How could Blake be so shy and unsure of himself? He was glistening with light perspiration and his muscles looked amazing in his tight training gear.

Elion angled his head so Blake would lean in. Then Elion closed the distance and pressed a swift kiss to his cheek. "Just wanted to wish you luck, baby."

Blake looked adorable when he blushed. "Um, thanks," he stammered.

He hugged himself and glanced around, obviously self-conscious at being kissed by a guy. They'd have to work on that. They were supposed to be boyfriends.

A few people were watching them, some scowling, some gawping. "Hey," said Elion. He snagged one of Blake's hands in his own. "Don't pay any attention to them. I've got you."

Blake glanced at the camera, then licked his lips. "Right," he said. He offered a shaky smile, then tentatively rubbed his thumb over Elion's knuckles.

It may have done nothing for Blake, but it made Elion shiver, head to toe. It wasn't exactly the red, hot romance the producers wanted for the viewers. But this was brand new for Blake, and it felt like a good step forwards to Elion.

"Knock 'em dead," he told him with a wink.

Some of Blake's confidence seemed to come back to him.

His smile became more assured and his back straighter. "Thanks," he said.

Then he was gone, into the throng, pulling the class to order and starting warm up.

From the corner of his eye, Elion saw Kala give him a thumbs up.

That was fun, but they were supposed to be loved-up boyfriends. Blake was cute as a rabbit in headlights. How long would that convince viewers they were together though?

There was a part of Elion that wanted to make Blake more comfortable around him for *him* too. Not just for show. But that was ridiculous. Blake wasn't into guys, otherwise he would have said something already. Imagining a scenario where he was comfortable stepping in close to give Elion a casual kiss was only going to hurt.

So Elion just needed to shelve his feelings. They weren't even feelings. They were lust.

Elion was used to that. Hook-ups over the weekend in Cincinnati were his usual style of things. That way they didn't have to see each other again and no hearts got broken. Live for the now. He'd never pined over a straight boy and he wasn't about to start today.

It had been a long time though since he'd had a real challenge. If he was going to keep himself in the game and on the show he'd need to step it up with the public displays of affection. But how far would Blake be willing to go?

His train of thought was disrupted by a cry from the left.

"Oh my goodness, you must be Elion?"

Elion turned to the woman who was now sitting next to him. She was the one who had cornered Blake a minute ago.

Unlike most of the other moms loitering in the studio, she wasn't done up to the nines. Her hair was naturally curly and mousey brown, sitting just at her shoulders. She only wore a little make up and her nail polish was chipped. Her pink blouse was nice but it clashed horribly with the beige pants she had on.

Her smile was wide and genuine though, and she had one hand placed over her chest. Elion switched to customer service mode and smiled back at her. He could never forget the cameras were rolling.

"Yes I am, nice to meet you, ma'am."

She carried on smiling, looking back and forth between him and Blake who was talking with Seth, presumably about how the lesson should go. The students were crossing the room in pairs doing high kicks. Blake would shout out encouragement or gentle critique whenever it was needed.

"I've never met a gay man before," the mom said. "It's funny, you boys look so normal."

Elion worked *very* hard to keep his smile screwed on straight.

"It *is* funny, isn't it?" he said cheerfully. "We look just like everyone else."

She shook her head. "Well, I guess when you see them on TV they act different, don't they?" She flopped her hand about with a limp wrist. "But you're as cute as a button. I love your hair." She reached out and ran her hair through it.

It took everything Elion had not to bat her away. "Why thank you. I can give you some conditioning tips, if you like?"

She missed the barb and just giggle behind her hand. "Well, I'm glad Blake's having fun. This bisexual thing's all the rage now." She sighed. "When Below Zero were over my heart did break a little. I'm so glad he had a friend like you there for him."

There was so much to unravel in that sentence, Elion wasn't sure where to start.

"We're a bit more than friends," he said, arching an eyebrow.

The woman went pink and shifted on her seat. "Well, I'm sure Blake's mom will want to see him married to a nice girl someday. But there's no harm in you two doing your thing while you're young!"

She patted his knee with a sincere grin, then turned back towards Blake.

"Better than being old and bitter for chances not taken," said Elion sweetly, then also looked over at Blake with a sigh. "He really is gorgeous, isn't he?"

The mom blinked, then apparently chose to ignore his last comment. "Oh yes," she cooed. "You know, my daughter Poppy and I were Below Zero's *biggest* fans. We drove all the way to Chicago to see them. She was just pleased as punch to get into this class. Weren't you, sweetheart?"

A gangly teenage girl glared in mortification at the woman. Then she turned her back on her mother in order to step-turn-leap diagonally across the room.

"We're just praying they get back together," said Poppy's mom with a sigh. "He's meant for the big old world, that boy. Not like you and me."

"I think Blake's happier dancing," said Elion stiffly, crossing his arms. He didn't need reminding that Blake was too good for him. That he was almost certainly going to leave again before long.

It was distressing the real pang that caused for him, though. Blake wasn't just hot. The sweet way he'd talked to that kid who hadn't made the class had stirred something in Elion's heart. He was kind as well as talented and gorgeous.

If there was even the smallest chance that Blake wasn't totally straight, Elion was going to find it. The show gave him the perfect opportunity to explore any possibility there might be. He just had to take it.

Poppy's mom prattled on in his ear, but Elion mostly let it wash over him. The class was moving fast, with the cameras zipping around to catch the action.

It was easy to spot the diva child Karyn that had been a part of his and Blake's set-up. She wasn't an especially remarkable looking girl. When she was on the sidelines, she didn't particularly talk, she just watched. But then she took to the floor and a hush would descend as people couldn't help but watch.

That was nothing though compared to when Blake stood in front of them all and outlined a two-count of eight he wanted them to try.

"Be sure and concentrate on your lines," he said after he completed the sequence once. "Finish every move with your fingers, toes or eyes. Nice long necks and think about your core. Do it with me?"

The kids complied, most of them picking up the moves easily enough. But Elion was solely captivated by Blake and Blake alone. There may as well have been no one else in the room.

Suddenly, the 'Feet of Flames' name didn't seem so ridiculous after all. He could take the simplest of motions and turn it into art. Every muscle of his perfectly sculpted body worked in harmony to deliver beauty and strength. He sizzled with raw energy. It was like he was leaving scorch marks in his wake.

He was aware he was leaning on his knees, eagerly drinking in everything Blake did. He didn't even care he'd tuned Poppy's mom out completely.

"I think we should change the double pirouette to a triple." Karyn stopped and placed her hands on her hips. A number of the kids around her stumbled in an effort not to crash into her. Blake also stopped dancing, making Elion scowl.

Nessa met Karyn's glare. "How about we learn the choreography first before criticizing it?"

"But it's dumb," argued Karyn, flinging out her hands. The cameras flocked around them.

Blake rolled his eyes in exasperation. Elion managed to catch his attention though and offer him a sympathetic smile. That seemed to help him calm down, which made Elion feel warm with pleasure. He wanted to be able to help and support Blake, in any way he could.

"Could you cut that out?"

Elion frowned and look around at another mom. This one was the more typical skinny, yoga-pants, frap-in-hand type. She sneered at Elion.

"There are children here, they don't need to see you acting perverted."

It wasn't anything Elion hadn't heard before, but the insult still stung. He could feel Kala and the camera on him though, so he swallowed the hurt and stuck his chin out.

"They don't need to see that cheap dye job either." He flicked his fingers towards her highlighted hair. To be fair, it wasn't bad, but the bitch had gone for him first. "However, it appears you're insisting on inflicting it on them anyway."

The chorus of gasps that earned him was extremely satisfying.

She wasn't done though. "Blake may think you're a cute publicity stunt, but I don't want my daughter anywhere near you."

Elion leaned back and narrowed his eyes. "Afraid she might learn some decent morals?"

The cat fight between Karyn and Nessa was reaching pitch. Several other parents started bickering around Elion. Suddenly it was becoming clear which were the homophobes and which were more accepting. He realized Kala was jerking her head towards the door.

Elion stood up, making those around him draw back and pause in what they were saying. "This is ridiculous. I don't need to put up with this."

He made sure the camera was looking at him, then glanced over at Blake before storming off. He felt utterly idiotic, but the camera stayed with him. Sure enough, within twenty seconds Blake was out the door and following him down the hall.

"Hey, what's going on?" The concern in his voice was real. Bless him, he was even worse at faking this drama than Elion. But that meant he actually cared, which lifted Elion spirits as well as his courage.

"Just some homophobic bullshit," he said with a shrug. Seth had said it was good to swear as much as they liked. "Sorry, I shouldn't have disrupted your class like that."

Blake huffed and folded his arms. "It was already disrupted," he grumbled.

Elion rested his hand on Blake's solid bicep. It was his natural instinct, but the cameras edged closer. So he hammed it up, stepping a little nearer, rubbing his arm.

"It's your first day, there was bound to be hiccups."

Blake scowled. "From the kids, yeah. I don't want people giving you crap though."

Elion couldn't help it. His heart melted a little. "I'm fine, babe," he murmured. They were almost brushing shoulders, eyes gazing into one another's.

This was it. This was his moment. He really hoped Blake wouldn't punch him. But the cameras were rolling and his heart was thudding in his chest. He couldn't let this slip through his fingers.

So he leaned in and pressed his lips to Blake's in a sweet, gentle kiss.

BLAKE

Blake had been wholly unprepared for Elion to kiss him. Of course he knew they were pretending to date, but he figured in reality they'd just stick with holding hands. There was a crazy part of him that had thought perhaps Elion *was* flirting for real, but he didn't think he'd act on it. Because Blake was straight.

Then Elion had gone and leaned in, touching their mouths together, and Blake couldn't deny he lost himself immediately. It was a chaste kiss, just a little tongue, lips tentatively exploring. But it was like fireworks on the Fourth of July in Blake's chest. Without realizing, he slipped his hands around Elion's waist and neck, drawing their bodies together.

It was Elion who broke the embrace in the end. He smiled and gave Blake another quick peck on the lips. "You ready to go back in there and face them?"

Blake couldn't explain it. He'd just kissed a guy. Surely he should he felt a bit wrong or freaked out. At the very least embarrassed that he was the one to deepen it.

Instead he felt like his body was singing. He was filled

with the kind of adrenaline you experienced after a great performance. It hadn't felt wrong at all.

"Uh, yeah," he said hoarsely.

Elion swatted his ass, making him jump. "Then what are you waiting for?"

BLAKE WAS way more tired that he'd have thought he'd be several hours later. Who knew teaching took so much out of you? He slipped gratefully into the shower in his en suite bathroom, letting the hot water pound against his aching muscles.

It was more than just the physical exertion. That hadn't been that hard at all. It was more the mental strain of concentrating for that long.

It had been a good day though, despite the cameras. Eventually Blake had been able to more or less ignore them. That was, until Seth or one of the producers started asking him to do stupid things like comparing the kids to make one cry. He'd loathed that, but Nessa seemed quite comfortable stepping in to be the bad cop. So he was happy to let her.

The real highlight of the day, aside from the moments when he'd been allowed to just get on and teach, had been Elion. Blake was still thoroughly confused as to what to think of the whole thing. Of course, the kiss had just been for show. But then Elion had stayed to support him the rest of the afternoon.

Seth and Kala had been all over it, getting plenty of shots of Elion. He hadn't done much more than watch after the catfight and their kiss. But the look on his face suggested he'd love nothing more than to eat Blake up. The guy exuded sexuality, totally not afraid of who he was.

The fact he was a man wasn't lost on Blake; quite the

opposite. But it had yet to freak him out the way it should have. He realized he liked the way he looked at him. And that kiss...

Blake struggled to remember the last time he'd kissed someone for real. Maybe New Year's, at a party a while back? The other guys in the band often talked about kissing like it was a gateway to knowing if you liked someone. As if that would help you get to know them better than talking with them. Blake never felt like that.

Except with Elion, it felt like he'd discovered a whole new side of himself. It was sensual and sweet and – *urgh!* Not real. He couldn't forget that.

It had felt real enough though. And hot. What might have happened if the cameras *hadn't* been there?

The thought lodged in his brain and wouldn't go away. What if Elion kissed him when they'd been alone? Would he have stopped there? He'd moved closer when Blake had slipped his hand on his waist. He couldn't deny how natural that had felt.

The shower cubical was full of steam and his skin tingled with warmth. He could feel his cock was perking up, stimulated by the memory of the kiss. Blake bit his lip. What would it be like to feel Elion's hand stroke him?

For a famous popstar, Blake had had a shockingly low number of hook ups. They hadn't interested him all that much. But now, as he reached between his legs and began coaxing his dick to attention, he couldn't help but wonder what it might be like to make out with Elion.

His devil-may-care attitude and easy smiles made Blake feel lighter. Comfortable. Maybe it wouldn't be so scary to try something new with him?

The water ran over his cock, making it deliciously slippery. With all the stress of the band break-up and the move and the show he hadn't jerked off in weeks. But now he was hard as a rock, the memory of Elion's lips fresh in his mind.

He steadied himself with one hand against the tiles and let his head drop back, moaning. All the tension from his body meant he was coiled like a spring. This wouldn't take long. His eyes closed, he pictured Elion smiling as he jerked him off, kissing his neck and begging him to come for him.

Blake rubbed one of his nipples between his finger and thumb, tightening the sensitive nub and sending sparks across his skin. He gasped against the water as his orgasm built. *'I want you,'* he imagined Elion whispering to him.

That was all it took to push him over the edge. He almost choked as he spilled against the tiles, the water washing away the evidence almost immediately. He took several ragged breaths while the dizziness dissipated.

He blinked as he got his breath back and his cock softened in his hand. "Whoa," he murmured. The water suddenly seemed very loud in his ears. He hadn't come that fast or that hard in years.

He didn't particularly remember finishing up his shower or rinsing the suds from his hair. All his thoughts were wrapped up in what he'd just done.

Had he crossed a line?

No, it was just an idle fantasy. He'd thought of far more depraved things like that in the past. But never about someone specific, someone he knew. The stars of his spank bank were always generic and faceless.

There was no denying how thinking of Elion had turned him on though. So what did that mean?

As if reading his mind, when he wrapped himself in a towel and checked his phone, he discovered a message from Joey.

'Is there something you want to tell me?'

"Fuck," said Blake out loud. He hit the call button without pause.

"I take that as a yes," Joey chuckled from down the other end of the line. It was good to hear his voice. Blake sat on the end of his bed and smiled to himself.

"Hey man. Sorry, I should have called earlier."

"Don't worry about it." There was a pause. "So, um. You have a boyfriend?"

Blake chewed his bottom lip. Shit. Was Joey jealous?

"I'm not jealous," he said unprompted. Blake laughed in relief. "I guess, I just thought you might have mentioned something. Before."

Blake tapped his foot. His hair was still wet and a few droplets were running down his skin. The ticklish sensation of the water reminded him of what he'd just done in the shower.

"There wasn't anything to mention," he said with a sigh. "It's all fake, dude. It's just for the show."

Joey was silent so long Blake almost said hello to check. "Really? Cuz, it doesn't look fake."

Blake scrubbed his face. "It's amazing what they do it editing. In a terrible way."

"How did you meet him?"

Blake explained how they'd been to high school together then reconnected at the coffee house. He became aware that he'd laid back against his pillows. Confessing to his gay best friend about Elion relaxed him, not stressed him further. Huh.

"I think we're friends for real though," he concluded. "At least I hope so."

More silence from Joey. That was unusual. Normally he would jump all over something as salacious as this.

Blake exhaled heavily and rubbed his eyes. "Do you hate me?"

"What? No!" Joey cried. "Why would you think that?"

Wasn't it obvious? "Because being queer is a reality for you," he said. "And this is just exploiting it for ratings."

"Blake," Joey said slowly. "Have you considered that you might actually be bi or something?"

Blake opened his mouth, the 'of course not' ready to go. But the memory of his breath-taking orgasm just now held the words hostage.

"Would it really be that bad?" Joey asked. His voice was small and that jump-started Blake's brain again.

"Absolutely not," he said. "No, I'm not ashamed or whatever you're thinking. I just…I don't think that's me." He didn't sound convinced, even to his own ears. He flexed his feet up, stretching his calves out. "I mean, wouldn't I have realized by now if I was bi? I'm twenty-three."

He practically heard Joey shrug. "Maybe. Maybe not. If you like this guy, would it really hurt to give it a shot?"

That was Joey talk for 'do it, you moron.'

"I'm not promising anything," he said. "But, let's just say I'll keep my mind open. Okay?"

Joey hummed gleefully.

They talked a little more about how he was getting on in L.A. Joey put on a brave front, but Blake could tell he was struggling. He dreaded to think what might happen if he had to go home. But that was a problem for another day. If Joey wanted to focus on matchmaking Blake with his already fake-boyfriend, he'd let him.

"Don't leave it so long to call next time, alright?" Joey insisted as they brought the conversation to a close. Blake promised he wouldn't.

He sat on his bed for some time after that, until his hair

had practically dried by itself. Did he really have feelings for Elion? He certainly liked him a lot.

He decided he would keep his promise to Joey. For the meantime, they could continue hanging out and playing things up for the camera.

And if something more came from that…he'd do his best not to shy away from it.

13

ELION

No matter how many times he told himself it was all a scam, Elion kept finding himself daydreaming about the kiss the day before.

It would be one thing if it had been awkward and sloppy, or stiff and dry. But it had been perfect. Blake's mouth had been soft and supple under his, responding with just the right pressure. His body had felt warm against Elion's hands. If the damn cameras hadn't have been there he would have one hundred percent slipped them under Blake's t-shirt to run over those deliciously hard abs.

The best part though was that Blake hadn't jerked away or slugged him. If anything, he had leaned *into* it, pushing them closer together. If Elion was honest with himself, it was the best kiss he had had in a long time.

He wouldn't push Blake on the straight or bi issue unless he brought it up. But it was hard to deny that there hadn't been heat to that kiss.

"Oh my God," said Devon with a fake gasp. "It's Elion Rodriguez!"

Elion shook his head. "What?"

"You're burning the milk, superstar," she said with a wink. He yanked it out and cursed. "So. You're like famous now?"

He scoffed. "No," he said firmly. He meant it. "It's like a two-minute thing. They'll all forget they ever heard of me in a week's time."

Although he couldn't deny that his Twitter had blown up at a terrifying rate. He'd turned off the notifications and only checked it every now and again since the first episode of Feet of Flames had aired.

Sure, there were some great messages on there from what he'd glimpsed. But there were also an awful lot of people telling him he was going to burn in hell for being a sodomite. Not to mention the 'enthusiastic' Below Zero fans. It didn't matter if they were screaming about how Elion had corrupted Blake or screaming about how the two of them were cute enough to make them barf. There always seemed to be screaming and Elion could only take so much of it.

"This will be, like, one of those stories I can tell my kids about the time Daddy did something really stupid."

Devon snorted behind her hand. Elion raised an eyebrow at her. "You said Daddy."

"Oh grow the fuck up," Elion shot back. He was laughing though as he slung a cup lid at her like a Frisbee.

She rubbed her nose and folded her arms. "That's cool, isn't it?" She shrugged at him, then started wiping the perfectly clean counter down. "That you can talk about having kids. Like, that's a thing that you can do."

Elion was stunned by the sincerity. Apparently, so was Devon. He felt a rush of warmth. Yeah, it was amazing. He loved the idea of being a dad someday. In fact, he was pretty set on it.

Rather than say any of that however, he lightly flicked Devon's ass with a dish cloth. "Everything about me is cool," he said.

"Well, you've certainly made the big time," Devon teased. "At least now you're screwing a popstar."

"He's a dancer," said Elion automatically. "And we're not screwing. Yet. Believe it or not, I can be a gentleman."

That wasn't really the truth. Realistically, he'd probably never get that chance with Blake. But it made him feel better to pretend out loud that that was where they were heading.

"I'm glad to hear it," said someone from the counter.

For a second, Elion's blood ran cold. But then he saw it was Blake's sister Jodi and he grinned in relief.

"Naw girl, when I bone your bro, you'll *definitely* be the first to know."

She stuck her fingers in her ears. "La la la!" she said loudly.

The brown-haired guy next to her sniggered. He was older than her but they were both wearing Panthers t-shirts. He didn't look the most athletic of men, but not all ball players were buff. He caught Elion looking at him and stuck his hand out with a smile.

"Hey dude, long time no see."

Elion drew a complete blank. He didn't want to be rude, but he couldn't have picked this guy out from a crowd if there was a thousand bucks on the line. If he had to guess from the shirt, Elion would hazard that they'd gone to school together. But if they'd been in the same year he really couldn't say.

He suddenly felt very honored that in the same situation, Blake *had* remembered him.

The guy registered his lack of recognition before Elion could save it. "Rob Matherson," he said. He withdrew his hand with a slight scowl. But then it was gone. "We had Advanced Chem together?"

"Oh sorry man," Elion said shaking his head but also chuckling, hoping to save face. "That explains it. I've purged that whole class from my mind." That was sort of true. He'd not minded science as a whole, but the teacher had been a real dick.

"Tell me about it," Rob agreed.

Now he remembered. Robert Matherson Sr. was the softball coach – Jodi's coach. Rob was only the assistant because his dad gave him the job. He wondered what Jodi was doing hanging around with him.

Now he looked closer though, she was slightly turned away from him. The arm closest to him was crossed protectively over her body. His instinct told him this wasn't a date and he was glad.

As if proving Elion's point, Rob nudged Jodi with his elbow, and she rolled her eyes.

"So Jodes here was just telling me all about how Blake's come back. Isn't that crazy?"

Elion flicked his eyebrow. "Yeah, *Jodes,* super crazy."

She hid her smirk behind her fist.

"I mean, it was obvious he was gonna be famous, right?" Rob laughed to himself. "Homecoming King and all that. And now he's with *you.*" He shook his head. "That's crazier than running off to be in a boy band."

"Not really," said Elion with a small frown. "I *am* pretty awesome."

Jodi and Devon laughed. But Rob threw up his hands. "Oh, no, I didn't mean that – like – I meant like it's just so cool he's come home. It's great for the town." He cleared his throat. "And, you know, I fully support you people and everything."

"Aww, thank you so much," said Elion through his best smile. "So, what can I get you folks?"

"A flat white and a cappuccino," said Rob.

Jodi shook her head. "Oh, no, I'll get my own."

"Don't be silly," Rob retorted. He pulled his wallet out and handed over a credit card.

Elion took it and awkwardly placed it by the till. "Okay. I'll just leave that there…for now. Hang on."

He hastily started throwing the coffees together. But Rob was obviously star struck and propped himself on the counter.

"So, you and Blake, huh?"

Elion couldn't help but feel a small bit of camaraderie with him. After all, they had both gotten stuck in this uninspiring town when everyone else had gone on to bigger and better things.

"Me and Blake," he agreed with incredulity.

Rob chuckled. "You know, I thought he was with that girl Lola Jenkins in Senior year?"

Elion was so proud of himself. He didn't even flinch. "Oh, no, this was *after* she left for college," he said. "It wasn't really even a thing, just a…test run. This feels like the real beginning."

God help him, he was getting lost in his own lie. But he absolutely didn't want to have anyone think Blake was a cheater. Or Lola, even though he barely remembered her. Blake and his ex were good people.

"Was it a secret?"

"Rob," said Jodi. She'd checked out and was on her phone, but she looked up at him for that. "Stop interrogating Elion. He doesn't have to answer that."

She offered him an apologetic look, but Elion didn't mind replying.

"Yeah, of course it was a secret," he said resolutely. "Other kids are generally shitheads to queer kids. Blake was just discovering himself, he didn't need that."

He still didn't need that. Fuck, even if he really *was* bisexual, what on Earth would it be like to try and figure that out in the public eye? Elion could make a good guess judging from the vitriol on social media.

"Well," said Rob as Elion handed him his coffees to-go. "I guess it's lucky that he had you. That he's *got* you," he amended with an awkward laugh.

Devon had finished serving her customer and came to stand by Elion with her arms folded. "Thanks so much for stopping by," she said fluttering her eyelashes.

Without looking up from her phone, Jodi grabbed her cappuccino from Rob's hand. "Thanks guys," she said, saluting with her drink as her thumb flew over the keypad. She reminded Elion of his mother in that moment, glued to the screen and her cyber friends. He smiled.

"It was so great seeing you again," Rob enthused. "Hey, tell Blake I said hi, yeah? It would be cool to see you both around."

Elion made some non-committal noises and waved them both out the door.

"Well that was quite desperate," said Devon, popping the last 't'.

Elion swatted her again with the dish rag. "Don't be mean. Nothing happens around here. You can't blame him for getting excited over a celebrity."

"You?" she asked with a wicked smile.

He glowered. "You know I mean Blake. He's...special."

"Uh-huh." She'd picked up her lollipop again from the dish where she'd rested it. Now she sucked on it like the picture of corrupted innocence.

"Will you cut that out," Elion said irritably.

He wasn't really irked at her though. He was pissed because Blake *was* special.

And unless there was some miracle, Elion was never really going to have him.

Maybe it was time to create a miracle then?

14

BLAKE

"What is this?"

Blake flinched as the iPad slapped down on the kitchen counter in front of him. Such as his life was, it wasn't overly unusual to see himself as the subject of a magazine article. However, seeing him kissing Elion was anything but run of the mill.

It wasn't any kind of a secret. The cameras had been rolling and it had aired in that week's episode. But Blake's hands still shook as he reached down and picked up the tablet.

"This," said Jodi brightly in response to their dad's question. "Is lunch. That meal you normally have between breakfast and dinner?"

Blake's dad scowled at her. It was a Sunday, so he was in casual wear, but he still had a way of carrying himself that meant nobody forgot he was a lawyer. Jodi didn't seem fazed though as she picked at the quinoa salad their mom had made her and Blake.

"I'm not kidding around," said their dad sternly. He jabbed his finger at the iPad.

"Oh it's fine, Richard," said their mom from the other end of the island counter.

She was happily opening up fan mail Blake's agent had forwarded over. In the age of social media, Blake still found it fascinating that people actually bothered to send mail. But they did. He had no interest in looking through it, but his mom loved it, so he let her handle it.

It wasn't that he was ungrateful for his fans. It was just a bit much sometimes. She would make sure he saw anything important. Also, she wanted to make *absolutely* sure she didn't miss any letters addressed to her.

"Seth said it was ratings gold," she carried on about the kiss. Naturally, that was what she cared about the most.

Blake's dad shook his head. "So you don't care that your son is being made to look like a fool?"

"How is being bisexual looking like a fool?" Blake snapped. Only afterwards did he realize what he'd done.

His father slid his eyes back over to him. "But you're not bisexual."

"But he *could* be," Jodi joined in. She was blatantly feeding Watson the carrot from her salad, but their mom was too engrossed in the fan mail to protest. "And then it's just a kiss, right?"

"You know very well it's not just a kiss," their dad retorted. He was still standing, looking over the rest of them on their stools. "People feel very strongly about this sort of thing."

"You mean they're homophobic," said Blake. He wanted to add that he didn't give a good God damn what bigoted assholes thought of him, but he didn't want to push his dad that far.

He shook his head. "They're entitled to their opinions."

Jodi snorted. "They aren't opinions. They're hate speech."

Blake's dad curled his hand into a fist. "None of that matters," he said coldly. "It's bad for our reputation."

"Not for the LGBT community it isn't," said Blake.

It wasn't like him to go head to head with his dad. Whatever Dad said generally went in their house. But he couldn't help but feel like this was an attack on Elion as much as anything else. He wasn't having that.

"If you care so much about our reputation," he carried on. "Why did you agree to this ridiculous reality show? They make up stuff and twist everything. Elion and I can't 'date' " – he put the word in air quotations – "without acting like a couple."

"The show isn't ridiculous," his mom piped up.

His dad glowered, but Blake didn't back down. "You need to remember how hard we worked to get you where you are today, young man," he said. "You should be grateful."

"I am," Blake cried in exasperation. He looked between his parents. "Of course I'm grateful. But you can't have it both ways! The show set up a story where I'm with Elion, so of course people are going to talk about it. And…" he added. He couldn't seem to stop his mouth in time. "Would it really be so bad if I *was* bi?"

There was a moment's silence. "But, you're not," said his mom.

He felt hot all over, like he had a sudden fever. "But…if I *was*…would that be something you couldn't live with?"

His mom rolled her eyes and went back to her letters. "I'm not sure why hypotheticals matter so much to you right now."

His dad was considering him very carefully. "It's important to support the LGBT community," he said slowly. "So if that was the case, it would be something we could discuss. But you must always remember you're in the public eye."

Blake dug his fingernails into his palm. He needed to keep his cool. "So it would be fine to date a guy. So long as you thought they'd get good approval ratings?"

"Your father has a point," said his mom with a shrug. She sliced her letter opener into the next envelope. "Maybe we should swap Elion for someone a little more marketable?"

"What's wrong with Elion?" Blake demanded. A wave of nausea passed through him at the idea of having to pretend to date some random guy. It was more than that though. He was furious at the implication that Elion wasn't good enough.

"Yeah, what's wrong with Elion?" Jodi echoed. "Not white enough?"

"Don't be so dramatic honey," said their mom with an eye roll. She shook out the letter she'd just pulled free. "Although I would be interested to know where his family is from. Is he local?"

"He's not an illegal immigrant," Blake ground out. "If that's what you're asking."

"And you too, with the drama," she replied. "I'm just trying to figure out if I know his mother."

"He works in a coffee shop," his dad cut in. He folder his arms across his chest. "He has pink hair."

"He's also kind and makes me laugh," Blake shot back. "I actually think it's great he doesn't care what people think of him all the time." *He's not full of shit*, was what he really meant. But if he was going to come out of this even remotely intact, he'd need to watch his language. "In fact-"

"Richard?" Blake's mom had gone extremely pale. The letter she was staring at in her hand was shaking. Her whole body was trembling.

In a flash his dad was by her side. But then he saw the contents of the letter and sighed. "It's just a prank, darling."

Jodi craned her neck to try and see the message. "What?"

Wordlessly, their mom handed over the sheet of paper. Blake almost laughed when he saw it. But then he realized it was genuine.

Someone had constructed an old-fashioned stalker note out of cut-out letters from magazines. It was quite artistic, in its own way. But then Blake read the message.

Blake,

You thought you were better than everyone but you're just like the rest of us.

Now you'll see. We belong together.

That boy is bad for you. No one can love you as much as me.

Blake sighed. Yeah, it was creepy, but the style of the letter was actually more evocative than the message itself.

"I think that can safely go in the trash," he said.

His mom snatched the letter back. "No. We have to hang on to it. We shouldn't really have touched it. Hopefully the police can still get fingerprints off of it."

"Mom, no," he said firmly. "We're not going to the cops. Keep it if it makes you feel better, but it's not like it was delivered to the house." He rubbed the back of his neck. "They don't know where I live any more than those trolls on Twitter, and they've said *way* worse stuff."

Jodi nodded. "As unsettling as that is," she agreed. "It's nothing compared to being told that someone wants to kidnap you and inject you with AIDS."

"Oh that's awful," his mom said, hand on her chest.

Blake shrugged. "That's the internet," he said. It wasn't like he was used to it. But he had got better at tuning the nastiness out.

"This is what I'm talking about," said Blake's dad, shaking his head. "By carrying on with this boy, you're attracting the attention of violent people. What if they hurt us, or one of the students?"

"Elion has to live with the risk of suffering a hate crime

every day," Blake countered. "If someone attacks him, or us, that's up to them. We're out there now for everyone to see. I'm not going to drop him just because things got a bit hard." He jabbed his hand towards the letter. "We may not really be dating but he is my friend now. I'm going to support him. You can't stop people from being obsessed."

"Besides," said Jodi. "Crazy is crazy. If it wasn't about Blake being queer, it would be about him breaking up the band. Or the way he has favorites in his class. Or some other stupid thing that people fixate on with celebrities."

"Blake is in the public eye," said their dad sternly. "And he needs to take responsibility for his actions."

"Maybe," Blake said, getting to his feet, "I want to just live my life for five minutes. I managed just fine by myself on the road and in L.A."

"You're in my house," his dad growled. "You'll abide by my rules."

"Whatever," Blake snarled. "I'm not a kid anymore. I don't have to put up with this."

He stormed around the island counter and down the hall, heading for the door. His mom and dad called after him, but he ignored them. He needed to stop letting them talk to him like a child. Storming off like one probably wouldn't help things, but he was too angry to stay.

Thankfully, there were no cameras present this time to watch him stomping away. He pulled his phone from his pocket as he reached the street and unlocked the screen. He tried calling Joey, but it went to voice mail. His thumb then hovered over Elion's number.

"Oh what the hell," he said out loud, connecting the call. "He'll probably be at work anyway."

Elion wasn't at work though. He answered the phone on its third ring.

"Hey man, how's it going?" he answered cheerfully.

Blake smiled. He felt the tension seep from his shoulders almost immediately. "Yeah, not bad," he said, not wanting to go into details. "Listen, uh, did you maybe want to hang out, or something?"

God, when did he become so pathetic? He used to have so many friends. Now he sounded like a needy loser.

But Elion didn't seem put off. "Yeah, sure," he said brightly. "At the studio?"

"Actually," Blake said, hoping this wouldn't dampen his enthusiasm. "I was hoping we could do something, just the two of us. No cameras or performing. Just…be normal."

For a split second he considered that maybe Elion wouldn't be interested. That he was enjoying being on the show rather than hanging out with Blake himself. But his response was immediate.

"Oh thank fuck," said Elion with a laugh. "Let's go have some real fun. When was the last time you just goofed off?"

"It's been a while," Blake agreed. He missed playing video games with Joey, or hitting the dry slopes with TJ. He missed the guys in general, if he was honest. But getting to spend time with Elion felt like it might fill that hole in his chest. "What do you want to do?"

"I'll come pick you up," Elion said. There was a hint of devilment to his voice.

Blake liked it.

15

ELION

ELION WATCHED WITH AMUSEMENT AS BLAKE AGONIZED OVER his food order. "Dude," he said, leaning in to murmur by his ear. "It's just burgers."

Blake looked bashful. "Sorry. I'm not used to eating stuff like this."

To be fair, that was probably why he had a body like a Greek god. But Elion figured he could most likely do with letting loose and being just a bit bad for once. "Take your time," he said. He didn't mind waiting.

They were at one of the takeout joints in town. Nothing all that fancy, but the food was so tasty it was Elion's go-to comfort eat. He always got the double cheese burger with extra onion rings, slaw, fries, strawberry milkshake, the works. When he told Blake this, it seemed to spur him on with his decision. He got a quarter pound burger topped with bacon and barbecue sauce, then all the same sides as Elion.

Elion was going to suggest eating in, but Blake was getting attention from some of the other diners and had already signed someone's burger box.

"Oh my God," said a burly guy in a trucker cap as they made to move away from the counter. "You're that guy, the one from the band, aren't you?" He laughed as he eyed Blake up and down and pushed the brim of his cap up. "Sing that *'Oh oh oohh'* song!"

"I'm so sorry," said Elion with his brightest smile, grabbing Blake's hand. "But I'm afraid I have to whisk him away. You have a great day now."

He steered Blake around the guy. He opened his mouth to say something else, but then the man noticed their entwined fingers and his curiosity quickly turned to a scowl. *"Faggots,"* he grumbled under his breath as Elion hurried them out of the front door.

Outside in the sunshine, Elion glanced at Blake. "Sorry," he said. He made to take his hand away, but Blake tugged it back.

"Fuck him," he said. He squeezed Elion's fingers. "Thank you for saving me from having to sing that God awful song again."

His voice was a little shaky, but he obviously wanted to put the insult behind him. Elion wished he could protect him from homophobic assholes like that. But the best he could do was look after him now.

"Yeah," he said with a laugh, allowing the conversation to move on. "Why do people always want you to sing Hearts Bound?"

Blake narrowed his blue eyes at him as he finally let his hand go and walked around to the passenger side of the car. "You know Hearts Bound?" he asked with a grin.

Elion shrugged, trying to gloss over the fact he'd been looking into the Below Zero back catalogue. "It's the most popular song you had, right? The one that made you famous?"

Blake nodded and slipped into his seat. "Yeah. That's why

people always sing it. It's mega catchy, but I never really liked it." He dropped his head back against the seat. "Fuck, it's good to say that out loud," he admitted. "We were never allowed to be honest like that, ever."

Something warm curled in Elion's chest. The fact that Blake was being truthful with him felt special. Even if the relationship was a sham, it would be worth it for little moments of authenticity like that.

"I think Cherish is my favorite," Elion said. As soon as it blurted from his mouth, he regretted it. That was an album track, from their very first album five years ago. Blake was going to think he was a fanboy.

Instead though, he turned and smiled at Elion. "I love that one," he said softly. "Raiden helped write it, even though they didn't credit him for it." He rolled his eyes. "It's beautiful."

Elion wasn't sure what to say, so he started the car instead. He'd asked for the food to be double bagged, so he wasn't so worried about it getting cold as he pulled out of the lot to start the short drive.

"Where are we going?" Blake asked.

"Surprise," said Elion. Then he winked over at his passenger. "I've got a secret spot."

He expected Blake to grill him further. Instead, he just gave Elion a curious smile, then looked out of the window. It was a beautiful day, warm but with a pleasant breeze. Perfect for eating al fresco.

After ten minutes driving he pulled his old car off the road in a dirt parking lot next to some woods. "Take a walk?" he asked. Blake raised an eyebrow at him as he unclipped his belt.

"Sure," he said.

They followed a track through some trees, then found themselves on a grass pathway through long grass as tall as Elion's waist. Power cables strung between telephone poles crisscrossed overhead, creating the feeling of being under a web. The sky was a beautiful azure blue and Elion breathed the fresh air in deeply.

"This is nice," said Blake appreciatively.

Elion nodded. "I used to come ride my bike here when I was a kid. It's peaceful."

"Peaceful is good," Blake said with a shaky laugh. "No cameras or fans." He mimicked Elion and inhaled a long breath. "Just a moment to step back and…I don't know, just be."

He seemed a bit embarrassed at admitting that to Elion, but what he said made sense to him. "Your life must have been quite the circus the past few years," he said. He was leading them down the path he knew all too well, towards a little patch he liked to think of as just his own.

Blake ruffled his blond hair. Christ, did he even know how gorgeous he was?

"Yeah," he admitted. "I don't want to complain. I've had an incredible experience that so many people would kill for. But some days, it's like I forget who the hell I even am."

Elion smiled at him. It wasn't flirty. It was something warmer than that. "I'd like to get to know the real you a bit better," he said. "We can coax him out away from civilization, perhaps?"

They rounded a corner and Blake stopped, his eyebrows raised. They were at one of the junctures of the grass paths. But there was also an old oak tree whose branches spread out overhead and a little babbling brook that ran beside it. If they sat down, like Elion intended, the long grass would obscure them from view. It was his favorite getaway from reality.

"Wow," said Blake. "This is…" He trailed off and looked around. After all the things he'd probably seen around the world, Elion couldn't really believe his hideaway was all that great. But the look of awe on Blake's face did make him feel the smallest bit proud. He was smiling so much the dimple made a reappearance. Elion gave himself a mental high five.

"Picnic?" he asked. He held up the brown paper bags scrunched in his hands.

Blake smiled. "Sounds awesome."

He'd seemed agitated when Elion had picked him up. He'd not been at home, instead giving him a street corner nearby for Elion to find on his maps app. He'd planned on making a Pretty Woman joke about the kind of guys that he normally picked up from corners. But Blake hadn't looked in the mood to be teased.

Whatever had been bothering him seemed to have lessened as they got comfy and spread out their feast. Blake moaned in a highly sexual manner as he bit into his burger. Elion had to shift his weight slightly as his cock threatened to perk up a bit too much.

"I can't remember the last time I had a burger and fries," Blake said with his mouth full. Elion laughed at him as he swallowed and grinned sheepishly. "Sorry, but that is really good."

Elion popped a fry into his mouth and chewed, licking the salt from his lips. "I know, right?" He unwrapped his own burger and raised an eyebrow. "Go on then. What's the best meal you've ever had? The fanciest restaurant?"

Blake nodded thoughtfully as he took another bite and swallowed. "Not really a restaurant, but there was this place in Tokyo that sold bento boxes in this mirrored, psychedelic, cyborg themed joint. It made you feel wasted before they even brought out the sake." He smiled to himself. "I had incredible cheese fondue in Budapest. Tea at the Ritz in London. For my twenty-first birthday TJ got me into this faux speakeasy in New York. We drank thirty-dollar cocktails from tea cups and jam jars and did shots with these girls from Puerto Rico."

He was staring fondly into the grass, lost in the memory. For a second, Elion allowed himself to just watch him. He looked so beautiful and relaxed.

"You must miss it," he said softly.

Blake stirred himself from his reverie and took another big bite of his burger. He licked barbecue sauce off his fingers. Elion waited patiently, giving him time to order his thoughts. "I do," he said eventually.

"But," Elion prompted, sensing it was already coming.

Blake laughed. "But," he repeated. "It was never my dream. Joey wanted to be famous since the moment he was born," he said with affection. "Raiden just has this incredible voice. It's like he sees music everywhere, he's so talented." He chuckled and shook his head. "TJ was put on this earth to live every second like he's going to die tomorrow."

"Cheers to that," Elion agreed, saluting with his burger. "TJ's the 'bad boy,' isn't he? The ripped one with all the tattoos."

Blake shook his head. "He wasn't as much trouble as the tabloids made him out to be," he said. "But yeah, that's him. He could really sing though, loved his classic rock." He laughed, scrunching up his pretty nose. "And Taylor Swift."

"No!"

"We'd try and tease him over it, but the man did not care." He sighed. "Then of course, there's Reyse."

Elion toyed with his milkshake straw. "Are you jealous?" Reyse Hickson already had a new single out, after all.

"No," said Blake. He licked his lips and frowned as he thought. "I had a lot of fun in the band, but it was also exhausting. Never ending, sleeping on tour busses, a different city every few days. We worked our fucking asses off to make it. But, well, you know already I had the weakest voice. I loved dancing on stage, putting on amazing shows. But the constant TV appearances and interviews and long hours in the recording studio…" He shook his head. "I don't miss that."

Selfishly, that made Elion happy. "So, you don't mind being home so much."

Blake's face clouded. Elion realized too late he must have hit a nerve. "Home is driving me nuts," he admitted. Then he glanced over at Elion. His expression was warm. "But Perryville isn't so bad for a change of pace."

The moment hung and Elion couldn't seem to tear his gaze away. "Sing something for me," he blurted out.

Blake blinked, then laughed. "What?"

"Come on," said Elion. "They put you in a band, you can't be terrible."

His cheeks were adorably pink. "You'd be surprised," he said, swallowing his mouthful of fries. Elion batted his eyelashes at him. "You're not going to quit until I do, are you?"

"Nope," said Elion gleefully.

Sighing, Blake brushed salt and grease from his hands and drank a swig of lemonade. "You're a tyrant." He cleared his throat.

"You're the light in my dark,
You give me that spark,
But you don't even see it.
You have my heart,
You're a work of art,
But you can't see, it's you I cherish."

For a moment Elion just stared, his skin tingling. Hearing Blake sing his favorite of Below Zero's songs by himself, a cappella, had a strange effect on him. Like it had been written just for him, no one else.

After a second he gave Blake a round of applause. "You're

so full of shit, you have a great voice." Blake smiled, but carried on eating rather than respond. "So, how did they make the band in the first place?"

Blake grinned, dipping an onion ring into the splodge of ketchup Elion had made in his burger box. "When the rumors started that a certain *other* five-piece boyband were on the rocks, Sun City threw us together as fast as possible. The official line is that we met on the circuit in L.A. But the truth is none of us are from there. We were auditioned individually by scouts for the label, then they had a weekend where they made sure we clicked. There was a couple of other guys who didn't make the cut."

"Wow, harsh," said Elion.

Blake shrugged. "The band worked really well with the five they chose, so I can't complain." He balled up his empty wrappers and began tidying up the picnic. Elion worried for a moment that was because Blake wanted to leave, but then he flopped on his back on the grass.

Grinning, Elion made sure his trash was back in the biggest bag too, then laid down beside him. They looked up between the branches at the sparse, fluffy clouds drifting overhead in the blue sky.

"You guys were close, then?" he prompted.

"Like brothers," said Blake softly. "I've not spoken to them much since the split. Aside from Joey. I think it's too raw right now. It all happened so fast."

Elion wanted to comfort him, but he wasn't sure how. "Once you're all back on your feet, I bet you'll all talk again."

Blake turned his head and smiled at him. "Yeah, you're right."

Elion pillowed his arm under his head and looked back at him. It felt comfortable between them. "So, I take it the show wasn't your idea?"

"Fuck no," said Blake. "I just want to dance, and teach, and my mom turned the whole thing into a freak show. Which you have obviously fallen victim to as well."

"I don't know, Elion admitted. "It's been sort of fun. Certainly the most interesting thing that's happened to me in a long while."

Blake chewed his lip and regarded him. "Can I ask you something?"

"Sure."

He mulled over his thoughts another moment or two. "How come you're working in a coffee shop?"

Ah. He should have seen that coming. He shrugged, a little embarrassed. It was pitiful in the shadow of international stardom, he had to admit.

"It's a job, it pays the bills. They haven't fired me. Yet."

"But it's not what you want?"

If it had been anyone else probing him, Elion might have gotten irritated. But Blake didn't sound like he was judging him and he hadn't exactly followed a conventional path himself. He hadn't gone to college either.

"Life's just so short, you know?" he said. He pulled at the blades of grass by his hip. "I don't know what kind of career I want, if any. So for now, I'm just happy earning a buck so I can enjoy my free time. Why worry about tomorrow when it might never come? Have fun today. Take risks, be brave. All that stuff."

He looked back over to find Blake looking at him with a slight smile. "My life's been one long plan," he said. "Win this dance show, get that agent. Work on this move, learn that song. Eat and work out to schedule so my body is always photograph ready. Tour, record, promote. I thought I'd get some freedom moving home, and then within five minutes I'm back on schedule." He bit his lip. "Christ, I'm so ungrateful."

Elion scoffed. "Dude, it's okay to want some freedom. No offense, but your parents are kind of intense."

"That's one way of putting it," Blake mumbled.

"So, rebel a little," Elion told him with a laugh. "You're your own man now, you can tell them to fuck off and do your own thing every now and again. You don't have to be indebted to them forever because they made you famous."

Blake tilted his head and regarded Elion. His pale blond hair flopped towards the ground and he shifted to his side, his face resting on the crook of his elbow. "I'm sorry we weren't friends before," he said. "At high school."

It wasn't what Elion had been expecting him to say. "Oh," he said. He was taken aback, but pleased nonetheless. "Well, I'm a pretty firm believer of things happening the way they're supposed to."

"Yeah?" Blake asked. "So I was supposed to walk into your shop. And Seth was supposed to come along and film us."

"I guess," said Elion. "No use stressing over what has been, or what will be. Now's the thing that matters. Today."

"Live for the moment," said Blake, like he was trying the words out on his tongue. "No regrets."

He had a small frown on his brow. Elion wasn't sure what was going through his mind, so he just waited, letting him process.

"If I ask you something," Blake ventured. "Can you not ask why? Just…say yes or no?"

Elion raised his eyebrows. "Uh, yeah, sure." He had no idea where this was going.

"If you say no, it's totally fine."

Elion grinned at him and rolled his eyes. "Dude, just ask. I'm pretty hard to shock."

Blake lowered his gaze and bit his lip, letting it slowly pull through his teeth. He appeared to be wrestling with himself.

Elion reached over and touched his elbow, just briefly. But he hoped it was reassuring.

"Ask," he encouraged.

Blake closed his eyes, then looked up, locking his gaze with Elion's.

"Can I kiss you again?"

16

BLAKE

Elion's eyes went wide. Blake forced himself not to squirm.

He meant what he said; he didn't want to analyze why he wanted this. But there was a hot, writhing ball of need in his belly that had become fixated on trying this when the cameras weren't around. Joey's advice was ringing in his head, pushing him to explore whatever he was feeling.

"Like, you want to practice being boyfriends?" Elion asked.

Blake looked away. "I guess. You can say no, I don't want to make things weird for us."

He looked back up when Elion shifted closer to him. Blake's breath stuttered as Elion cupped his cheek with his warm palm. "I'm up for anything," Elion whispered. "You probably don't know how hot you are. We can experiment however you like, no strings attached."

Blake's stomach rolled with nerves and want. He hadn't felt like this since Lola at school. That desperate need to be as close as possible to somebody else. But the thought of admitting that out loud was terrifying. That would mean he really *was* bi, or something like that. For now, just experimenting sounded safer. If it was for the sake of their fake relationship on the show, he could keep his emotions out of it. Or at least try.

Elion was looking at him with such naked hope, he couldn't help but be moved. His thumb moved in little circles against his cheek. He'd just confessed that he wanted Blake. Badly. Irrespective of anything else, that was extremely flattering.

It wasn't just ego that urged him to move closer, taking their lips millimeters apart. He felt Elion's breath ghost over his mouth and he knew in his heart he wanted to kiss him for its own pleasure. Not for practice.

He let his actions speak for him though, closing the gap and pressing their mouths together. Elion moaned and deepened the kiss immediately, moving his lips and letting his tongue slip through to seek out Blake's. He cupped his face with both hands and maneuvered them so their bodies were now pressed together lengthways.

It was obviously different to making out with Lola. Elion was a lot less soft. But he had a lovely dip where his waist met his hip and Blake rested his hand there, feeling the warmth of his skin through the material of his t-shirt. He had a light bit of stubble that rasped against Blake's jaw, but it wasn't unpleasant. Just different.

The kiss was sweet, but Blake could feel the heat behind it. "You don't have to hold back," he mumbled when they broke apart for air. "I'm living for the now, remember?"

Elion groaned and ran his hands through Blake's hair. By using his hips and thighs, he nudged Blake onto his back and started kissing him with fervor. He straddled his waist and Blake raised his hands to grip his t-shirt at the shoulders.

"Holy fuck," Elion rasped. He pulled away, panting. His

dark eyes were blown wide with lust. "Look, if you start to freak out or need to stop, just say the word."

"I don't want to stop," Blake said. He wrapped his fingers around the back of Elion's head, carding his fingers through his hair. "I don't want to think. I trust you."

He realized he meant it. He didn't especially trust himself in that moment. He couldn't decipher if this was primal lust or real emotion. But he trusted Elion, and believed what he'd said. Life was for living, for taking chances. And it felt so fucking good with Elion's lithe body lying on top of him.

Elion looked down at him with an unreadable expression. "Okay," he whispered. He cradled the back of Blake's neck and the small of his back. "Okay. You're in charge though. I want you to feel good."

Hot shivers fluttered over Blake's entire body. He nodded. He wanted that too.

Elion's kisses were possessive. He claimed Blake's mouth with determination, molding his lips and sucking his tongue. Just as Blake was struggling for breath, Elion moved to the side, tracing fiery kisses down his jaw. The hand that had been gripping his back slid around the front, underneath Blake's shirt.

He gasped and moaned. It was like Elion's fingertips were scorching his skin, branding his flesh. He ran his own hands over Elion's chest, feeling the firmness of his torso. It was odd, not to have breasts to fondle. Not in a bad way. Like the kissing, it was just different.

When Elion's hand snuck between them and massaged his thickening erection through his jeans, Blake gasped. Elion paused.

"Too much?"

Blake shook his head. "Just a long time since anyone but me has done that," he said with a shaky laugh. God it felt good though. He pushed up into Elion's hand.

Elion's eyes went wide and he grinned. "Oh yeah?" he asked, leaning down to kiss him again. "Do we need to check it still works? I think we need to check."

Blake couldn't help but laugh. That quickly changed to a moan though as Elion laced open mouth kisses down his throat and against his collarbone. Then he shoved Blake's shirt upwards, exposing his stomach and pecs.

"Sweet baby Jesus," Elion groaned. He nuzzled his nose and cheek against Blake's abs. "You're like a sculpture."

"Shut up," said Blake, feeling himself blush. That just spurred Elion on.

"I've been with a lot of guys," he said between kisses from his belly button to his right nipple. "Not to brag, but I have. And you have *got* to be the hottest. This is a dream, I'm dreaming."

Blake wanted to tell him to shut up again. But Elion's lips wrapped around his nipple and he began to suck and lick and all coherent thought flew from Blake's mind. Him and Lola had never tried this before. That was a real shame.

"Christ, you're sensitive, aren't you?" Elion sounded utterly delighted.

Blake whined. "Don't tease."

"Teasing's the best part," said Elion.

He flashed Blake a wicked look as he moved over and latched onto his other nipple. He sucked and laved his tongue over it until Blake was shuddering and mumbling nonsense. The only words he seemed to be able to muster were 'yes' and 'Elion' and not much else.

His dick was rubbing painfully against his jeans. Elion was on top of the situation though, his hand back to groping the bulge between his legs. "Can I?"

Blake wasn't entirely sure what he was asking for. All he knew was he needed *more,* so he nodded. Elion carefully unzipped his fly and Blake let his head drop back down onto the grass.

The thought of *'What the hell am I doing'* flitted briefly across his mind. But then he felt his cock released into the fresh spring air. Then Elion's lips kissed the tip.

"F-fuck," Blake stammered as Elion swallowed him deeper. He gripped at the ground, his eyes screwed shut against the bright sunshine. Everything was reduced down to the sensation of Elion's hot, wet mouth and his fingers as they tightly squeezed the base of his shaft.

He was vaguely aware that Elion had his own cock out, and he was jerking himself off. As much as looking scared him – it would all seem very real then – he couldn't stop himself. The sight of his cock disappearing into Elion's mouth over and over as he touched himself was hotter than any porn he'd ever watched. It was like a rush of fire through his veins.

"I'm not-" he stuttered. "Gonna – Elion!"

Elion ignored his attempts at a warning though and just sucked harder. Blake buckled as he came, his orgasm tearing through him and blinding him temporarily. He shot his load down Elion's throat as he cried out.

Only as he flopped back onto the grass did he remember in his bleary state that they were outside. He was too wrung out to panic though.

Elion sucked gently on his softening cock as he came himself. He angled his dick so he sprayed on the grass, not Blake's jeans, which was oddly sweet and considerate.

Blake was still gasping for air as Elion crawled back up and dropped beside him. "Yeah, your cock still works," he said with a sleepy grin.

Blake covered his face and laughed. He was slowly coming down from his high though, and doubts were creeping in.

Elion was one of his only friends in town. Were things going to be weird now? If Elion wanted more, he wasn't sure if he was ready to give that. If he didn't want to look at him again he was sure that would hurt like hell. He tried to tuck himself back in his jeans as subtly as possible while thinking of what he should say.

"Hey," said Elion, causing Blake to look once he was done. "You okay?"

Elion's light brown skin had taken on a rosy flush and his pink and black hair was in disarray. Blake hadn't thought of a guy as being beautiful before, but Elion was. His smile was warm and kind too, making Blake relax.

"Um, yeah," he said. He could hear the slight tremble in his voice, but that couldn't really be helped post orgasm.

Elion was already back in his pants, so there was no awkward flopping about as he stretched and rolled on his side. "I meant what I said," he told him. He held Blake's gaze, not ashamed or shy in anyway. "You don't have to overthink this or make it a big thing. We're supposed to be dating, so it's good to explore a little. Make it more authentic."

He licked his lips. Blake realized with a jolt that he was tasting the remaining flavor of Blake's most intimate body part. A small bit of him panicked that it was way out of his comfort zone. The rest thought it was extremely hot.

"I like you," he said hastily. "I like being friends. And that was, uh, fun. Nice."

Elion arched an eyebrow. "Just nice, huh? I'm going to have to up my game."

Blake definitely blushed at that. "No, I didn't mean-"

"I'm teasing," said Elion gently. He poked his chest lightly then pillowed his hands under his head. "I like being friends too. This doesn't have to change anything. I'm happy to be your bisexual experiment." He shrugged. "I can take you out into the city to one of the gay bars if you like. See if anyone else sparks your fancy?"

"Oh, no," said Blake quickly. A little too quickly. He didn't know what he was thinking, so it wasn't fair to put any pressure or expectations on Elion. But he didn't like the idea of fooling around with anyone else. Elion was safe. And lovely. "We're supposed to be dating, right? I wouldn't want anyone to accuse me of cheating."

Elion gave him a searching look, but he didn't ask for anything more. He just gave a slow, half smile. "Sure. And if that was too much, we don't have to do anything again, or even mention it. Equally," he added, looking at Blake through his long, dark lashes. "If you ever want to try anything else, I'm up for anything."

The way he said 'anything' made Blake's pulse race. But this was absolutely what he wanted; to take it slow and at his own escalation. Maybe he might want to try something else in the near future. But for right now he just had to process how he was feeling.

"Thank you," he said.

They looked at one another for a moment that stretched on just a little too long.

"So," said Elion loudly, rolling on to his back. "What's the most outrageous thing the band ever got up to. Any trashed hotel rooms? Hookers and coke? Stolen pieces of art or running from one of those fancy restaurants before paying the check?"

Blake's laugh startled him. Yeah, talking about something else would be a very welcome distraction.

He had a lot to think about.

17

ELION

ELION RODRIGUEZ WAS A BIG FAT LIAR AND HE KNEW IT.

For all his reassurances to Blake that their hookup didn't change anything, he couldn't stop thinking about how amazing it had been.

If it was just a case of great sex, he'd probably be able to shake it off and get over it soon enough. But they'd spent all afternoon talking and getting to know each other better. He was passionate and kind hearted and made Elion laugh.

Elion had meant what he said about being there if Blake wanted to try out his newly found bisexuality. Even if he wasn't ready to label it, Elion was sure it was real attraction he was experiencing, not just the desire to have his dick sucked by a willing mouth.

But Elion had also implied that he could do that without getting attached. And he was pretty certain that ship had already sailed.

If he wasn't thinking about Blake he was texting him. Unlike a lot of guys, Blake actually texted back, unless he was teaching class. And when he was teaching class, Elion spent any hours he wasn't working just hanging around with the moms, watching his not-boyfriend like a love-struck teen.

At least he'd made sort-of-friends with Poppy's mom, Julie. Poppy liked to act like her mother was dead to her from the moment she stepped into class, but Julie didn't seem to notice. She had also latched on to Elion as her new token gay friend and was keen to ask all sorts of wildly inappropriate questions as well as feed him cookies. But she was fun in a harmless sort of way.

Elion had a kind of fan club now. Moms who would flock around him to watch the class together. Some were bitchy, some were dorky, some were shy. But they were more confident as Elion's little posse, and generally kept the polished, super rich, homophobic prom-queen moms away. That was fine by Elion.

He was driving to yet another evening of lessons. Tentatively, he had a plan to ask Blake out to dinner after he was done teaching. He didn't care if the cameras came too. He just wanted to show Blake how good a boyfriend he could be.

There was no sense lying to himself. If there was any chance he could switch this from being a fake to a real relationship, he'd take it.

But would that be something Blake wanted? It was hard being queer most of the time anyway, let alone in the limelight. Elion had to brace himself for the event that even if there was something real between them, it might just be easier for Blake to go back to girls after this fling was done.

What was wrong with him? Normally Elion was fine with wham, bam, thank you ma'am. Now the thought of Blake being with somebody else made his chest ache like a knife to the heart.

"You're being dramatic," he grumbled to himself as he

pulled into the parking lot. He wasn't in love. That would be ridiculous.

A familiar face greeted him from the steps of the community center. And a familiar tail. "Oh hey," he cried. He pocketed his keys and dropped to the tarmac to let Watson bound over and lick his face. Jodi laughed at him.

"It's official, you have no dignity," she said.

Elion grabbed the beagle's head and shook it playfully. "She said you had no dignity, Watson! How rude!" Watson let out a distinctive beagle howl, her tail wagging so fast it looked like it might propel off her bottom.

"Good to see you," said Jodi when Elion finally offered her a hug as well.

"You too," he agreed. He did his absolute best not to think of sucking her brother's magnificent cock a few days ago. But of course, then that was the *only* thing he could think of. He cleared his throat. "So how come you're loitering around out here?"

"No dogs allowed inside," she said with a shrug. "I'm off to training in a minute anyway. Rob's giving me a lift."

"Oh," said Elion.

He'd looked up Rob after their meeting the other day. Sure enough, he'd been in the yearbook, with a funny quote thanking the school for all that useful chemistry he'd be sure to use out in the real world. Elion could agree with him on that one. He did sort of remember him now.

"You get a ride with him often?"

"Oh, no," she said lightly. She kicked up her foot to her butt and idly stretched her quad out. "My tire got a flat, so it's in the shop. He offered to help me out."

"That's nice," said Elion genuinely.

It was stupid, him feeling protective over Jodi. She wasn't his sister and she could look after herself, judging from the way he knew she could swing a bat.

"Well, I better get in there. It was cool seeing you both again."

Watson threw herself down over his feet though in a bid to get him to stay. He and Jodi laughed at her determination.

"Come on you lump," she groaned, hauling her off of his sneakers. "We're going to the ball park. They actually let dogs in there."

Elion waved to her then went inside while she waited for Rob. The a/c was cool on his skin and much appreciated. His car was sadly lacking.

He was just unsticking his hair and fanning his button down away from his chest when Kala strode up to him with purpose. Marcus was behind her with a camera and shotgun mic attached.

"Hello, handsome," she said. She slipped his mic into his pocket and hooked him up. "Don't you look pretty today?"

He frowned at her. "I always look pretty," he pouted. At her arched eyebrow, he relented. "Alright, thank you. I took your advice and I think I'm going to ask Blake out to dinner tonight. I assume you guys will want to tag along and make it awkward as fuck."

"You assume correctly," she said looping her arm through his. She was up to something. "This is actually perfect timing. You're good at this, Rodriguez, you know that?"

She tapped him on the nose and steered him towards the main dance studio. That was funny. Even though it was the half hour break before the elite adult class, there would normally be younger students and parents still milling about. But the corridor was empty.

As they approached the doors, Elion could see through the glass that the lights were slightly dimmed. Not so much they wouldn't be able to film, but definitely more dramatic than usual.

"Um, what's going on?"

Kala rolled her eyes. "Nothing to be afraid of. I just thought I'd give you a hand kick-starting that date."

Before Elion could ask what *that* meant, she opened the door and pushed him inside. She and Marcus followed with the camera right behind.

The lights around the edge of the studio were indeed dimmed, leaving pale pink spots angled towards the center. There was only crew inside, several cameras rolling, and Blake stood in the middle looking mildly uncomfortable. Or at least, his expression did.

His body was clad in black boots, skinny jeans and vest, like Patrick Swayze in Dirty Dancing. Elion had been obsessed with that movie when he was a kid. And now here Blake was, looking like he'd stepped right out of it.

A single red rose dangled from his fingers. He was chewing his lip, his eyes down cast. But at Elion's entrance his whole face lit up. "Um, hi," he said. His eyes flicked briefly around the crew, but then they settled on Elion.

"Wow," Elion drawled. "What's all this?"

He guessed Kala had been a bit more forceful with her suggestions to Blake that they go on a date.

Blake ran his fingers through his blond hair. "Um, I realized I've been so focused on work that I've been neglecting you." He held out the rose, smiling shyly in the soft pink light. "Would you dance with me?"

Elion tried not to gulp too audibly. Sure, he could move in a club to the beat. But that was more about grinding up against a pretty guy until the need for sex became unsurmountable. When it came to actual choreography, Elion was pretty sure he had two left feet.

But Blake moved like liquid power. Elion had seen him teaching and training enough to know. And now he was holding his hand out, offering to guide Elion through this.

He had trusted Elion the other day with his body, which

he had tended to reverently. Now it was Elion's turn to trust Blake with his body in return. So he took a cautious step forwards and accepted the rose.

"This is beautiful," he said, careful of the thorns against his fingers.

"So are you," whispered Blake.

It was just for the sake of the cameras. They were right in their faces after all. But it still made Elion shiver.

Kala deftly stepped to his side and slipped the flower from his grasp, allowing Blake to step into his space. "May I?"

His hands hovered by Elion's hip and shoulder. He was unbearably hot this close up. Elion was glad he'd worn a short-sleeved shirt, but he felt stuffy compared to Blake who was essentially oozing sex-appeal.

"Uh, sure," he managed to utter.

Blake smiled, resting his hands on him and pulling their bodies closer. "Don't think about them," he said, flicking his gaze at the crew. Elion's hands drifted up to mimic Blake's positioning. "This will be fun. Just follow my lead, okay?"

Elion nodded, slightly dazed.

Blake leaned in to murmur in his ear. "If we want to talk, they can't play music. Too hard to edit around. Also, can get tricky with copyright issues. But I want a beat. You need a beat to feel rumba." He placed his hand over Elion's heart. "Do you think you can do it without talking? Just following me?"

Elion felt dizzy. For someone who wanted to take things slow and wasn't sure of his sexuality, this seemed pretty damn sexual. His heart was thumping in his chest, he wanted this so badly.

"Music," he rasped with a nod. If he was going to have any chance of not making a fool of himself, he needed something loud to spur him on.

One of the P.A.s took Blake's cue and pressed play on the

sound system, pumping out a sultry, slowed down version of a Rihanna song that Elion couldn't quite name in that moment. He was too busy trying not to get a boner from his proximity to Blake as he started to move.

He began slowly, encouraging Elion's feet and hips to mirror his. Elion didn't realize he was staring at the floor until Blake squeezed his ass, grabbing his attention. He smiled and tilted his head, telling Elion to look at him instead.

Elion swallowed and nodded. His grip on Blake's body tightened slightly. The adrenaline was coursing through him, making him want to fly. He needed Blake to keep him on the ground.

They moved their way over the floor. Blake took one of his hands and spun him away, then whipped around several times to reclaim Elion back into his arms. He pressed his hand to Elion's lower back and swung him gently, encouraging him to lean back and expose his neck.

He reeled him back in with a few more basic steps. Elion knew the cameras were all around them, but with the darkened lights it was easy to think they were all alone in the world. Blake smiled and bit his lip. Christ, Elion was going to need a cold shower after this.

Blake slipped his hand behind Elion's neck, his other arm extended. He tilted his head and flicked his eyes up and down to tell Elion to copy him. He did so, clumsily, but then they were spinning. Elion's whole world was reduced to looking into Blake's eyes, following his every move.

He knew he was still sort of clumsy. He almost tripped over his feet several times. But Blake was there to steady him every time. The music started to fade. They were so close, breathing heavily. Elion didn't care about the cameras, he wanted to kiss Blake again so badly.

The lights blared to life, dazzling Elion's eyes and surprising him enough to jerk away from his almost-kiss.

"What the hell is this?"

Elion blinked and stepped away from Blake. The doorway which had previously been closed was now open and filled with several people. Nessa was the one who'd spoken. She had seemed alright when Elion had briefly interacted with her over the past couple of weeks. Now she was looking at the two of them distinctly unimpressed.

Beside her was the black guy from the elite group. His name escaped Elion for the time being, but his smirk suggested he was a bitch-queen if ever there was one. Jodi and Rob were also next to him, and several moms including Julie seemed be hovering behind them.

Great. So it was a set-up. Blake looked just as shocked. Apparently dancing for the cameras had been okay for him, but having people burst in on them had evidently not been a part of the deal. He screwed his hands into fists and clenched his jaw.

"Um, hi guys," said Elion with an awkward wave. "We were just having a bit of fun. Oh, look at the time, it's elite's class already." He leaned over and pecked a kiss on Blake's cheek. "Don't let anybody fuck with you," he whispered so quietly even the mic wouldn't pick it up.

Blake looked at him as he drew away, then nodded. Some of the tension left his shoulders.

"Come on in guys," he said brightly. "Jodi, are you staying?"

She shook her head. "No, Rob just wanted to say hi, but we'll leave you to it. Watson's tied up outside anyway."

She pulled on Rob's arm and Elion almost felt sorry for him. He'd obviously wanted a chance to remind Blake that they'd been at school together, but Jodi wasn't having any of it. Some people just got so star struck.

The crew had already swarmed like ants to reset the room for the elite group's training. The lights were back up to their usual bright white and chairs were set up in rows so Elion and others could watch.

The elite group were going to do the closing number for the big show in several weeks' time. It was what Feet of Flames was gearing towards for its finale too, so these sessions were pretty intense. It was also when Blake did his best dancing. There was no way Elion was missing these classes.

Not even when Nessa glowered at him on her way to set her bag down. She flicked her hair and rearranged her top so her boobs were even more on display. "Hi Blake," she said sweetly.

Elion felt jealously flare in his guts. This was an issue he hadn't anticipated.

18

BLAKE

BLAKE HAD BEEN A FOOL TO THINK HE COULD HAVE HAD AN actual, private moment with Elion. Somehow, the cameras didn't seem that bad. He'd just wanted to repay him in his own way for their wonderful afternoon lying in the grass by the brook and the oak tree.

Then everyone had tumbled in on them just as they were about to kiss and turned the whole thing into a spectacle, as usual. Now Nessa was flirting with him and everything felt so exposed.

He'd not stopped thinking about making out since it had happened. Images of Elion kissing him or going down on him would pop into his head all the time, often at the most inconvenient moments. He hadn't jerked off this much since he'd been a teenager.

And it was always Elion in his mind now when he did. If this were a girl, he wouldn't be fighting it as hard as he was. He'd just ask her to start dating for real. There was a part of his brain that argued that as far as the world was concerned, they already *were* dating. So what the hell was this block holding him back from truly crossing that line?

There was no going back, he supposed. His parents had made it pretty clear that they weren't happy with the idea of him actually being bi, and if he was, someone like Elion wouldn't be good enough.

Not someone. Elion. Blake didn't want anyone else. And if being real meant his dad was going to try and force some pretty WASP type guy on him, he would rather keep it fake. That way he could keep seeing Elion while he sifted through his feelings.

He had only felt this attraction with two people in his whole life. Lola, and Elion. Was that enough to make him bi?

The guys had often riled him about being a prude. During their time in the band Blake had been propositioned by girls non-stop. Hell, most of his fan mail was still declarations of love and marriage proposals. But Blake wasn't interested in hooking up with someone he didn't know. In fact, he found the concept almost revolting.

Did that mean there was something wrong with him?

He shook his head as he moved away from Nessa and over to Elion again. The issue was null and void so long as he could stay exploring what he had with Elion.

"Sorry about that," he said quietly as the cameras finished setting up. "Nessa's normally pretty chill unless Karyn's here to wind her up."

Elion shrugged. "It doesn't matter," he said.

He looked at him through those long lashes. Blake hadn't noticed them before they'd spent the afternoon out in the sunshine. They practically swept over his cheekbones and made Blake's insides swoop.

"I liked our dance," Elion said in a sultry tone. "Maybe we could rumba again sometime?"

Of course the cameras were on them, but Blake was getting better at tuning them out. It was probably why he thought Kala's idea was a good one earlier. He smiled at

Elion like he was the only one there, and gave him a quick, swift kiss on the lips.

"I'd like that. You staying to watch me dance?"

"You bet," Elion replied, swatting his ass.

Blake's good mood was almost spoiled by Nessa's blatant scowl. But if she'd decided to make a move for him, let her. He wasn't interested.

Tyler was soon there to distract him. He was the only other dude in their six-piece group and out-and-proud gay. He sashayed over licking his glossed lips and swinging a pair of black stiletto heels from his fingers.

"Size eleven, right?"

Blake raised his eyebrows at him. "You want me...to wear those?"

Tyler shrugged. "We were all going to wear them. Why? You too *manly* for that?"

He gave him a shit-eating grin, but Blake didn't rise to the bait. He knew men dancing in heels was an art in its own right and he respected it. In fact, he'd been wanted to give it a go for a while. But he knew *precisely* what his parents would have to say if he put those on.

He glanced over at Elion. He was grinning from ear to ear and gave him a nod of encouragement.

This was living for today, seizing the moment. It would be no shock if his parents freaked out over this, but Blake wanted to try.

"It's a technical dance skill," he said, snatching the shoes from Tyler and slinging them over his shoulder. "Gender doesn't come into it. I'll still be the best in the room."

Kala threw an air punch from behind the camera and one of the other P.A.s gave him a thumbs up. Tyler arched an eyebrow then swished away and pulled his own pair of heels from his bag.

Blake had planned different choreography for the day, but

it seemed Nessa and Tyler had been prepped to take the class. He'd show he could do anything they threw at him though. So he dropped into the chair beside Elion and set about swapping his boots for the heels.

"Um," said Elion scratching the back on his head and staring forwards. "So you know this is going to be super-hot, right?" He cleared his throat and shifted in his seat. "There's a reason chicks wear heels; it does incredible things to your ass."

Blake smiled slowly at him. "Is this turning you on?"

"Kind of," said Elion, still staring straight ahead like he couldn't cope with looking at Blake just then. "Also, the way you got all alpha reminding them who's school this is."

Blake glanced at the camera, then back to Elion taking a detour to glance at his crotch. "Are we going to have to check certain things are working again later?"

Elion froze. Maybe it wasn't fair, flirting with him like this. But the less Blake overanalyzed it, the more he simply enjoyed it. If pressed by his dad he had the fallback of being able to say it was for the show. But in that moment, Blake knew it definitely wasn't.

He liked the way Elion was hot for him. Lola had been different, so cool and impressive. She'd not really been one to get fazed. But Elion wasn't shy about showing how much he enjoyed sex, or how much he wanted Blake. It made it easier for Blake to want him back.

"Go dance, you prick tease," Elion growled. It was full of playfulness though, making Blake tingle with anticipation.

The first few steps in the heels were a little strange. But thanks to Blake's core strength and leg muscles he was able to keep his balance and get used to the sensation pretty quickly.

Honestly, he thought he might look a bit of a fool in them. Like he was playing dress up with his mother's wardrobe or he was an unfinished drag queen. But his all black ensemble and shock of blond hair made the look powerful, otherworldly. He almost wished he was wearing black eyeliner.

Maybe next time, he thought with a smirk to himself. His dad would *love* that.

Nessa took up the head of the class. He and Tyler were joined by the three other young women in their troupe; Maddie, Kim and Coral. They were all in their early twenties and had serious talent. That meant they came from neighboring towns and even Cincinnati, but it was worth it to get the caliber of dancers Blake had wanted in one place.

Teaching was an amazing reward in itself. But there was nothing quite like dancing flat out with people who challenged him. Until today, there had been relatively little drama in their group. But of course Seth couldn't let that last.

Blake lost himself in the choreography. It was a lot of isolation and hip rolls, but he relished that. He was extremely conscious to keep the moves for the kids non-sexual. Now was a chance for him to let lose a little.

It didn't hurt that he knew Elion was watching him either. He wasn't ashamed to admit he was showing off.

That was, until his heel snapped away from the shoe taking his ankle along with it and sending him crashing to the floor.

He cried out at the sharp stab of pain that shot up his leg and he immediately grabbed at it. His mind was already panicking, trying to establish if it was just a sprain, or a break, or-

"Here, let me see." Elion was already beside him before anyone else. He must have launched himself from his seat. His nimble fingers were undoing the strap, freeing the foot and touching gently at bones in his ankle.

"I think it's just a sprain," Blake said through gritted teeth. "Nothing snapped."

"Except for this piece of shit," Elion said, holding up the remains of the heel. He was right, it had broken clean off. Tyler threw his hands up in a 'not guilty!' sort of way, but Blake wasn't so sure. He looked over at Kala, but she just shrugged at pointed back to Elion.

Of course she wanted him to pay attention to his hot 'boyfriend' and not question what had happened. Fuckers. Absolute *fuckers.* If they'd messed with that shoe to injure him on purpose, if they'd ruined his career and his ability to dance just for a bit of drama, he'd kill them. He'd sue the shit out of them. He'd-

"Hey, hey," said Elion, cupping his face in his hands. "Take a breath. This is fine. Don't worry. Although we do need ice, can someone-"

"Here," said Nessa breathlessly. She'd obviously sprinted to get one of those single-use ice packs. He and Elion both gave her similar incredulous looks, but she just dropped to her knees and peered at Blake's foot. "It's not swelling yet."

"No," Elion agreed. He grabbed someone's spare t-shirt lying near them and wrapped the ice in it before applying it to Blake's ankle. "Is that where it's hurting?"

Blake nodded. "Thanks."

"What's going on?" a shrill voice rang through the air, and Blake cringed. Of *course* his mom would show up at just this moment. Had Kala kept her waiting in the wings? He wanted to hit something.

Instead, he grabbed onto Elion's hand and held on tight. The cameras could loom over him all they liked. This was his actual fucking ankle and ability to dance on the line. He wasn't going to act like it didn't matter.

But then, that's probably what they wanted.

"Blake – *Blake!*" she shrieked. The bystanders all stepped

away aside from Nessa, but the crew remained. "What the hell have you done?"

"The shoe broke. Mom," he said.

He watched with dread as he picked up the stiletto and then turned her gaze to his other foot still wearing its partner.

"Why were you wearing women's shoes?"

Elion raised his hackles. Like an actual dog. "Because the show runners *put* them on him," he hissed. "And one of the heels was obviously tampered with. Your son is injured here. Do you care about that?"

"Of course I do," his mom cried, clutching his chest. "Blake, what do you need?"

"Ice, pain killers, elevation, compression," snapped Elion. "Also rest, but that's going to be tricky." He rubbed Blake's calf in a soothing manner. "This is fine, don't worry."

"And are you a doctor as well as a barista now?" his mom sniped.

Elion's expression turned stony. "I'm first aid trained," he said coldly. "Are you?"

She pursed her lips. "Blake, why the hell were you on camera cross dressing?" she hissed.

He'd been prepared to deal with that when he'd been fighting fit. But he was staring at his ankle and imagining the end of his career right there and then, all thanks to a fucking pair of shoes.

"I don't know," he uttered.

"Because they were all wearing them," said Elion filmy. He jerked his head towards Nessa, Tyler and the others. "Only Blake's were faulty. You can take him for an x-ray if you want, but it's probably just a sprain and rest will be the only thing to heal it."

"I'm taking you to Urgent Care," said his mom with a curled lip. "Honestly, what were you thinking? Some stunt this turned out to be. What if you've damaged your ankle for good?"

Blake gritted his teeth. "It was just a new dance technique and an accident, Mom," he said firmly. He knew full well what could be at stake.

Elion's stormy expression suggested he still thought there had been foul play, but they couldn't really prove anything then. Blake just wanted to get his ankle checked out.

He looked at Elion. "Come with me?"

His mom tutted. "I don't think so," she snarled. "I have this in hand." She pushed Elion's hand with the ice pack away and insisted Blake use her to stand.

He wanted to protest. But he was under his parents' insurance now he was living with them again and he was frightened of doing anything that would delay his treatment by even a minute.

"I'll text you as soon as I know anything," he said. He grabbed for Elion's hand. "Thank you."

"Sure baby," he said.

Baby. Blake bit his lip.

No one had ever called him baby before.

19

ELION

Blake kept his promise and texted as soon as he'd been examined at Urgent Care. Elion had been right, it was just a sprain. No broken bones or torn ligaments. The relief Elion had felt at hearing the news had been startlingly sharp. Whether he liked it or not, he cared deeply for Blake now and was invested in his wellbeing.

As soon as Elion had finished his morning shift the next day he had driven over to the Jacksons' place to see him. He doubted Blake's mom or dad would want to let him in. That's why he'd brought in reinforcements.

"You alright?" Kala said as she met him in the driveway. It was just her today, as they were trying to keep things on the down low. She had a handheld camera with a shotgun mic attached to the top and a concerned look on her face.

"Depends," said Elion. The weather was a little more breezy today and he shoved his hands in his jacket pocket. "Did you tamper with that heel?"

She blinked at him. "Did I fuck with the cash cow? Is that what you're asking?" She tsked. "What do you think I am, an idiot? Yeah, the footage and drama were great. But *only* because he's fine and going to be dancing again in a week or two."

Elion scrutinized her. He felt she was telling the truth, but he was pretty sure they couldn't trust anybody involved with this show. No one said what they really meant.

"Maybe it really was just a fluke break," he said for the sake of making peace.

She hummed at the back of her throat. "How about you keep your eyes open and your wits sharp, okay? You hear about those letters?"

Elion raised his hands. "You're going to have to be more specific," he said.

"Blake didn't tell you?"

That stung, but rather than let her get to him, he just crossed his arms. He realized she hadn't wired him up yet and the camera cap was still over the lens. It wasn't like her to miss a chance to capture something on film.

"Okay, so Blake's had a couple of old school stalker type letters," she said practically, like they were discussing last night's football game. "You know, like you see in the movies, where someone's cut letters out of magazines."

"How delightfully creepy," said Elion. Privately though he didn't like the sound of that one bit. Why go to all the effort when a nasty tweet was a thousand times easier? "What did they say?"

Kala bit her thumbnail and narrowed her eyes at him. Perhaps deciding whether or not to tell him. "That Blake and this person are 'meant to be together, that no one else can love him, and now he's been dragged down a peg or two there's no stopping their love.' Shit like that."

"What the fuck?" Elion's throat went dry. "Did...did they threaten him?"

She tilted her head in thought. "Things like 'you'll see' and 'it's only a matter of time,' but, no, no actual violent threats. Otherwise they'd have to go to the cops."

"They haven't already?" Elion was stunned, he would have thought Mrs. Jackson would be all over that drama.

Kala shrugged. "It seems your boy put his foot down. Doesn't want to cause a fuss. He does get a lot of crazy flying around him; this isn't much different."

Elion considered her a moment. Then why mention it to him at all if she didn't think it was particularly anything to worry about?

"Maybe I'll bring it up with him?"

She shrugged again and hoisted her camera up to get it rolling. She also fished out a mic set from her back pocket and handed it over. By now, he knew how to set the thing up himself.

"It might be a good idea to talk it over, just so you're in the loop." The light started blinking to show the camera was recording. "Now, with his ankle. The important thing is that he's already recovering." She jerked her head towards the door. "You want to head on in? Our woman on the inside is expecting you."

Elion shook off his worries about the letters and smiled. At least there was one other member of the Jackson family who was on his side.

Kala filmed him as he knocked lightly on the door. It opened almost immediately, but as usual he wasn't given the chance to greet Jodi first. "Oh yes, good girl," he cooed as he bent down to cuddle and stroke Watson, her long ears flapping around her head as she scrambled to say hello. She was on her best behavior though and didn't bark or howl.

"Hey dude," said Jodi as she ushered him into the foyer. Elion still wasn't getting over this place. This entire hall was probably half the size of his and his mom's whole house.

Jodi quickly hurried him upstairs with Kala in tow. Elion

suspected they were going for a forbidden romance storyline for this episode, but he didn't care. He'd play along so long as that meant he could keep seeing Blake.

Urgh, he was pathetic.

Jodi saw him to Blake's bedroom door. "I'll leave you to it," she said. With a flick of her signature long ponytail she headed down the corridor, presumably to her own room. Watson stayed behind though, wagging her tail and looking up at Elion's expectantly.

Kala nodded towards the door. So Elion knocked.

"Come in," Blake's voice sounded from the other side.

Elion pushed the door open. Blake's bedroom was large and looked like something out of a magazine. Varying shades of grey and metal finishes gave it a hyper-masculine feel and there were almost no personal touches to be seen in the decoration. A framed portrait of his family hung on the wall as well as an official shot of Below Zero winning their Grammy for best music video a few years ago.

"It must be hard to jerk off with those guys all watching," he said with a grin, pointing at both frames. It was easier to crack a joke than acknowledge how good it was to see Blake propped up in bed, fully washed and clothed, his left foot resting on three extra pillows. It was wrapped and Elion could see several discarded ice packs on the nightstand, so he was reassured that he was looking after it properly.

Blake laughed at his joke and smiled warmly at him. "You made it," he said. He patted the bed, encouraging Elion to come sit beside him.

Although he was wearing sweatpants and a t-shirt, it still felt strangely intimate. Obviously, Kala and her camera were on hand to help diffuse any real tension they might have felt. She followed Elion, and another camera operator that had already been set up in the room rearranged themselves to point at Blake.

"How are you feeling?" Elion asked. He rested his hand on Blake's thigh. As annoying as having the camera there was, it also meant he could get away with flirting more.

"Honestly alright," said Blake, the relief clear in his voice. "It's going to be fine. Oh, hey Wats!"

He leaned down to pet Watson's head. She had her front paws on the side of the bed and was obviously asking to get up. Elion was almost certain that wasn't something Mrs. Jackson would allow, so when Blake reached over to pull her up, he immediately helped.

Now happy she was not missing out, Watson circled once, then dropped between Blake and Elion so they could both pet her.

"So you'll be fine to dance again?" Elion asked.

Blake's relief became even more evident. "Absolutely. This ankle has gone before, so I know how to ease it back up to strength. I'll wear a support for training and thank God it's not my fouette foot." Elion looked at him blankly. "You know when I turn on one foot round and round with my other leg held straight out? That."

"Oh." Elion nodded. That was a good thing then. That was one of Blake's most impressive moves.

He glanced over at Kala who gave him the smallest of nods.

"Uh," he said, feeling awkward. "So, um, I heard you got some letters. Like, creepy ones?"

Blake sighed and stared daggers at Kala. "Did you now?" He didn't seem mad at Elion though. Instead, he took his hand and held it tight. "They're nothing, I didn't want to worry you."

Elion looked at him, reading between the lines. "They're just dumb letters, aren't they? I mean, I don't like the idea of someone threatening you. But they're just stupid. Right?"

"They don't seem to like you very much," Blake said

heavily. He reached into one of the drawers by his bed and pulled out a couple of letters. "This one came this morning. I didn't…I didn't want to hurt your feelings."

You can do so much better than that fence-hopper spic.

Baby we belong together. Don't make me beg.

Soon you'll see. I've always loved you.

"Well, she's obviously not the whole nine yards, is she?" Elion said brightly, handing the letters back.

Blake blinked at him. "You're not upset?"

Of course he was upset. There was a lump in his throat from the fact that even though he'd only been to Mexico once in his whole fucking life, people still called him and his mom names like that. He was enraged that some deluded woman out there was so angry at the idea of him and Elion being together that she'd wasted her time making these awful notes. It burned that everything he was feeling was unjustified, because after all, they weren't *really together*.

But the way Blake was looking at him with such concern made it better. The game wasn't over yet. There was still a chance this could become something real.

He smiled at Blake and rubbed his leg. "It's not the first time someone's called me names, believe it or not."

Blake scowled. "Yeah, but they're using me to insult you."

Elion was genuinely touched. It was beyond awful, having someone call you names based on nothing more than the color of your skin. Elion had been born in America, he was a damn American. But some people always wanted to treat him as less.

But with Blake looking at him like that, it became fractionally more bearable.

"It's fine, baby," he said.

There it was again. He thought Blake's face had lit up at the pet name yesterday evening, and it did it again now.

"So," he said, swiftly changing topics. "Until you're better, are you going to be cooped up here? Because I had hoped to take you out last night before you threw a diva fit and pretended to break your leg."

Blake laughed and poked him playfully on his arm. "Actually," he said. He stopped fussing over Watson and picked up his phone. "I was just talking with Joey. His agent, Martha, has a proposition for me."

"Yeah?" Elion waggled his eyebrows suggestively and Blake slapped his knee.

"Get your mind out of the gutter." He scrolled though his phone. "Okay, so in a few days it's the Nickelodeon Kid's Choice Awards in L.A. Joey is already going to present an award, but his partner dropped out last night. They wondered if I'd step in. I'll definitely be able to walk by then," he added as if sensing Elion's question.

He smiled. "That's great," he said. "Keeps your face out there and gives you a chance to see your buddy again." He rubbed his thumb against Blake's leg in a comforting gesture. "You going to say yes?"

Blake bit his lip and looked at his phone screen. "Well, since you ask, I wanted to check with you first. I get a plus one to the awards."

It took a second for what Blake was asking to register. "You want me to go with you? To California?" He'd hardly ever even been to Indiana, let alone the West Coast.

Blake occupied himself stroking Watson's head again. "I mean, only if you want to?"

"Are you kidding?" Elion cried. "I'd love to! Do we get to walk the red carpet? Will I need a tux?"

Blake beamed at him. "Yeah, all those things," he said. "When I feel better we can go shopping if you like? Find something together."

Elion was almost bouncing with excitement. "Yeah. Yes, I'd like that." Suddenly, the next few days were looking very exciting indeed.

20

ELION

N<small>ATURALLY</small> B<small>LAKE'S</small> <small>PARENTS WEREN'T WHOLLY KEEN ON THE</small> two of them running off on a trip together. But Joey's agent had only secured two event and plane tickets and just the one hotel room for him and Blake. For a while, Elion seriously thought Mrs. Jackson was going to rebel and book her own trip. But Elion had a suspicion the show runner Seth managed to say something to convince her to stay behind.

Whatever it was, Elion was extremely grateful. He was beyond excited to be going away with Blake. They could have been going anywhere and he would have been psyched, but the fact it was to a glitzy awards show in sunny California was even better.

As promised, Blake had taken him shopping and they'd gotten complimentary suits. Blake's was a darker purple and Elion's more of a lilac, with white shirts, grey-ish purple accessories and fancy Italian leather shoes.

Blake insisted on paying for everything. Ordinarily, Elion liked to try and contribute his fair share. But there was no way on Earth he'd be able to afford those prices, so his pride had stepped aside and he'd allowed Blake to treat him. Who knew if it would happen again, anyway? Elion was okay accepting a gift if it was possibly the only one he was ever going to get from him.

The plane journey was just four hours but he and Blake had been granted seats in first, whereas the crew were confined to economy and their camera equipment to the hold. It wasn't like he and Blake could do anything surrounded by people anyway, but it was nice to relax and not feel like they were being recorded for once.

They chatted quietly about nothing in particular and half watched an action film on the small screens from their arm rests. Elion reveled in how normal and uneventful it was. Like they were a real couple. Even when a teenage girl came running up to Blake as they were exiting the plane it didn't burst his bubble. Because when she tearfully asked for his autograph on the back of her boarding pass, she then also asked for Elion's.

"You guys are so awesome," she managed to choke out, her voice slightly lisped from the braces she wore. "I started taking dance classes because of you, contemporary *and* ballet."

Blake's face was pure delight as Elion scribbled his signature on the cardboard next to his. "That's amazing, you keep at it honey."

"Thank you, thank you," she stammered as she ran back to her folks.

Elion couldn't stop smiling as they went to get their bags from the carousel. "That was pretty neat," he admitted. Knowing Blake had inspired someone to pursue their passion almost made all the shit they got online worth it.

"I know," Blake agreed. Then he took his hand.

Elion was sort of aware of people looking and some taking photos. Kala got her smaller camera out of hand baggage and was obviously filming them. But Blake's hand felt like a shield between Elion and the world. He clung to it and leaned into his body, letting everything else blur into the background.

They were only there for just one night and in no time they were in a car getting whisked off to their fancy hotel to get ready for the awards. It showed how nervous Elion was as he didn't try to flirt or make a pass even though the both of them were running around having showers and grooming with nothing but towels around their waists.

He wasn't totally brain dead though. So he did register how stunning Blake looked with his shirt off, glistening with droplets of water clinging to his golden skin. He just didn't have the energy to do anything about it.

It hadn't really occurred to him that he'd actually have to walk the red carpet. That he would be there as Blake's boyfriend. That there would be reporters and bloggers and people scrutinizing them. Fuck. He wasn't anybody. He wasn't famous. He was just some guy who worked at a coffee shop that happened to go to school with a dude from a boy band. It was by accident he'd got himself on the show.

As he fumbled with his tie for the third time he was just about ready to throw the damn thing across the room, when he felt deft fingers slip around his collar and Blake appeared behind him. "It's going to be fine," he murmured in his ear as he expertly knotted the tie. He felt warm and reassuring with his chest pressed against Elion's back. "I'll be right there with you, I promise."

Elion took a shaky breath and gave him half a smile. "You must be used to this by now," he said.

Blake shook his head. "Just learned how to deal with it." He smoothed the finished tie down and turned Elion to take in his finished look. They were about the same height; Blake was an inch or two taller, but it was easy for Elion to look into his eyes. "Perfect," he said, holding his hands.

Elion was a bag of nerves. Part of him wanted to seize Blake and kiss him senseless, demanding that they date for real and take him to bed to utterly ravish him. The other was so scared that he was about to set a foot wrong with some unknown etiquette that he thought he was going to puke.

"Shall we go down to the lobby?" he asked, stepping away and rubbing his hands on his thighs.

Blake blinked then smiled at him. "Of course."

On the car journey over, Blake explained how it would work. They would walk the carpet – orange, not red in this instance – and talk with reporters. "You don't have to say anything if you don't want to," Blake assured him.

Elion knew he was being uncharacteristically quiet, so when Blake took his hand again, he let him.

Then they'd mingle for a cocktail reception, take their seats, and enjoy the show. Blake's award was about halfway through, so that was the only time he would leave Elion's side. In the safety of the auditorium though, Elion didn't think he would mind that so much.

Then there would be the inevitable after parties. As the ceremony was starting in the late afternoon, there were apparently several events Blake was expected to attend. But Elion would deal with that when the time came. For now, it was time to get out of the car.

The cameras started flashing as soon as the door opened. Elion's heart raced in his chest as he slid out after Blake. He didn't let go of Elion's hand as they stood, waving to the crowds with his other free hand.

The show was being held at the Galen Center in Los Angeles. It was a big, square, red and cream building with palm trees swaying along the exterior walls. The carpet was indeed orange and stretched out before them towards the main entrance of the arena.

Blake's laughter as people screamed for him was

infectious and Elion felt himself relaxing. People were chanting for their attention. There was a chorus of *'Oh oh oohh!'* that dozens of people sang at the top of their lungs.

Apparently, their 'ship' name was Belion. As they slowly made their way along the carpet, Elion could see people had made signs.

"We love you Belion!" some tearful girls screamed at them. Blake ignored the first few reporters hanging over the railings and took Elion to go say hi to the fans.

Like at the airport, the sobbing, shaking girls wanted both of their autographs, which Elion couldn't quite believe. But he followed Blake's lead, talking to each girl in turn and giving them a hug once he'd signed whatever they had in their hands.

"It's so great to meet you," he said over and over, meaning it ever time.

The reporters were still calling out to them. But before he and Blake had a chance to move over to them, there was a hurtling ball of black suit and curly hair that launched itself onto Blake's back.

"DUDE!" the excitable ball screeched. Blake roared back in his face as he turned and hugged him with lots of back slapping. The cameras – both from Feet of Flames and all kinds of other shows – swarmed around them to capture the moment Blake and Joey from Below Zero reunited.

Elion stepped back gracefully. He was happy for them as they talked over one another, saying how much they'd missed each other. The reporters and bloggers were keen to ask them many questions and the guys stood with their arms slug over each other's shoulders to answer them. The crowd started singing *'Oh oh oohh!"* again.

Elion had never asked about Joey. He was openly gay and by all accounts Blake's best friend. Was there more to it than that?

Joey was cute, there was no denying it. He had a mop of blond highlighted curls and green eyes that sparkled. Smaller in almost every way than Blake, he also had a baby face and had always been marketed as the 'cute' one of the band.

Maybe that was who Blake would rather be with if he was actually bi. At this juncture, Elion was convinced it wasn't a case of 'if' but 'when' he felt able to come out. So, when he did, was Elion just the warm up so he could go back to Joey?

The thought stung and made his nausea come back in full force. But if that was the case, he resolutely promised himself that he'd accept that with humility. He was here to support Blake through the show and his self-discovery. The chances of Elion being his 'happy ever after' were never very high.

Except Blake suddenly looked around confused, ignoring the reporter who currently had a microphone in his face. He stopped searching once he spotted Elion. "Come here," he cried, waving him over eagerly.

Elion almost checked behind himself to see if Blake meant somebody else. But he didn't. He was looking right at Elion.

So he eased his way through the small throng that had gathered and stood by Blake's side. He didn't hesitate to wrap his arm around his waist and kiss him on the temple. "Joey, this is my boyfriend, Elion."

Joey managed a handshake before the questions started up again. This time, some were even directed towards Elion. They were mostly what he thought about Blake and his dancing, rather than about himself. But that was fine. Because Blake's hand didn't leave his hip the entire time and his thumb rubbed in little circles, reassuring Elion that he wasn't going anywhere.

The rest of the orange carpet was a whirl. Elion lost track of the number of truly famous people he saw. Some even came over to say hello, which stunned Elion into silence most of the time. Blake did a great job mingling with everyone though, and his hand only left Elion's waist to take his hand so they could move around more easily together.

Joey stuck by them, not close enough to be intrusive, but near enough to pop back in whenever people wanted Below Zero photos. He was good at playing the crowd.

Eventually, they made it into the Galen Center building and out of the sunshine. Elion had sort of wished he'd brought shades with him, but apparently that would look bad in photos. Better to squint and have your face seen. But the a/c was a nice relief as much as the champagne flute pressed into his hand by a waitress.

"Cheers," said Blake, holding up his own glass.

Elion licked his lips and lightly chinked the two flutes together. *"Salud,"* he toasted back.

They mingled for a little while but then Blake was accosted by a biracial girl he was sure was from a British girl band. He was about to follow them as he had been doing for the rest of the afternoon, when he felt a tug on his arm.

"I'll entertain him for a minute," said Joey brightly, shooing Blake and the girl away.

Elion suddenly felt nervous. He chewed on his lip as Joey steered them to swap their empty glasses for full ones.

"So, you know what I'm going to ask," he said once they were a little away from anyone who might overhear.

"How I get my hair so shiny?" Elion suggested, attempting to cover up his nerves. "Because it's just coconut oil, my friend."

Joey's mouth twitched at the corner, but he didn't smile. "Blake said it was all fake."

Elion threw up his free hand and darted his eyes left and right to see if anyone had heard. "Look, it wasn't our fault, okay. We were tricked. But we have to keep it up for now. Please don't make Blake out to be a liar."

Joey watched him for a moment, then sipped his champagne. "So it's true?"

Elion took a larger gulp of his own drink. "It's...complicated."

"Because," said Joey, leaning in and slipping his hand across Elion's back. "He looks at you like you hung the moon."

Elion just stared as Joey moved away again and smiled at him. "Huh?" he uttered.

"Are you telling me you two haven't..." He let the pause do the talking. "At all?"

Elion obviously had a terrible poker face, because Joey grinned at him. "Okay," he said hastily. He had no idea if he was making a terrible mess of things or not. "Blake's figuring some stuff out, and I'm helping him. He's my friend and I want him to be happy, but he needs to do some soul searching and work out some things about himself."

"He's bi," said Joey bluntly. "And I'm almost certain he's demi too." He touched Elion's arm affectionately. "You must be pretty special."

Elion couldn't help but look over to where Blake was taking photos with the girl band. "Really?" he said faintly.

Joey shrugged when he turned back to him. "I've known him a pretty long time. I've never seen him get like this with anyone." He rolled his eyes fondly. "He talks about you *all* the time."

That made Elion laugh, but also he felt like firecrackers were going off in his chest. Did this mean he really had a chance?

"Question is," said Joey, arching an eyebrow, "how do you feel about him?"

"Oh man, I'm crazy about him," he said in one rushed breath. He probably should have kept his fat mouth shut, but if what Joey was saying was true, he didn't want Blake's BFF to be in any doubt of his intentions. "I can't…" He shook his head. "I'm going along with this fake thing because I don't want to lose him. But…do you think I really have a shot if I made a move? For real?"

He could hear the desperation in his voice, but he had a feeling that went in his favor as Joey slipped his arm around his shoulders. "I think you do. Don't let that ridiculous show get in the way of something real. Blake might need just a bit of help to be brave for this one."

Elion looked him square in the eye. "And I wouldn't be getting in your way if I did that?"

Thankfully, Joey laughed loud enough to get the attention of several people around them. But he kept his voice low to talk to Elion. "He's my brother. I love him more than pretty much anyone on the planet. But no, you're not getting in my way. In fact, you have my blessing," he said with a wink.

Relief coursed through Elion's body. "Thanks, man," he mumbled.

Joey shook his head. "Don't mention it. Now how about we go rescue your *beau* before those girls eat him alive?"

Elion fully endorsed that plan.

21

BLAKE

BLAKE HAD BEEN A LITTLE NERVOUS AS TO WHY JOEY HAD wanted to talk to Elion alone. But the two of them had come sauntering back over with smiles on their faces, relaxed and happy. So it couldn't have been that bad.

Shortly after they'd been able to take their seats. The inside of the auditorium was decorated like some sort of Dr. Seuss wonderland, with whacky shapes and bright colors forming the basis of the stage and the areas around it.

"Wow," said Elion, craning his neck to take it all in. Blake squeezed his hand, so happy he was able to share this with him. It was funny. He would have sworn that when the band had split, he wouldn't miss this side of things. But here with Elion and Joey he was having a wonderful evening.

"Thank you," he whispered in his ear. "For being here."

"Thanks for inviting me," Elion replied a little bashfully.

He sat in between Elion and Joey, who was on the aisle end. That was so the two of them could slip out easily enough when it was their turn to go present. He was a little nervous, but that was always the way when he wasn't just dancing. He was sure he could read the tele-prompter okay without fumbling.

As the lights dimmed and the show started Elion watched everything with the eagerness of a child at Christmas. Blake found himself paying attention to him over the performers and presenters half the time. His joy was infectious. Blake felt his heart swelling.

All too soon, Joey nudged him. "We'd better go."

He was practically bouncing with excitement at the prospect at getting on the stage. Blake hadn't had the heart to ask how his latest round of auditions had gone. The fact he hadn't told Blake about any successes spoke volumes. Blake hoped desperately that he'd get something soon. He was made for the limelight. Mundanity would make him wither away.

He shelved those melancholy thoughts as he jogged up the steps backstage. This night was about having fun, not about stressing over the future.

He and Joey were shuffled from mark to mark and given the envelope with the winner of their category. They brushed shoulders with Hollywood actors and sports stars as P.A.s herded them all where they needed to be. A Canadian rock band were currently tearing up the stage.

"It's good to be doing this again," he said in Joey's ear. He turned and grinned at him.

"Hell yeah, bro," he said, slapping his shoulder.

As their names were called by the presenter, Blake winked at Joey and they stepped into the glaring lights, smiling and waving to the screaming crowd. Blake couldn't see Elion, but he looked where he thought he was probably sitting anyway.

They jogged to the podium and waited for the applause to die down. "Hello!" Joey read from the tele-prompter. "Good evening California. Thank you for having us!"

Blake beamed and glanced at his cue. "And thank you for helping us get the band back together. Two out of five ain't bad, huh?"

The crowd obediently laughed, thank God.

"We're here to present the award for Best Squad," said Joey, showing them the envelope in his hands. "Blake and I were lucky enough to be part of a kick ass squad. So we're proud to announce the awesome nominees."

Blake looked at the tele-prompter. He could see the words perfectly clearly. But something took over him.

"You know what though?" he said.

He felt Joey stiffen beside him for going off book. But he didn't care. He had a platform, and he had something to say.

"Our incredible days with Below Zero may have come to an end. But Joey and I are part of another squad now. A... squad that's new to me."

He could feel the tension in the room. People were probably wondering what the hell he was doing.

"I recently came out as bisexual," he said. And by 'recently' – to himself – he meant right that very second. It was time to stop pretending. The crowd started clapping. He used that to galvanize him. "And it was tough. But it's something kids all over the world have to do every day.

"I don't know if I could have managed it without my friends." He looked to Joey, then out where he hoped Elion was. "Not every kid has that." The applause was really mounting now. People were cheering and he felt himself shaking. He leaned closed to the microphone.

"So while we're thrilled to announce which amazing squad has won the award this year, Joey and I are also part of the LGBT Plus Squad. It's got millions of members. They speak a hundred different languages and are every skin color you can think of. They're rich and poor. Some of them have religion to guide them, and some..." Fuck it. He was going there. "Some of them have religion working against them. Whoever you are, if you're queer, you're part of our squad. Right, Joey?"

"Hell yeah!" Joey practically shouted into the microphone. The crowd was deafening now.

"Thank you for all the support you've shown me. I hope you'll show it to the rest of our squad too. Today, and every day."

Joey was applauding him, shaking his head. Blake grinned. He felt like he might pass out.

"Now how about those nominees, huh?"

The crowd cheered again over their applause. But before he or Joey could read out the names, he was hit over the head with a downpour of cold, green slime.

He screamed and so did Joey as the audience went wild. Getting slimed at the Kids' Choice Awards was one of their highest honors. It meant that you mattered. But it was also absolutely disgusting.

Blake could only laugh as Joey, ever the professional, wiped his eyes and read out the contenders. Blake cleaned his eyes and spat out gunk and tried to pay attention. But he was shaking too badly.

Adrenaline was making him giddy. He'd just come out, officially, to the whole world. People could argue that he'd already done that on the show. But that hadn't been real. This…this was him finally giving up the fight.

It was going to be hard, and there was no going back now, but holy shit he was glad.

All he could think about was getting cleaned up and getting to Elion.

The winners – the cast of some dystopian young adult film – were crowding onto the stage, giving air kisses to him and Joey and trying to avoid the slime. Within minutes they were waving their way back stage once again as the crew raced onto the stage to clear up the goop before the next act performed.

As soon as they were in the wings Joey launched himself at Blake for an extremely squidgy hug. "Are you kidding me? Are you fucking kidding me?" he wailed. "That was one of the most awesome things I have *ever* seen!"

"Yeah?" Blake said, feeling like he was asking the question Joey was already answering. "It was okay?"

"It was fucking epic," Joey cried as P.A.s attacked them towels so they at least weren't dripping goo all over the place. "So?"

"So, what?" Blake asked. He was still trembling and his brain wasn't working all that well.

"Sooo," said Joey. "Are you going to go get your man now?"

Warmth blossomed in Blake's chest. "Try and stop me."

MOST PEOPLE who got slimed were escorted to a shower area and offered a clean and dry set of clothes for the rest of the evening. Blake had skipped that. As soon as he was no longer saturated with gunk, he tore from back stage into the auditorium. Elion was engrossed in watching Little Mix as he approached.

Blake leaned over the seats. "Hey handsome," he said, making Elion jump. He went from surprise to mirth as he took in Blake's disheveled appearance.

"Oh my God," he sniggered, slapping his hand over his mouth. "Don't *you* look gorgeous?"

"What a coincidence," said Blake. His heartbeat was slamming in his ears. "So do you. Do you want to get out of here?"

Slowly, the amusement fell from Elion's face. He looked up at Blake with confusion, disbelief, then finally, he gulped.

"Uh, yeah," he rasped. Hastily, he rose from his seat. He checked that neither of them had left anything behind, then followed Blake from the arena.

Their car wasn't that hard to locate once Blake had made the call. Unlike when he left with everyone else at a normal event, their car was the only one to pull up to the curb when he and Elion trotted down the steps of the venue.

"I'll pay for any damage to the upholstery," he said by way of a greeting to the driver. "Is that okay?"

The guy shrugged. "Sure man, whatever you say."

Blake let Elion slide in first, then took his jacket off, turned it so the dry side was on the seat, and sat himself on the backseat. Elion kept looking at him throughout the drive, but Blake didn't trust himself to say anything when they weren't alone. Instead, he offered his hand which Elion took, and held it tight until they reached the hotel.

Staff gave him an alarmed look as they crossed the lobby. Blake saluted at them. "I promise I won't touch a *single* thing," he said. He felt like he was drunk. But those couple of glasses of champagne had been ages ago. He was completely in his right mind as he led Elion into the elevator and jabbed the button for their floor.

They still didn't speak, but it felt like electricity was sparking between them. Crackling off the walls. Promising what was to come.

Luckily Blake had been instructed to leave his wallet and phone backstage with a P.A., so their hotel key card had been safe from the slime. He felt absolutely vile. His clothes were stiff and sticky from dried goo, his skin was itchy and his hair actually hurt where it pulled against his head. Yet none of that mattered.

All that mattered was the heated look Elion gave him as the door blissfully swung inwards.

"Did you mean that?" he asked. He grabbed Blake's hand and pulled him into the room. "What you said. On stage."

"Yes," rasped Blake. Elion was still tugging him along. The door slammed shut behind them but Elion's was focused on his destination. The bathroom.

"So, you're feeling up for a bit more experimenting?" Elion asked. He bit his lip, which looked difficult considering how broadly he was grinning. "A little bit more education?"

"Please." Blake's voice caught in his throat. Elion was already undoing his tie as they stumbled into the bathroom. Blake tried to copy him, but everything was gooey and uncooperative. He growled at his shirt buttons when they refused to do as they were told.

Then Elion captured his mouth in a kiss.

"We've got all night," he said. His voice was laden with promise. "No stress, okay?"

Blake was breathing heavily. "Okay," he managed as, together, they unraveled the tie and dropped it to the tiled floor with a splat.

Blake leaned over and seized Elion's mouth for another kiss. Despite the fact they were both in a frantic struggle to get out of their clothes, despite the fact that Blake knew his skin still carried the plastic taste of goop, he had to kiss him.

He'd never shared a shower before; he imagined it would be really awkward. But like everything with Elion, it felt easy and fun as they pulled off their clothes and stepped under the hot water.

"That was pretty awesome," said Elion between kisses. "Your little speech. I bet that'll be *all* over YouTube by tomorrow."

Blake's skin was already flushed from the heat of the

shower, and the provocation of being naked and rubbing up against Elion's lithe body. But he blushed again at the praise.

"I just," he mumbled, "said what was on my mind. For once."

"I liked it," said Elion. He showed Blake how much he liked it by sliding his hand over his already hard cock.

Blake uttered something obscene. He wasn't even sure what, he was too focused on Elion and his gorgeous body and what he was doing with his hand. Tentatively, he reached out and slipped his fingers around Elion's own shaft. He buckled immediately, only just catching himself from dropping completely by slamming a hand on the wall tiles.

"Oh, fuck, yes, baby."

His cock was slightly longer and thinner than his own, and it curved a little upwards. But really, it wasn't too dissimilar. They were both cut and there were the same thick veins and ridges. It was hot to the touch and had a velvety softness to it despite the rigid core. He stroked it, absolutely loving how it made Elion come undone.

"What do you want?" he asked Blake, despite his distracted state. "We can do anything."

The prospect was daunting. Blake had no idea where to start with a guy. If it had been Lola he probably would have fingered her – she always loved that – then taken her to bed and made love, slowly, until they couldn't hold back and it was all over in a few frantic thrusts.

The idea of actually fucking with a guy though seemed too much. He almost wanted to wilt at the prospect. Try as he might, he couldn't really see how you'd get a cock in an ass.

Something must have shown on his face, because Elion let go of his dick and cupped his jaw, kissing him tenderly under the waterfall. "Hey," he whispered. His face was full of delight and excitement. "You don't have anything to be worried about. We don't have to do anything you don't want. Or you can ask me for whatever you desire."

The word 'desire' short circuited his brain. "I don't know," he stuttered. He blinked water away from his eyes and looked into Elion's brown ones. "I don't – I-"

"How about," Elion suggested with a tone akin to a purr. "We get you cleaned off, then I take you back to that big, warm, comfy bed, and we just cuddle." He wiggled his eyebrows. "Naked."

Blake smiled. He felt ridiculously inexperienced, but Elion didn't seem to care. "That sounds lovely," he admitted.

To speed things up, they stepped apart and washed their hair and bodies. But then Elion captured his lips again, hot and needy. It took Blake a second to realize that while they were kissing, he had his fingers between his ass cheeks, cleaning himself.

Blake still wasn't sure he was up for anything that advanced, but it wouldn't hurt to give himself a freshen up either. So while Elion was preoccupied, he made sure every inch of his intimate areas were rinsed. That way he was ready for anything.

By the time they shut the water off they were both painfully hard and slightly breathless. Blake dried off in record time, and soon Elion was once again leading him by the hand. This time they were stripped entirely bare, and headed for the bed.

Blake chuckled as they ripped the comforter back and scrambled between the sheets, damp hair splaying over the pillows. They lay side by side and tangled their bodies together as they kissed. Elion used his right hand to capture both their cocks, wrapping his fingers around the shafts and rubbing them together.

Blake spluttered. "Oh God, oh fuck."

"Good?" Elion was grinning like the Cheshire Cat.

Blake managed to nod. "So good."

This was exactly what he wanted. Nothing complicated, but still so intimate. Elion stroked them as they kissed deeply. He tasted of sweet champagne and something uniquely Elion. A kind of spicy muskiness. Blake moaned.

Elion pulled away, just an inch, and squeezed their cocks in a sinful manner. "Can I try something?" he asked. "I've never done it, but now seems like a good time and if you don't like it we can stop, like, right away."

His eyes sparkled in the dim hotel light. Blake touched his fingertips to his cheek. "You really love sex, don't you?" he marveled.

"When it's done right," Elion said. He gave them a gentle stroke, just enough of a tease to make Blake shudder. "It's the best way to talk to someone without the bullshit."

Blake didn't really get that, but he was having a magnificent time, so he didn't question it further. "What do you want to do?" he asked. "I'm not sure...I mean. I don't have any condoms."

Elion shook his head. "We don't need that. It's something I like guys doing to me, but I've never done it to someone else." He pressed their foreheads together, their panting breaths mingling. "I want to eat you out."

Blake wasn't sure he heard him right. But...they had just had a shower.

He remembered how amazing the blow job had been, and Lola almost always wanted him to go down on her. She preferred that more than sex half the time. Maybe it could feel good, to have Elion's tongue and lips working his ass?

"Yes," he managed to rasp out. "Yes, we can try that. Please."

Elion groaned and kissed him hungrily. "Just lie on your front and relax. Let me do the hard work."

Blake nodded and they shifted positions. He was

trembling with anticipation, but like before, he trusted Elion. What was the worst that could happen, after all? He was pretty sure it couldn't hurt. If it felt unpleasant, he'd just ask Elion to stop.

As Elion pulled the covers down and rubbed his hands over his ass cheeks, he did feel horribly exposed. But it was just the two of them, and Elion was soon soothing him by trailing little kisses up the inside of his thigh, inching closer to his hole, tingling with anticipation.

He moaned into the pillow. "Baby," he gasped.

Lola hadn't been keen on pet names in the slightest, but he *loved* it when Elion used the term of endearment on him. It made something warm blossom in his chest and saying it back to him only intensified the feeling. It gave him a sense of belonging, of being complete.

He felt Elion smile against the crease where the top of his thigh met his ass. "Hmm, baby," he agreed.

Blake did his best not to flinch when Elion pulled his cheeks apart, exposing his hole to the air. He took his time though, massaging his hands into Blake's skin as he kissed around the puckered flesh.

There was nothing that could have contained the filthy groan Blake let loose as Elion licked his tongue over the entrance. "Holy shit, that's incredible," he whimpered. He wouldn't have even thought to suggest doing this, let alone had the courage to, if Elion hadn't voiced the idea. Fuck was he glad he had.

"Yeah?" Elion asked, doing it again, kissing and sucking his flesh.

Blake thought his string of profanities was probably proof enough he was enjoying himself. "Yes, feels amazing," he said. He rutted his throbbing cock against the sheets. There was a good chance he could come like this.

Elion hummed against him. He began to probe with his

tongue, slipping it through the rim of Blake's tight ring of muscle.

"Elion," he gasped, clutching at the sheets.

Elion kept at it for another few minutes until Blake could hardly remember his name. Then he pulled away, crawling up the bed. "I want to come together," he said through swollen lips.

Blake didn't need any encouraging. He grabbed Elion's shoulders as he moved to face him, hauling their bodies back together and slinging his leg over Elion's. He wanted to claim all of him.

Their kisses were messy and lips bashed against teeth, but it was perfect. He knew what to do after Elion's earlier demonstration, so wrapped his larger hand around both their pricks and began to thrust. They were both slippery with pre-cum and it felt even better than before.

Elion's fingers dug into his back and side. He grunted and gasped and wailed.

"Yes, baby, yes," Blake begged him. He rolled them over so Elion was on his back and Blake loomed over him. He felt like he was getting the hang of this now and his confidence made everything even more intense. Elion arched up into him, rubbing his cock desperately against Blake's and his hand gripping them tightly.

"You're so fucking gorgeous," he moaned. He leaned up and kissed Blake once before dropping his head back to the pillow and looking up at him wantonly. "Are you going to make me come?"

"Yeah," Blake grunted.

"Do it, baby. I'm all yours. *Fuck* I'm all yours."

A possessive wave of lust rolled over Blake. Elion *was* his. And he was Elion's. The rest of the world didn't matter in that moment. It all came down to the phenomenal pleasure they were giving one another.

"I'm going to come," he panted.

"Yes," begged Elion. "Come all over me."

The idea of his spunk over Elion's body woke up something primal in Blake. It tipped him over the brink, his orgasm exploding and robbing him of his sight as he rode it out. Elion came just a few thrusts later. But Blake didn't let go of their cocks until they were fully soft again and exhaustion covered him like a blanket.

He almost flopped on top of Elion but he managed to roll to one side before he hit the mattress. They were a sticky mess, but he didn't care. Instead he took Elion's face in his hand and kissed him softly. "That was incredible," he whispered.

Elion smiled sleepily back at him. "I want to say that we're only just getting started. But, damn, yeah, that was awesome."

Conveniently, there were boxes of tissues on either side of the bed. So they didn't have to move far in order to get something to mop up their mess with. Once they were dry enough, Blake leaned down to pull up the blankets again over their bodies.

"Come here," he said. "Turn around."

Elion allowed himself to be spooned. "I love it when you get bossy," he said, wriggling against him so they were pressed together as much as possible.

"Yeah?" Blake asked, his eyelids already drooping. He felt like he'd just done a serious work out.

"Yeah," Elion repeated. "Maybe next time we can try a little more of that."

Next time. Blake realized that wasn't as scary as he thought it might be. He wanted more of this with Elion, no question. Sex didn't feel like an obligation with him in the slightest. It felt like a gift. Something he yearned for.

He wanted Elion in his bed and in his heart, as much as he could possibly manage.

From his steady breathing, he figured Elion must have passed out already. Sleep wasn't far off for Blake either. He had no need to fight it.

He felt content to his bones with Elion snuggled tightly in his arms.

It was too soon and he didn't want to jinx anything. But as he drifted into unconsciousness his last thought was that maybe, perhaps, he was falling in love.

And that it was wonderful.

22

ELION

ELION WAS AWOKEN SUDDENLY BY THE OBNOXIOUS RING OF THE telephone. It took him a moment to orient himself and remember where he was…and what had happened.

He had a split second to indulge in the dizzying joy at realizing it hadn't been a dream. He and Blake really *had* had sex last night. Then his fumbling hand latched on to the receiver and he plucked the phone from its cradle, thankfully killing the ringer.

"Hello?" he mumbled. What time was it? Where was his phone?

"Mr. Jackson?"

"This is his room, yes," said Elion. He sat up and rubbed his face. Mr. Jackson himself was stirring beside him. Elion couldn't help but reach over and stroke his lovely blond hair back. Fuck. How had he got so lucky? Did this mean things had changed between them; were they really dating now?

The guy at the end of the line was still talking, saying something about calling from reception.

"Sorry, what was that?"

"I said this is a message to let Mr. Jackson know his car has arrived."

"Huh?" He looked around for his cell again, but neither his nor Blake's were in sight. Presumably, they had got dropped along the way during their hasty striptease. "What time is it?"

"Eleven o'clock, Sir."

"Fuck!" Elion yelped. He didn't bother saying goodbye to the concierge. He just slammed the phone down and shook Blake's shoulder. "Baby, we gotta go," he cried, laughing. "We're late, we have to get to the airport!"

Blake blinked at him, all ruffled and cute like a baby owl. Elion couldn't resist swooping down for a quick kiss. "Wha-?" he mumbled.

"We overslept," said Elion, throwing himself out of bed. There was no need to be shy at his nakedness now. Blake had already seen it all. He hauled his suitcase from the corner where he'd stashed it and yanked on the first pair of briefs and jeans he laid his hands on.

"Oh shit," Blake grumbled. He rolled off the bed and stumbled towards the bathroom. "Give me a minute."

Blake was apparently one of those people who was slow to surface and grumpy while he did it. Elion loved that he knew that now. He didn't have time to dwell on it though. Instead, he helped him out by packing while Blake managed to pull on sweatpants and a t-shirt.

His body felt like it got more gorgeous every time Elion glimpsed it. He hoped beyond hope he was just at the start of seeing it a hell of a lot more.

He wasn't used to the desperate want that had settled in his chest. He was craving Blake now, like he imagined drug addicts did. He *needed* him. The feeling was new and completely terrifying.

This is why he stuck to hookups. Far safer to just deal in

sex and guard your heart. But there wasn't much use fighting the way he felt for Blake now. Not after last night.

As they flew around and packed up their toothbrushes and discarded suit pants, Elion reminded himself he still didn't know where they stood. Sure, Blake may have come out quite spectacularly last night. But just because he'd accepted he was bisexual didn't mean he wanted to seriously date Elion. For all he knew, he was still Blake's guy experiment, his gateway into dating other guys. For real.

There was no time to even contemplate discussing how he felt as they zipped their suitcase shut and headed out the door. Blake laughed at Elion as he suddenly dropped to his belly and checked the floor under the bed.

"It's always worth looking," Elion said, grinning as Blake tried to tease him. Wherever they were at, at least it wasn't awkward. They'd had sex twice now, and Blake still grabbed his hand as they hurried down the corridor towards the elevator. Blake limped slightly on his bad foot, but on the whole, he had made a great recovery so far.

Doubt was circling Elion like water round a drain though. The way those people had *cheered* for Blake as he'd given his speech. They'd loved him. They were his peers and they'd been proud of him. Elion hoped nobody had seen him surreptitiously wiping his eyes at the end.

But they wouldn't want him dating some Hispanic coffee barista with pink hair, surely? They'd want to see him with an actor, or singer, or someone else in the public eye. They'd want to ship him with other all-American hunks and write Fan Fiction about them.

"Hey?" said Blake quizzically as they stepped out into the lobby. "Are you okay?"

"Uh, yeah," said Elion hurriedly as they rushed to their car. "Just worried about the flight."

Blake stopped and pulled him in for a kiss. Elion was so stunned he just froze and let it happen. Several people stared.

"Obviously we want to make it," said Blake, tugging on his hand to get them moving again. "But if we miss it, we'll just get the next one, okay?"

Something clenched in Elion's chest. He wasn't used to anybody looking after him, not like that. His mom and him did things as a team usually, but lately, he'd been the one doing a lot more of the caregiving. It felt really nice to have Blake just assure him he'd fix a problem if it arose. It didn't hurt he was rich and didn't have to think about wasting money like that.

"Let's still try and make it, yeah," said Elion. He didn't want to take Blake's generosity for granted. He squeezed his hand to show his appreciation though.

He didn't feel comfortable talking about personal stuff in the cab, so he and Blake just sat listening to the radio. At least their hands were still entwined. They had to run through the airport check-in and security, only stopping for a couple of different fans who wanted photos.

No matter how stressed they were, Blake always stopped for them. It made Elion's heart swell.

He tried to think about how many guys he'd been with in the past were actually *kind.* He wondered now if that was why he'd never really got anywhere far with anyone before.

They never got a moment just to themselves. There was always other people in earshot, forcing the questions Elion had burning inside back down his throat. *What does this mean? For us?* That's all he wanted to say.

His hesitancy meant that before he knew it, the taxi from Cincinnati International was dropping him off outside his mom's house. At least Blake gave him a kiss goodbye.

"I have class," he said as he escorted Elion out of the cab.

He sounded genuinely sorry for leaving Elion alone. "Are you sure you don't want to come?"

"It's okay," he assured him. "I have to do some house stuff and probably sleep." He laughed and was pleased to see Blake's cheeks flush a little. "Text me later?"

"Of course."

With another kiss, he was gone.

THE DANCE SHOW was fast approaching, which meant extra lessons so the kids would be ready. Elion had also had to pick up extra shifts to cover the ones he swapped when he'd gone to L.A. Therefore, he and Blake didn't see each other for three whole days after they'd parted ways on the curb by his house.

There was a part of Elion that knew he could always *text* his questions. Or arrange a time to call. But this felt like something he wanted to discuss alone. Face to face, without any cameras.

So when Blake asked if he would like to get together for dinner, Elion let his hopes get up for all of thirty seconds. Then Blake had messaged back to explain Seth wanted him to come over to Elion's house and meet his mom for a family dinner. With the crew.

Part of him wanted to say no way. He'd never agreed to getting his mom involved with this shit. But there was a little voice in the back of his head that pointed out that he'd *love* for his mom and Blake to meet. And, so what if the cameras were going to be there? Maybe afterwards he'd get a chance to talk to Blake and clear some things up.

They set the date for the evening after next.

Elion had been apprehensive asking his mom what she thought of inviting a TV crew into her home. So far, she had been pretty cool about him being on the show to a point. She'd always been one to grab opportunities with two hands and have some fun. But whenever Elion mentioned Blake her eyes narrowed.

"You deserve a *real* boyfriend," she had argued more times than he could count. The more she said it, the more it hurt. He wanted Blake to be his god-damned boyfriend. But now the prospect was dangling right in front of his nose, he was too chicken shit to ask.

The opportunity of being allow to meet and – more importantly – feed Blake had perked his mom right up. Especially when Blake told him Seth had specifically asked for traditional Mexican food. Elion had a horrible feeling they might have an ulterior motive and were going to play some racism card. But Blake assured him it would be alright and that he was really excited about home-cooked enchiladas.

He hadn't brought up the sex in L.A., but then neither had Elion. He was pretty sure Blake had loved it as much as he had. It had been utterly thrilling going down on him like that. But at the moment it was feeling like the elephant in the room. He hoped again that at some point during this dinner, they would be able to sneak a moment to themselves.

"Do you think it looks okay?" his mom asked for the sixth time, biting her thumbnail. The kitchen-dining area was gleaming. She'd spent the two-and-a-half-days since the date had been set cleaning like a woman possessed and cooking up enough food to feed an army.

He slung his arm around her and squeezed. "It looks great," he assured her. They had the best plates out and the fancy little dishes for appetizers that normally only served as decorations. The room had smelled of lemon and pine before scents of dinner overpowered it, and the windows and mirrors were sparkling. Elion had helped as best he could, but his mom had taken it as her own personal point of pride to make her home camera and boyfriend ready.

Elion *had* washed his own bedsheets. Just in case.

He stood with his mom a minute without speaking as they listened to the radio softly playing in the background. He wanted her to feel relaxed, but he was nervous himself.

"Is he nice to you?" she asked in a quiet voice.

Elion sighed. She was the only person aside from Joey who knew the whole thing was a total sham. Devon at work might have had her suspicions, but Elion couldn't help confessing to his mom as soon as everything went down. She didn't know the steps they'd made in taking their relationship closer to something real.

She didn't know Elion was falling in love for real.

"He's great, Mom," he assured her. "It started out wanting to help him out after what the show did to us, but now..." He sighed. "We're friends, I'm sure."

She bumped him with her hip. "Maybe more than friends?"

"Mom," he protested, rolling his eyes.

"What!" she cried, swatting his arm. "I watch the show. I know you say they edit it a lot, but it looks like there's something there."

He bit his lip. "How about a beer?" he asked, going to the fridge.

"You're not distracting me that easily," she scoffed. She folded her arms and pursed her lips. "He's handsome and rich."

"And sweet and talented," Elion jumped in a little too quickly. But he didn't want her thinking this was superficial. "Alright, yeah. I'd really like there to be something more between us. More than just the show. But this is all new to him. At the start he didn't think he was actually bi."

"With you as his fake boyfriend?" His mom tutted and

took her beer from him as he held it out. "So he's stupid, but at least he's pretty."

"Mom," he growled as his ears went hot. "Please don't say stuff like that to him, okay? His parents can be kind of dicks."

Her face softened. "You really do like him, don't you?" Instead of answering, he took a swig of his beer. She sighed and reached up to rub his back. "Well, we'll show him a great time tonight, okay? I'll be the best mother-in-law he ever saw. He'll have no choice but to fall head-over-heels in love with you."

He definitely blushed at that. "Oh God, why did I ever agree to put you in front of the cameras," he wailed in mock anguish. "If you get out any baby photos I'll never speak to you again."

She pinched his cheek then stood on her tiptoes to plant a noisy smacking kiss there. "Don't be ashamed of your mother. I brought you into this world."

He felt a rush of strong emotions, all tangled up together. He was so thankful for his mom's support and in knots about him and Blake. He didn't really know how to articulate any of that though. So instead, he just pulled her over for a hug.

She patted his back. "It's okay, buba."

Before they could say anything more, the doorbell rang. Elion took a deep breath and stood up straight.

"Okay," he said. He and his mom looked at each other. "Here we go."

23

BLAKE

BLAKE STEPPED BACK FROM THE DOORBELL AND FIDDLED WITH Watson's leash in his hands. Kala stood beside him with the half a dozen crew laden down with cameras, lights and sound equipment. She gave him a wink.

"Excited to meet the in-laws?" she asked.

He rolled his eyes. "It would be much better without you lot," he said. She just grinned broader.

Elion lived in a fairly typical neighborhood for Perryville. The one-story houses were all set back behind neat front yards that were all just one long continuous run of grass. Telephone poles and power lines ran the length of the street on both sides. Every other house had a great oak tree standing proud and tall by the sidewalk.

Elion – or more likely, Elion's mom – had pots of pretty pink flowers lining the exterior wall out front. They waved cheerily in the warm evening breeze.

The door flew open and Blake's heart jumped into his throat. Having not seen Elion for a few days he seemed extra beautiful today, even though he was just wearing a simple Henley and jeans.

"Hey," he breathed out. Watson strained on her leash and barked.

Before they could even think about embracing, Kala and all the crew but one camera operator pushed their way inside. "Nope, you know the rules. Let us set up then you can do that again."

Blake blinked as the door was slammed in his face. Watson looked up at him with a quizzical expression. "Yeah, I know, it's dumb," he grumbled. She wagged her tail and head butted him in what was undoubtedly a show of support. He smiled and scratched between her soft, floppy ears.

The camera operator angled himself in front of him and Blake zoned out while he waited for the all clear again. He was nervous, which was kind of stupid. But he and Elion hadn't had any time together since L.A. and it was undeniable things had changed.

His heart ached at them being apart. Like an actual strained muscle. Blake found himself absently rubbing his chest to try and make it go away. His ankle was all but healed, and in comparison didn't hurt half as much.

Now he had to stand there and wait for the stupid cameras and lights to get in place before he could give his damn boyfriend a hug.

He loved referring to Elion as his boyfriend. Not like before, where the word scared him. Now it made him feel secure and wanted and...loved.

He was probably going to have to accept the L word soon enough, but one step at a time. Tonight, he just had to get through dinner.

Eventually the door reopened. This time there was nothing stopping him hopping eagerly up the front step and slipped his arms possessively around Elion's waist and back, breathing his scent in deeply.

"I missed you," he mumbled into his neck. The mics would pick it up, but he didn't care. Let them.

Elion pulled apart and smiled brightly at him before pecking a kiss to his lips. "I *am* adorable," he said.

That was all the greeting he was allowed though before Watson's demands became too incessant. Elion laughed as he reached down and gave her a cuddle. "Do you want to meet my mom? Do you?"

They untangled themselves from her leash then let her off. She went charging down the corridor, past the rest of the crew, into the room on the left. There was music playing quietly, but as he and Elion got closer, someone turned it off. The sudden silence felt slightly awkward.

The room on the left turned out to be a kitchen/dining room combination, and a middle-aged Latina woman was waiting for them with her hands clasped anxiously around the neck of a beer bottle. She was plump with an angular face and cropped hair immaculately cut and styled. She had nice pants and light-knit buttoned sweater on with boots that Blake guessed normally wouldn't be worn inside her pristine house.

As soon as she saw Blake walk in, lead hand in hand by Elion, she put down her beer and covered her mouth with her hands. "You must be Blake," she said once she'd regained her composure and stepped over to greet him. He held out his hand, but she only used that to pull him down into a hug.

"It's nice to meet you, Mrs. Rodriguez," he said. He wasn't used to being manhandled into an embrace like that, certainly not by his own mother. It took him by surprise.

"Now, now, none of that," she said releasing him. She held him by the shoulders and inspected his face. "Call me Luciana, or Lucy's even better." She had a slight accent, but not strong. She certainly didn't seem to struggle with speaking English.

He smiled at her. "Okay," he said. He could hear the nervousness in his voice.

He'd met Lola's parents a couple of times, mostly when he'd picked her up for homecoming and prom. But in some ways that felt more forced than this. He'd just been a kid then, trying to impress her dad under some ridiculous social pretext that he was 'allowing' Blake to take his 'baby girl' out.

He was an adult now, and he just wanted Lucy to like him. Respect him. So this did feel more authentic, despite the camera crew hovering and the P.A.s hastily adding decorations all around the room. They had come armed with brightly colored Mexican pottery pieces, pillar candles and cacti in pots to dress the set. As much as it pissed him off they wanted it to obviously look as 'ethnic' as possible, he had to admit it did look stunning under the lights they'd set up.

It also reminded him that one of the girls was holding something for him. "Oh," he said, searching for what he was looking for. "These are for you."

He handed over a large bunch of flowers made of so many colors they were practically a rainbow. Blake suspected that might have been Kala's aim. Lucy's eyes widened in genuine surprise. "Oh, you didn't need to…" she began.

Blake shook his head. They may have been the show's idea, but he'd wanted to bring something nice. "Don't be silly. Wow, it smells wonderful in here!"

Lucy beamed as she put the flowers in a vase. After that, she couldn't ignore Watson any long as she ran around her legs. "Who have we got here?" She laughed and crouched to pet her. Blake noticed she kept looking self-consciously into the cameras, but hopefully she would get better once she got used to them.

Elion had never mentioned his dad, although he said once he was an only child. Seth had been pissed, wanting a big

Mexican family get together to film. But apparently it was just Elion and his mom. That was fine by Blake; he just hoped Kala wouldn't probe too much.

As usual since the show had got into its own stride, Seth was elsewhere watching the footage on several monitors. He had a dedicated room at the studio now, but Blake thought he had a van set up on the curb for this location shoot. He'd be talking to Kala in her ear no doubt, egging her on.

Lucy was besotted with Watson, having sat completely on the floor now, tickling her belly. Elion smiled and sidled up to wrap his arm around Blake's waist. "We could never afford a dog," he said sadly.

Blake had the sudden rash idea of buying them one, or he and Elion having their own little pup and coming regularly to visit Lucy with her. But that was definitely jumping the gun. Instead of saying anything, he just pulled Elion a bit closer and kissed his temple.

Kala soon herded the two of them into the seats and got Lucy dishing up divine smelling food, chatting to her about the dishes she'd made. One of the P.A.s had already poured them three large glasses of the wine from the crate they had brought with them. Blake didn't drink it much, but he figured it would be perfect for a nice relaxing dinner. Or, at least it would give him a bit of liquid courage for whatever stunt Seth had in mind, because there was bound to be one.

Blake was soon distracted by the mountain of food that was placed before him. He recognized the enchiladas right away, his mouth watering at the spicy tomato aroma. There was also half-moon shaped crispy things, which turned out to be shredded beef empanadas. Guacamole, beans and rice, several different colored salsas, and of course, lots of cheese.

"This looks incredible, Lucy," he said. Good manners would have meant he'd have said that regardless, but he did mean it. "Did you really make all this?"

"Absolutely," she said proudly. "Except for the croquettes." She pointed towards the bowl of deep fried balls. "Martha's deli does them way better than I ever could, so why bother to compete?"

Blake laughed and reached to dig in. But he found his hands being grabbed by both Elion and Lucy.

Oh, right. They wanted to say grace. Blake wasn't sure he was comfortable with that.

Church and religion was always used as a kind of punishment in his house. Something other people used as a yard-stick to measure your worth. He didn't realize Elion was religious. He'd never mentioned anything before. But he seemed perfectly happy joining in with his mom as they intoned a few words.

Kala loved it. She got Marcus and the other camera guy to zoom in on them with their eyes closed. Blake liked that he was seeing a glimpse further into Elion's everyday life, but he was still glad when it was over.

Elion and his mom didn't seem to mind that he hadn't joined in. Instead they let his hands go with smiles.

"What are you waiting for?" Lucy asked happily. "Dig in!"

24

BLAKE

KALA SAT HERSELF IN THE FOURTH SEAT SO SHE COULD produce them from off camera while they ate. She tried to decline when Lucy offered her a plate laden with a bit of everything from the feast she'd prepared. But Lucy wouldn't hear of it.

"Don't be ridiculous," she said, putting the food in front of her. "Like we could just sit here and make you watch us eat."

Kala tried to explain that that was their *job*. But Lucy wasn't happy until all the crew had at least taken an empanada each. Watson was very happy chewing on a stick of celery by Elion's feet. He must have slipped it to her. Blake smiled. The two of them certainly had bonded.

Finally, Lucy settled herself down. Blake had already finished his first enchilada. He hadn't realized how hungry he was until he'd started. He felt bad as Lucy made him take another before she had one herself.

"You must burn a lot of calories, with all that dancing you do," she said, shaking her head. "Gosh, I just love watching you on the show. No wonder Elion fell for you."

Blake chuckled as Elion threw her a 'shut up now!' look.

He couldn't help but feel it was a bit late for that now though. He'd be pretty upset if Elion *didn't* like him like that.

"How's your ankle doing?" Elion asked instead, changing the topic.

Blake nodded as he sipped his wine. "Much better, thank you. I should be back to normal next week."

"Thank God," said Lucy, scowling. "Nasty business if you ask me. Elion told me about the stalker letters you've been getting. Do you think they're related?"

He hadn't actually considered that until now. He still firmly suspected it had been the crew creating drama for the show. He didn't want to say that on camera though. "I'm sure it was just an accident," he said, dipping a tortilla chip into one of the brown salsas that he assumed was made from beans.

The spice hit the back of his throat and he coughed immediately. Elion and his mom laughed good-naturedly at his suffering. "Sorry, I should have warned you," said Elion, rubbing his back.

He wanted water, but there was none on the table. Kala passed him his newly topped-up wine instead. In fact, they all had full glasses again. When had that happened?

"So you're a fan of the show, Mrs. Rodriguez?" she asked.

Lucy nodded. "Oh yes." Kala prompted her to address Blake directly, so she repeated herself for the camera's sake. "I wasn't sure about Elion getting involved at first. But you boys seem to really like each other."

Elion tensed up beside Blake. Was he worried she might say something bad? Like what?

A cold, nasty thought slipped into his brain. Maybe he didn't like Blake the way he liked him? What if it was all just an act, to stay on the show? He'd admitted he liked sex for its own sake too. Was there no emotion behind it? He chewed his lip. Surely Elion wouldn't do that to him, would he?

He wanted to assure Lucy that, yes, they did like each other very much. But doubt held the words hostage in his throat.

"How do you feel about your son being gay, Mrs. Rodriguez?" Kala jumped in instead.

Blake's eyes went wide, wondering if she'd just opened a can of worms. But Lucy snorted and took another mouthful of red wine. "Poor thing," she said, taking her son's hand. "He got himself in a bit of a state when he told me. How old were you, *chulo?* Fourteen?"

"Thirteen," said Elion. He'd gone a bit bashful, which was unlike him. Blake leaned over and took his other hand, squeezing it tightly.

Lucy shook her head. "He tells me, like it's this big thing. 'Mama,' he says. 'I'm gay.' So I tell him. 'I know, *lindo.* You wanna go get ice cream?'"

Blake couldn't help but laugh. There was a lump in his throat which he tried to swallow and he caught Elion's eye. "That's pretty cool," he said. He thought about trying to come out to his own parents, then squashed it down. Tonight wasn't about them.

"Of course I didn't really know what that meant; I worried a lot. But then I joined PFLAG." Her eyes went wide and she grabbed Blake's wrist. "Do your parents know about PFLAG?" He shook his head, he'd never heard of it. "Oh, it's this *wonderful* organization for parents of gay kids and allies and all that."

"Mom made most of her friends there," Elion said fondly before taking another bite of his food. Blake had got so wrapped up talking he'd forgotten to keep eating. He took another mouthful of the delicious enchilada so Lucy didn't think he wasn't enjoying it.

"I can take your mother," she said excitedly. Her eyes

sparkled the same way Elion's did when he was happy. "You tell her I'd love to do that."

Sadly, Blake knew his mom would never be caught dead in a place like that unless it was for a photo op or something. But he thanked Lucy profusely all the same. She chatted on for a while about all the different kinds of people she'd met there. Elion was right, it seemed like it had formed her core social group. Blake thought that was pretty damn amazing.

Her stories allowed him and Elion to eat a fair bit of food. She picked at things, but her wine went down at a quicker rate. The P.A.s never let the glass get more than half-empty though.

Blake tried to slow down to begin with. But he figured, as long as he didn't get wasted, it couldn't really do any harm. He was having a nice time after all, and the wine felt good thrumming through his veins.

When he'd had his fill of food, he swapped his glass to his other hand and linked his free one with Elion's. He rested them on the table so the cameras could see.

"Oh," said Lucy resting her hand on her chest. "You two do look sweet together."

Blake smiled, blushing a little thanks to the heat of the lights and the wine.

"Elion," said Kala. Blake had almost forgotten she was there. "How does your dad feel about you and Blake dating?"

Elion snorted into his glass. "Never met him, never will. Don't care. He probably wouldn't even know it was me if he ever watched the show."

Lucy was shaking her head. "His father never even knew Elion's name," she explained to Blake. "Took off the second he knew I was pregnant. Just like the rest of the family." She leaned over in her chair and squeezed her arm tightly around Elion's shoulder. "It's always just been us two."

Blake felt like he'd been hit with a bucket of water. Lucy's family had disowned her? All of them? He looked at her again and tried to work out how old she might have been when she had given birth, learning to be a mother. He wondered if she might even have been a teenager.

How utterly unforgivable, to leave her to that by herself. And Elion, did they even know him at all?

If they didn't that was wholly their loss. "They're all idiots," he said a little more forcefully than he meant to. But as far as he was concerned, anyone who shunned Elion wasn't in their right mind.

Lucy smiled, her eyes bright, and she stood up to hug him from behind. "They are idiots, you're absolutely right. But it's fine, we don't need them. We have each other."

"And me," said Blake thickly. He saw Elion's face mouth drop slightly and his eyebrows raise. Maybe he shouldn't have said anything. "And PFLAG," he added to lighten the mood.

Lucy cheered and lifted her glass. "Here's to good friends and boyfriends," she cried as she took her seat again. Blake and Elion copied the toast. Blake couldn't read Elion's expression and he didn't want to ask with the cameras rolling. The best he could do was to take his hand again and rub his thumb across the knuckles.

Elion smiled back at him, allowing his nerves to calm little. He wasn't sure what he'd do if this wasn't real for Elion. Be heartbroken, he suspected.

"Blake, Elion," Kala said.

The cameras shifted around from where they'd got Lucy's hug. Watson moved to avoid getting stepped on and trotted off to lap at the bowl of water Lucy had put down for her.

"How do you feel about the negative reaction you've received?"

Blake shook his head stubbornly, noting that the P.A.s were yet again topping up their glasses. "The positive *far* outweighs the negative," he said firmly. He cradled Elion's hand in both of his. His head was swimming from the alcohol, despite all the food he'd eaten. "There's no way to make everyone like you," he continued. "Not everyone's going to be a fan. And sometimes, people like to spend their time spreading hate rather than investing in things they love." He shook his head. "I don't get that, but there's nothing we can do to change it. We'd just rather focus on the people supporting us and the ones we're helping."

He looked at Elion who nodded at him. "That's right. We get messages all the time from kids who say we've helped them come out, or even just accept who they are." He rolled his eyes. "I mean Blake, not me. He's the famous one."

Blake scowled. "I wouldn't even know this side of myself if it wasn't for you though," he said. He held Elion's gaze. Didn't he see that? He was more special than any of the famous celebrities he'd ever met in his whole career.

He was going to elaborate, but Kala interrupted from behind the camera. "What about this stalker though? Aren't you worried about the threats you're getting?"

That sobered Blake up faster than a cold shower and a cup of coffee. Seth had told him that he'd had a word with the police, and that the safest course of action would be to not draw attention to it on the show. What the hell was she doing?

His expression must have showed what he was thinking, because she went on to elaborate. "Your mom told us all about it. She showed us the letters and we had someone from the F.B.I. come in and analyze them with us." As she spoke, she pulled out a sealed envelope. By now, Blake recognized the style of it, the font type and the color and size of the envelope. His breath caught.

"When did you get this?" he asked. He didn't want to open it on camera, but there was no way he could wait either.

193

"This morning," Kala admitted.

Blake flashed her a glare. "And you're only just giving it to me now?"

Kala jerked her chin forwards. "We thought Elion might want to open it with you. It seems like this concerns him too now."

They glanced at each other as Blake opened the letter. If the F.B.I. were *really* involved, there was no way they would let him open this unsupervised without gloves on. So they'd probably just got some college professor in to act the part with his mom. Or, hell, even just an actor full stop. That didn't mean he wasn't nervous though.

The last time he'd been tricked into having the letters on him when Elion asked about them. Now, they were opening this one together. Blake couldn't even vet it first. Even worse, Lucy was right there watching, too.

Blake willed it to just be about him. He didn't care how disturbing or vile it was. He just didn't want it to involve Elion.

The universe wasn't that considerate though.

Why do you do this to me, Blake? the familiar mismatch of cut out letters read.

We could be so happy, I could give you everything.

It's him or me. Don't make me chose for you. This doesn't have to get ugly.

"What does that mean?" Lucy stammered in alarm. She got to her feet, pointing at the note.

"Mom, it's just a stupid thing, don't even worry about it," said Elion hastily. He got up too, so Blake followed. The cameras moved around them like a choreographed ballet.

Lucy was shaking though, tears in her eyes. "No, no," she cried, jabbing her finger. "They're threatening you, they want to hurt you."

"No one's going to hurt me," Elion tried to assure her. But

she'd had several glasses of wine and probably wasn't thinking rationally. Besides, Blake had to agree. That sounded horribly ominous.

"I won't let anyone hurt him, Lucy," he said vehemently. "I promise."

Watson was grousing and began winding between his and Elion's feet.

Lucy was hugging her son and starting to cry though. "You have to protect him," she snapped angrily at the crew. "This isn't funny, this isn't a game. Do you have *any* idea how wonderful he is? The kind of man he is?"

Kala was standing with them now, her hands raised in the face of Lucy's angry tears. "I promise you Mrs. Rodriguez, we'll do everything we can. I didn't know the letter was going to threaten him-"

"But it has," she snarled. She scrubbed her face and hiccuped. "He isn't just some extra in your little show! Do you know what he did when he was just a boy? Do you know how amazing he is?"

"Mom, please." He tried to grab her hands and calm her down. But she was like a tiger, riled up and baring her teeth.

"When his mother got cancer, when he was supposed to go and live his life and go to college and get out of this town," she stammered. "He gave up everything we'd saved his whole life to help pay for my treatment. I'm still *alive* because of my boy, so don't you dare, don't you *dare-*"

She became too upset to speak. Kala grabbed her by the shoulders and hugged her, then steered her from the room promising they would call the police right away. Half the crew followed them. The other half stayed with Elion and Blake.

Blake turned as Elion slumped in his chair. He looked utterly miserable. Blake's insides were churning.

So that was why he'd taken a job at a small town coffee

house, why someone so full of life and potential had chosen to stay here rather than go find his place in the world. Why he worked all hours and still lived at home.

Blake felt wholly inadequate as he dropped into his own chair and took Elion's hand. He didn't even seem to notice him doing it. How could he think his life had ever been hard? He had been inundated with privilege and opportunity at every turn.

Yet here Elion was. He'd chosen to give back all the money his mom had saved to send him to school so she could get the best treatment possible, and by the looks of it, beat her cancer. And still he faced each day with a laugh and a joke on his pretty lips, always seeing the best in everything.

"You're incredible," Blake murmured. His heart was swelling with pride.

Elion shook his head though and gently pulled his hand free so he could hug himself. "It's what anyone would have done," he said. Blake didn't believe that, but he didn't get a chance to say so. "Look, this stalker shit isn't funny. I don't care what your parents say. I want to go to the police, like Kala said."

Blake nodded. "Of course."

That's what he'd wanted to do from the beginning. Especially if Seth was stupid enough to air this. Surely that would just encourage whoever was behind it all. Unfortunately, Blake knew by now the great entertainment outweighed compassion and morals.

"I'm so sorry, I never wanted you involved in this."

Elion gave him a shrug and a half smile. "Look, I better go look after my mom. Maybe you should just head home?"

Blake swallowed.

Fuck. If Elion didn't really care for him, if he'd just been doing this for a laugh and a bit of fame, then a cloaked death threat would surely be enough to push him away for good.

Blake desperately wanted to assure him that this was all real. That he'd get this asshole arrested, whoever they were, and look after Elion and his mom to the absolute best of his means. That he loved Elion, no matter what.

But this seemed like the worst time to try and confess how he felt. So instead he just nodded. "Of course," he said again. "Come on, Watson."

Mercifully, Elion let him hug him, and he kissed his lips tenderly. There was no heat behind it, purely comfort. Blake was overcome with a roaring urge to protect Elion and his mom with everything he had.

But that would have to wait. For now, he was forced to leave them behind while he and his dog stepped out into the cool night air. The cameras followed them to the sidewalk, but then he insisted he wanted to walk home, alone.

He was grateful when they listened and went back to the house.

He had a lot to think about.

ELION

IT TOOK A WHILE TO CALM HIS MOM DOWN. ONCE SHE'D drunk some water she managed to see sense. When she started to get embarrassed at her emotional reaction, Elion refused to hear it. "You had every right to get upset," he assured her.

He didn't mind the cameras hanging around to get that on film, but after that he insisted they leave. Kala had wound his mom up with the wine and the letter, and they'd got their fucking drama for the show. Now everyone would know what a hellish time she'd been through, and what he'd had to do to get her through it.

There was no scenario where he wouldn't give up his every last cent to make sure his mom got the treatment she needed. It had been a shit couple of years, but the chemo had paid off and his mom had made it through without even having to get a mastectomy. Of course it hurt that he'd had to give up his dream of going to college, but he'd trade that in a heartbeat for keeping his mom with him.

He'd just rather everyone didn't know. He didn't want people looking at them with pity, or treating him like he'd lost something. These were the cards he'd been dealt in life and he'd make the best hand he could with them.

There had been times with Blake where he'd felt the difference keenly in their financial situation. Hanging around with someone who simply didn't have to worry about money, who never had, set his teeth on edge at times.

Blake had never once made him feel inferior. But now he knew. Now he understood that thanks to a crappy tumor his and his mom's pennies had been pinched to the point where they'd almost had to turn off the lights and water because they couldn't afford the bills.

But they were still here god-damn it, and they were doing just fine. He didn't need some rich popstar feeling sorry for him.

Especially not one who he didn't even know for sure wanted him to be his genuine boyfriend.

It was so awkward with the cameras around all the time. Elion wanted to believe what Blake said that evening had been from the heart. But how could he tell? He had to play the part of the doting boyfriend, and the response to his speech at the awards had been so amazing there was no way he could 'dump' Elion anytime soon without coming across as an opportunistic liar.

Was he hamming up his part now, so in a few months' time he could swap Elion for someone a little more Caucasian? Was that why the crew had brought all that crap into their house?

Elion was too tired to think about it anymore. He made them go pack it all up while he looked after his mom. She wasn't used to drinking that much and was feeling pretty sick, so he got her more water and urged her to brush her teeth. He was also a big meanie and made her take off her makeup despite her protests.

"We've got to keep you looking gorgeous, now, haven't

we?" She grumbled but he did manage to raise a smile out of her.

By the time he put her to bed and returned to the kitchen, Kala and the crew had all gone. They'd even wrapped up the leftover food and put it in the fridge, which he did appreciate. That was probably going to be his lunch for the next couple of days and he would have been pissed off if it had spoiled.

As he was washing up his phone dinged, so he dried his hands and pulled it from his pocket. His heart clenched when he saw it was a text from Blake.

'I'm so sorry that happened tonight. I feel like I've put you in so many awkward positions since you got dragged into the show. Do you want to meet tomorrow? We can sort this out, I promise.'

Sort this out? Well that sounded like the fake-dumping of the fake-boyfriend was probably happening sooner rather later.

Elion angrily fought back the tears that sprung in his eyes. What did he expect? Blake was getting threatened by a stalker if he didn't ditch Elion. Poor, brown, uneducated Elion. It was hardly rocket science.

'Sure, what time?' he messaged back. As soon as they agreed on four o'clock, he shoved his phone back in his pocket and finished doing the dishes. He ignored his reflection in the darkened window of the tears breaking free and slipping down his face.

HE FELT numb by the time he pulled into the parking lot the next day. He'd already worked a shift at Cool Beans with Devon calling him a zombie more times than he could count. He couldn't shake his funk though. No matter how many times he told himself that this was always inevitable, he couldn't seem to stop his heart from breaking.

He'd gone home and changed so he looked his best when he got his ass handed to him for all the world to see. He fussed with his hair in the rear-view-mirror until he admitted he couldn't put this off any longer.

"It's been real fun," he muttered to himself and swung himself out into the parking lot. He passed a few parents and students milling around on his way in. If Blake had any mercy at all, he'd at least do this away from them. The cameras were probably unavoidable, but he didn't want the kids to see him cry.

The young protégée Karyn was standing outside on her phone. Presumably, she was waiting for a ride having after a class from the way her fashionably baggy t-shirt was dark with perspiration. When she saw him her face lit up. It was enough to startle him into stopping. Since that episode where she'd filmed the fake witnessing of him and Blake, she'd pretty much ignored him. She only ever seemed to want to dance and fight with Nessa.

But now she ran over to him as he started walking again towards the front doors. "Elion," she hissed, delight clear on her face. "Elion, guess what?"

He stopped once more and raised his eyebrows. "Um, what?"

"I got cast in Reyse Hickson's new music video," she whispered with such excitement she couldn't seem to stop herself quivering. "This never would have happened without you and Blake!"

He couldn't really follow what she was saying. "It's Blake's show?" he said.

She shook her head. "When you guys got together, that meant I could get a solo part in the very first episode." She hugged him. "Thank you."

Pain lanced through Elion's chest. She must know that they'd never really got together, and now they were going to be over for good. But he was happy for her and her success.

"You got the music video all by yourself," he said, giving her a smile. "Congratulations, kiddo. You deserve it."

She grinned at him, then spotted whoever was picking her up. "See you later," she called over her shoulder.

"I doubt it," he muttered to himself. He wasn't going to have a reason to hang around here any longer.

As usual, a P.A. stopped him as soon as he walked in the building to wire him for sound. There was no point in fighting it, so Elion just stood and let it happen. Like a man walking to the gallows, he approached the main dance studio.

He couldn't remember what class was supposed to be going on. He thought maybe the elite group, which people often stuck around to watch as they were so good. Therefore, Elion was expecting Blake to be dancing when he pushed through the doors.

What he was not expecting was to see him doing some sort of sexy Dirty Dancing with Nessa's leg wrapped around his waist and her head draped back so her waterfall of hair cascaded behind her while she exposed her neck and breasts in all their glory for Blake to see.

Elion felt like his heart stopped. "Well isn't this just fucking perfect," he said too loudly considering there were small children everywhere. But their parents were letting them watch this pornography, so he gave precisely zero fucks what they thought.

He was getting out of here and never coming back.

He spun on his heels and let the door slam behind him. He didn't care that Kala and her cameras were on him. He was already trying to pull his mic off, but his hands were trembling too badly and he couldn't get them to work. It didn't help that his eyes were filling up with tears.

"Elion!" he heard Blake call from behind him. "Elion wait, where are you going? What the hell's the matter?"

Elion stopped and turned, hastily wiping his face with both hands. "Nothing," he spat, forcing a smile that was probably more of a grimace. "Nothing. I don't have anything to be jealous of, do I?"

Blake looked perplexed. And mouthwateringly good, of course. His damp clothes clung to his perfect body and reminded Elion of what he couldn't have any more.

"We were just dancing," said Blake slowly. There were two cameras on them now and several people watching from a distance. "Why would you be jealous?"

Elion shook his head. "No," he ground out. "I shouldn't be jealous because this whole thing was never real and you can hook up with whoever the hell you please."

Blake looked like he'd been smacked in the face. "You don't think it's real?"

Elion couldn't stop the tears now. "I don't want to play around anymore, I can't. I know I said no strings attached, but I lied. I can't pretend, so if you don't want me, I'll just-"

He probably would have carried on pouring his heart out if Blake hadn't grabbed his face and kissed him fiercely. Elion barely registered what was happening before it was over.

"I don't know what you're talking about, but this hasn't been an act since L.A. Probably before, if I'm honest. Unless you tell me differently, you're my *boyfriend* and I fucking *love you.*"

Elion felt the air rush out of his lungs. "W-what?"

Blake hugged him close and murmured in his ear. The mics would still be able to hear them, but at least the growing crowd wouldn't.

"I love you," he said again. "I'm so sorry this stupid show keeps getting in our way. This isn't fake, I'm not doing it for the fans or the ratings or anything. I want to be with you because when I'm *not* with you it feels like half of me is missing." When he pulled away, his eyes were glassy but he wasn't crying just yet. Unlike Elion, who felt like a total mess. "If that's not what you want," he said slowly. "I'll have to accept it. But if you want to be together, really together, then I'm in. One hundred percent."

Elion felt faint. He didn't have the strength to speak. He just pulled Blake back against him and hugged him with all his might, nodding into his neck.

"Oh thank God," Blake breathed, hugging him just as tightly. "Don't scare me like that."

"I'm sorry," Elion half-laughed, half-cried.

Blake shook his head. "I'm sorry. We should have cleared things up after L.A."

"It doesn't matter now," Elion said. He was so light with relief he thought he might float away. "Can we get out of here?"

"Hell yes," Blake growled.

As soon as he stepped away he expertly removed both his and Elion's mic packs in a flash. He handed them over to Kala, who, if Elion didn't know any better, he would have sworn she had tears in her eyes too.

"I take it you can edit something from that?" Blake asked as he handed the packs over.

"I've got *gold* from that," she said, grinning devilishly. "Now get out of here, and don't come back until tomorrow."

Elion allowed Blake to seize his hand and drag him out of the center, not caring that a couple dozen people were watching them. Some were mute, trying to work out what was happening. Others called out to them, but Elion honestly didn't hear a single word they said. Blood was rushing in his ears and his legs felt as wobbly as a newborn foal's.

As they broke into the afternoon sunshine Elion swung

him back around and cradled his face for a passionate kiss. "I love you too," he whispered. "In case that wasn't clear."

Blake sighed and kissed him back. "I hoped, but it's still really nice to hear." He laughed, that elusive dimple popping back into his cheek. "Oh Christ, come home with me. Please."

Heat flared through Elion's body. All his doubt and fears were banished in the face of pure lust. "Do you have supplies?" he asked. He wasn't holding back this time. He wanted Blake Jackson inside him and he wasn't talking no for an answer.

Adorably, Blake flushed pink. "I did some research, got some things. I hoped…"

"You hoped, right, mister," said Elion. He pulled him towards his car. "Is anyone home; do we need to be discreet?"

They threw themselves inside the small car and Blake shook his head. "We should have the place to ourselves."

Elion wasn't sure how he made the drive. The whole thing was essentially a blur. Before he knew it, they were parked in front of the Jackson's enormous house, scrambling outside. He wasn't even sure he locked the doors, but he didn't care. No one was going to steal his banged-up piece of crap in a nice neighborhood like this.

Watson met them with her usual enthusiasm when they entered, greeting them with a loud howl. But she seemed to pick up pretty quickly that they were busy, so thankfully scampered off as they headed up the stairs.

Like Blake said, none of his family appeared to be at home. Elion sent up a quick prayer of thanks. He had a detailed plan on being *very* noisy for the next half an hour or so.

Like he was going to last that long. His dick was already half-hard and his whole body burned with desire. Blake *loved* him. He was dragging him to his bedroom like a horny teenager. This wasn't fake any more.

He wondered, giddily, if it ever really had been.

As soon as Blake locked them in he launched himself at Elion, grabbing his face and kissing with tongue and teeth and delicious moans. Elion loved that Blake was big enough that he could jump up and wrap his legs around his waist and his arms around his neck.

"Take me to bed," he begged.

Blake was happy to oblige, depositing Elion on top of his mattress then crawling on top of him. "What do you want, baby?" he asked.

Elion grinned. "I want you to keep calling me baby," he said. He slipped his hand around the back of Blake's head, running his fingers through his soft blond hair as he pulled him down to kiss him again.

Blake nipped his lower lip between his teeth. "Is that so, baby?" he asked. His blue eyes were blown wide with want and it was all for Elion. He couldn't believe how wretched he'd felt only an hour ago. Now everything was perfect.

"I want you to fuck me," he rasped. He ran his hands up Blake's back, under his damp shirt, and rolled his evident arousal up against Blake's own erection in his pants. "I want it so badly, please. If – if you don't feel up to it we can do something else, but-"

"I want that," said Blake, his voice low and heavy with need. "I want you. Show me how you like it. I want..." He faltered and swallowed. "I want to be as good as the other guys you've been with."

Elion stopped rutting against him immediately. He propped himself up on one elbow and cradled his face with the other. "You're not competing with anyone," he said earnestly as he looked into his beautiful eyes. "None of those other guys compare to you, alright? You're the only one I want. The only one I've ever loved. Whatever we do will be perfect."

Blake regarded him for a moment before nodding. "Okay," he whispered. He leaned down and kissed Elion, but this time it was slow and gentle. "I'm so happy you came into my life."

Elion snorted, somewhat breaking the mood, but he couldn't help it. "I wish I could tell eighteen-year-old me I'd have you as my boyfriend one day," he said. His hands were roaming as the heat turned up again. "He'd never believe it."

Blake laughed. "Holy shit, did you have a crush on me?"

Elion rolled his eyes. "Of course I did you moron, I had *eyes*."

Blake tickled his sides, making him jerk, and used the momentum to roll them onto their sides. "Well, you can tell eighteen-year-old you we got there in the end."

"It was worth the wait," Elion whispered.

After that, clothes became entirely optional and the two of them hustled out of them in no time at all. Elion's face hurt he was grinning so much, but he wasn't about to stop.

"What do you want me to do?" Blake asked as they wrapped themselves around each other like octopi. It was so tempting to just frot like that and come in a few minutes, but Elion had been craving Blake's lovely, thick cock inside him for weeks and he could be moderately patient in order to get that.

"You've got condoms, right?" he checked before they went any further. "And lube?"

Blake nodded, bashfully. "I looked up the best ones online."

"Did you now?" Elion teased, feeling like he'd died and gone to heaven. "You've been thinking about fucking me a lot then."

Blake bit his lower lip, his gaze through his eyelashes positively simmering. "I've been thinking about making love to you," he said. "Slowly, until you're a trembling, gibbering wreck of a man begging to come."

Elion just stared at him for a full ten seconds. "That," he eventually managed to utter. "That, let's do that. Please. Now."

Blake laughed.

Elion watched as he reached over to his bedside drawer and removed a small grocery carrier bag. Inside was a fresh packet of condoms and a pump action tube of lubricant, still with the seal intact.

Elion leaned up and took that from Blake, and they each dispensed of the cellophane wrappers. "This first," Elion said, wiggling the lube.

Blake swallowed visibly and left the condoms on the side. Elion laid back on his pillows as Blake took the tube back and straddled him again. "So, I, um…"

Elion took his hand and kissed his palm. "You won't break me, it's not my first rodeo," he added with a grin. "You just need to stretch me a bit. You've got quite a package there."

They both looked down at their somewhat softened erections. Blake snorted. "It's pretty big, I guess?"

"Don't act all coy, it's gorgeous." Elion peppered several kissed up his chest and nipped at his clavicle. "But it does mean I need a little help, then you can come right on in."

"Okay."

He sounded like he was doing his best to relax. Elion had all day though. He was so happy, he could burst. Coaxing his boyfriend through their first time doing anal would be an absolute pleasure.

"I can do it myself," he said, pointing at the lube. "But that's a bit boring for you. Just give it a go. Two fingers. Have you ever done it to yourself?"

Blake bit his lip and nodded. "I like it."

Elion stored *that* lovely little nugget of information away from later. "It's better if someone else does it though."

He laid back, pulling Blake almost into his arms so they could half cuddle while he prepped him. He moaned as he pushed his fingers inside, allowing himself to stretch out.

"Like that?"

Elion wriggled and panted. "Exactly like that."

"Fuck, you look hot." Blake captured his lips in a kiss, pulling his hand back and forth, adding a third finger without even needing to be told.

"Oh, no, like *that*," Elion groaned.

He reached down and started stroking Blake's cock, bringing it back to life. He loved the needy little noises Blake made as he touched him, feeling his hot length thickening and beginning to weep.

"Suit up," Elion gasped. "I hope you bought extra-large."

Blake was too far gone to respond. He just pulled his fingers free, leaving Elion feeling devoid. But not for long. Blake wiped his hand dry on the bedspread and tore open one of the foil packets. Elion made a keening noise as he watched Blake roll it down his big, hard cock.

If this was going to be a thing, a *real* thing, Elion was marching them down to a clinic as soon as humanly possible. He'd never been with anyone long enough to fuck without protection, but he wanted that with Blake. He wanted everything.

He grabbed one of the spare pillows and shoved it under his hips for a better position. Blake angled himself, lining up the head of his prick to Elion's throbbing hole. Elion surprised him by pulling his knees up to his chest and slipping his heels over Blake's shoulders.

"Flexible," he marveled.

"Oh, baby," Elion purred. "You have no idea."

He pushed his hole against Blake's cock, impaling himself

and relishing the burn. Blake took the hint and began to ease himself inside. It was a tight fit, but it felt incredible.

"Holy shit," Blake whimpered. "Are you alright? Oh my God, you feel amazing."

"Don't stop," Elion begged. "Give me more."

With one firm thrust, Blake bottomed out. Elion couldn't deny it hurt, but he knew that would pass. He gripped onto Blake's large arms, feeling the firm muscles underneath. He took in several deep breaths, slowly getting used to the intrusion into his body.

"Please," he rasped once he was comfortable enough. He rolled his hips, and the tip of Blake's cock rubbed against his prostate, setting off sparklers in front of his eyes. "Oh fuck, give it to me, baby, make me come."

Blake began to move his god-like body, undulating over Elion. He grabbed Elion's hip with one hand and his hair with the other. Elion couldn't tear his eyes away from his face as he fucked him deep and hard. He reached down and began to jerk himself off, feeling entirely wonton.

"Not gonna take long," he gasped.

Blake shook his head. "Me either. Go for it. Wanna see you come."

Elion arched his back and put on his best show, moaning and writhing and generally having the time of his life. Blake pound into him. All he could hear was their desperate pants and the slapping of skin. All he could smell was Blake's musk. His sweat dripped down onto Elion's chest.

"Come for me, Elion," he begged.

The sound of his name on those perfect lips launched him over the edge. He gave his cock one last tug before he felt like his body shattered and hot cum shot all over his belly. Blake grunted, slamming into him a few more times before he went rigid, filling the condom deep inside Elion.

Slowly, Elion's senses came back to him. He dropped his

heels and Blake edged out of him, carefully pulling the condom off his softening dick. Elion looked around for something to clean up with and was amused to see that there was a box of tissues in the pharmacy bag too. He'd learned from L.A.

Despite his fatigue, Elion ripped the pack open and fished several sheets out. He took the used condom from Blake and wrapped it up while he flopped down next to him. Then he set about mopping them both up.

"You're so caring," Blake said sleepily. "And totally not inhibited," he added with a laugh.

Elion smiled and shrugged. "It's just bodies, everyone has them. Besides, sex is amazing and all, but I prefer non-sticky cuddles afterwards."

Blake growled. "Hmm, come here you." He pulled Elion so he was snuggled against his chest. He carded his fingers through Elion's hair. "I didn't really believe sex was amazing anymore," he said. "I was starting to think I'd imagined it with Lola."

Elion looked up at him. "Did Joey ever tell you he thinks you're demi?"

Blake blinked at the apparent non sequitur. "Um, no. What's that, and when did he tell *you* that?"

Elion grinned and ran his fingers lightly up and down Blake's sternum. "In L.A., at the cocktail reception. Around the time he tried to convince me you were already totally in love with me."

Blake groaned and covered his eyes with the hand that wasn't resting on Elion's hip. "We were such idiots."

Elion pulled his hand down and kissed his knuckles. "We were," he agreed. "But he said you're demi, and I think he might be right. It means you're not physically attracted to people unless you're emotionally invested in them first."

Blake tilted his head to gaze down it him. He slipped his

hand away from Elion's and gently caressed his face. "Unless I love them."

Elion's heart sang. He nodded. "Unless you love them."

They cuddled closer together, wrapped in each other's arms. Elion listened to Blake's heart beating in his chest, allowing it to lull him to sleep in perfect contentment.

BLAKE

BLAKE COULDN'T REMEMBER THE LAST TIME HE FELT SO relaxed and at ease. He and Elion dozed for some time on his bed, comfortable in each other's arms after their passionate tryst. When Blake wasn't sleeping, he lightly ran his fingers through Elion's gorgeous black and pink hair, appreciating how beautiful he looked sated and sleepy.

"Stop staring at me, you pervert," he mumbled with his eyes closed. Blake barked out a laugh.

"I can't help it," he retorted. He nuzzled his nose into the hair he'd been admiring. Elion smelled of sex and it was almost enough to get him horny again. "You're so pretty."

"I'd argue I'm something far more manly," Elion said as he turned in Blake's arms to face him. "But we both know I'm *hella* pretty." He batted his long eyelashes and Blake leaned in to kiss him.

He loved how natural it felt to just lie there naked together. There wasn't any pressure to have sex, or cover up to remove temptation. It was just easy and sweet. He traced his fingertips along Elion's side, making him shudder. "I love your body," he said.

Elion cupped his jaw and looked into his eyes. "I love you," he said. He placed a chaste kiss on his lips. "Your body's alright," he added, rolling his eyes.

Blake tickled him as penance, but after a minute's wriggling and shrieking they settled into trading lazy kisses.

"I'm sorry I lost my cool over nothing," Elion said. He focused on his finger tracing patterns on Blake's chest rather than look at him. "It was stupid and insecure. I don't want you thinking that's what I'm about."

Blake captured the wandering hand and kissed a couple of fingertips. "It's fine. Let's just talk to each other now when we're upset, alright?" Elion looked at him and nodded.

"Promise."

Blake got to kiss and cuddle for a little while longer, but all too soon Elion checked the time on his phone and groaned. "I have to go," he said. He shook his head when Blake protested. "I want to be home when my mom gets there. I think she's still a bit fragile after last night."

Blake felt a surge of guilt. "That was awful, I'm so sorry."

Elion kissed him and shook his head. "We know the show likes to play with us. No harm done, not really. Unless," he bit his lip and sighed. "I don't know, I guess you know why I didn't go to college now."

"Neither did I," said Blake quickly. "I don't care about any of that stuff. I *do* think it's incredible that you took care of your mom like that. But, now? I just want you to be happy." He caressed Elion's cheek then the back of his neck. "If that's at the coffee shop, amazing. If there's something else you'd maybe like to think about, we could talk it through?"

Elion's eyes flicked back and forth, searching Blake's face. "Alright," he said with a shrug. It wasn't like him to be coy or reserved. But Blake hoped that meant he'd heard what he'd said and would consider it.

Blake thought he might want to do more than just serve

coffees. Even if that was simply moving into management, he would support him. As long as he was happy, then Blake would be too.

Unfortunately, Elion really did have to go. They had a quick rinse off in Blake's en suite and found their clothes again. Blake almost caught himself getting melancholy, which was ridiculous. Elion was his *boyfriend* now, they could see each other whenever they liked.

"Call me later, okay?"

"Promise," said Elion with a wink and slipped out the door. Blake wanted to walk him out, but Elion insisted they'd just end up saying goodbye seven times over and make him late. So he gave him a filthy kiss in his bedroom then told him to stay, like a puppy.

Blake grinned to himself then turned to the window to watch for him to get into his car and leave. He was totally smitten and he didn't care. Which was a good thing. Because no sooner had he looked out into the front yard, a sudden noise behind him made him realize he was no longer alone.

He spun around to see his dad standing inside his room by the door, folding his arms. The noise he'd heard was him slapping a pile of mail onto the obviously disturbed bed. That, along with the wads of tissue on the floor, and lube and condoms on the bedside table, painted a pretty clear image of what had been going on the past couple of hours.

His dad's jaw was clenched and he shook his head. "This is your idea of a pretend relationship?" he all but sneered.

But something miraculous happened. Blake didn't feel guilty, or cowed. He just felt irritated.

"Nope," he said cheerfully. "This is my idea of a very real relationship, where very real sex just happened. It was great," he added in a mad fit of daring as his dad threw up his hands up in disgust.

"God damn it, Blake," he snarled. "Why are you doing this to us?"

"Doing-?" said Blake faintly. "This may come as a shock to you," he said, slipping his hands into the pockets of his sweatshirt. "But this isn't really anything to do with you."

"The hell it isn't," his dad fumed.

Blake shook his head. "You're pathetic. Were you literally lurking outside, waiting for Elion to leave? You have issues."

"We've discussed this," his dad said, jabbing a finger at him. "If you decide you want to be bisexual-"

"I didn't *decide* anything," Blake said loudly, but his dad just carried right on yelling.

"-then you can date someone respectable. Not some Mexican coffee barista!"

"Oh, fuck you," said Blake. He didn't even feel angry. He just felt tired. "He's a great guy. He's kind. There's something you wouldn't know much about."

"You ungrateful, disrespectful," his dad fumed, curling his fists. "How dare you talk to me like that in my house. You would be nothing without us, *nothing!*"

Blake felt like he was seeing his dad – both his parents, but his dad in particular – clearly for the first time. "Actually," he said calmly. "I'm exceptionally good at what I do. And you know I'm thankful for the opportunities you've provided me. But that doesn't mean you get to hold me hostage to your whim for the rest of my life."

"While you're under this roof, you'll do as you're damn well told," his dad said. He was pale and shaking.

Blake felt just the smallest bit sorry for him. "I know you've tried to make the best of a bad situation, Dad," he said with no small amount of disdain. "You wanted a football player and got a little faggot dancer. But it was okay, so long as I wasn't *actually* queer. Well tough luck. Play your sports fantasies out with Jodi, if she'll let you. I'm done with this crap."

"We'll see about that," his dad retorted, not denying the accusations. He gave him a twisted caricature of a smile. "That boy's mother came into this country illegally as a child. Did you know that? I'm sure her health insurance company would love to hear all about it."

Blake's blood boiled, but he gritted his teeth and kept a lid on his temper. For now. "Did you just threaten a woman who's survived breast cancer?" He gave him a slow clap. "What a man. If you or your firm's private investigator – I assume that's who dug up the dirt? If you come near Elion or his mom again, I will rip you to shreds." He glowered with all the force he had. "I'm not fucking around."

A part of him was terrified that his dad had very real power over him and Elion with that threat. But as usual, he was all bluster with no actual weight behind him.

"He's not to set foot in this house again," his dad said, like he was winning this argument.

Blake scoffed and rolled his eyes. "Whatever. I'm moving out. As soon as I find my own place, I'm gone. This place is toxic."

His dad started off on another tirade about how unappreciative Blake was and how he wouldn't get away with disgracing the family like this. But something had caught Blake's eye and the alarm that filled him drowned out his words.

"Where did you get this?" he demanded, interrupting his dad mid-rant.

He snatched up the top letter from the mail he had brought in with him and left on the rumpled bed sheets. It was another one from the stalker, he was sure. He recognized the typeface and style of the envelope. However, there was one crucial difference.

His dad looked perplexed. "It's just what you had by the front door," he said with a scowl. "It doesn't matter, you need-"

"Shut up," Blake cried, panicked. "Look at it – *look!*" He thrust the letter into his dad's face. "It doesn't have a postage mark, not like the others. If it wasn't mailed, how did it get into the house?"

His dad's eyes widened as Blake tore into the letter.

You had your chance' read the familiar magazine cut-outs.

I'm so disappointed in you

Don't say I didn't warn you

This is your fault

"Elion," he whispered. He spun around and threw himself at the window. His car was still in the driveway. "ELION!"

He ignored his dad's protests as he bolted around him out into the corridor. His room was on the third floor and he took the stairs two at a time, calling his boyfriend's name. He was probably being stupid. But the note sounded like he was out of time.

How had it got into the house? Had someone delivered it by hand? Had the stalker *been there?*

He reached the foyer and bolted for the front door. "Elion!" he bellowed again.

Just as he reached the handle, the glass in the windows either side of the door shattered, imploding all over the polished floor. The door shook and Blake threw his arms up over his face as he staggered backwards.

Disbelief froze him in place as the glass finished tinkling to the ground. There was smoke outside.

"ELION!" he screamed.

27

ELION

ELION WISHED HE DIDN'T HAVE TO BID FAREWELL TO BLAKE, but it was more than likely a good thing that he needed to go home. It would probably do them both good to have a bit of space and process what had been quite an emotional few days.

Unlike before when he'd had worry twisting in his gut over where they stood and what was going to happen, he jogged down the stairs with a ridiculous grin on his face. He just wanted a bit of time to bask in the joy of making everything clear and honest between him and Blake. Never in a hundred years would he have foreseen this outcome.

Blake Jackson was his honest-to-God boyfriend.

He heard voices above him as he reached the second floor and stopped to jerk his head up. Now he was paying attention, he could hear other sounds of life on the other floors too.

As much as he wasn't afraid of these people – certainly not Jodi – he had no wish to make life difficult for Blake by antagonizing his parents. No doubt if they were home they had more than likely registered his car in the driveway, but he didn't need to have a face to face confrontation as well.

Unfortunately, he didn't get much of a choice as he crossed the second-floor landing and almost ran straight into Mrs. Jackson coming out of what looked like hers and Mr. Jackson's room.

"Jenna," he said brightly. She would be seeing a lot more of him now, so maybe it would be a good idea to ingratiate himself a little. "Hi, I was just on my way out."

She narrowed her eyes at him. She had a pair of skinny jeans on that hugged her flat stomach, pink, sparkly pumps, a floral camisole and diamond jewelry probably worth enough to pay his mom's mortgage for a year. Or longer, what did he know?

She looked him up and down. He decided in that moment that she didn't hate him. She just didn't know him. She bit her painted nail and seemed to consider what she wanted to say.

"Some of the moms said there was a bit of a scene at the school today," she said, just when the pause was threatening to get awkward between them. Now it was absolutely awkward.

Of course the yoga-latte brigade had sold him out. They probably had a whole social networking system in place for all the best gossip.

"Oh, yeah," he said with a laugh, hoping to brush it off. "I can be such a drama queen sometimes," he said. "Blake calmed me down though. You know what it's like when you're still getting to know each other. Hopefully that should be the last fit I throw for a good long while." He waved his hand in Jenna's direction. "Blake is such a good influence on me."

Jenna shifted on her three-hundred-dollar shoes. "But Blake's not gay though," she said with a shrill laugh. She fiddled with the sparkling necklace sitting on her prominent collarbones. "This is just a bit you're doing for the show."

Elion licked his lips. "You have an incredible son," he said, stepping closer and resting a hand on her slim shoulder. She allowed him to do it and didn't flinch away. Just looked up at him with wide blue eyes. The same eyes as Blake had. "I think you should talk with him. But he means the world to me and I respect him so much. All I'd ask is that you keep that in mind." He smiled and turned to jog down the next flight of stairs. "Oh," he turned to add before he rounded the bannister. "I think my mom would really love to meet you. Let me know if you'd like that too?"

To her credit, Jenna Jackson didn't dismiss him out of hand. She did pout in confusion though, looking down at the carpet with a frown as she opened and closed her mouth a couple of times.

Elion left her to mull it over. As much as he thought they'd never really be friends, he loved Blake and he wanted to build as many bridges as he could with his family.

He checked his watch as he trotted down into the foyer. He should still beat his mom home. It wasn't that long a drive between their two houses. This town wasn't really big enough to manage that.

"Oh, hey man," a vaguely familiar voice sounded. Elion paused for the second time, frowning as Rob Matherson stepped out from the den. As usual, he was wearing a Panthers sweatshirt and the same workout shorts as the team wore.

It was easy to feel sorry for him, but it was hard not to find him annoying too. Had he even played on the team when he'd been at school? The guy had graduated five years ago and he was still relying on his dad for a job with the softball team and hanging out with Seniors like Jodi, trying to reclaim some kind of glory days.

Elion was one to talk. But he'd not really had much choice about sticking around this place.

He had a moment's private pause where suddenly, that didn't seem like such a burden anymore. In fact, with Blake by his side, the idea of getting settled together around here seemed pretty appealing.

His pleasure and joy was undoubtedly showing on his face. He tried to temper in down. It would be uncouth to announce to the world how thoroughly well fucked Below Zero's Blake Jackson had left him.

"Oh hey," he said. "You waiting on Jodi again?"

"Yeah," Rob said. He was giving Elion a once-over, he was sure. He was almost certain his dick wasn't hanging out his pants, so he decided whatever he was seeing he could deal with. Elion wasn't bothered.

"Well I better get going," he said, moving towards the door.

"You here with Blake?" Rob asked, making him pause.

Elion shrugged. "Yeah, just hanging out," he downplayed. The first person he was going to talk to about the magnificent fucking he'd just had was not going to be this guy. "Anyway-"

"You know he's still never spoken to me," said Rob, shaking his head. "Not at school, not since he's been home. Even though Jodi and I are friends. Isn't that crazy?" He laughed, but Elion detected a hint of bitterness there. Man, some people were just so fame hungry and celebrity obsessed. It was like he thought Blake owed him a conversation or a selfie or something. He needed to let it go.

"I'm sure it'll happen," said Elion as kindly as he could. After all, this guy didn't have the most exciting life, of that he was already sure. "Just play it cool, he'll totally come say hi soon. He's a good guy."

Rob chuckled and nodded. "That's why he's your boyfriend, right?"

Elion distracted himself by pulling his car keys out. "Yeah," he said. He didn't really feel like going into it. Blake was his, he was special and it felt like this guy just saw him as a meal ticket or shiny prize to be idolized. "I have to head out I'm afraid. But catch you later, okay?"

"Sure buddy," said Rob warmly. "Take care."

Elion blinked to himself as he headed towards the door. Maybe Jodi would make him a little bit more chilled? Though, to be honest, he wasn't sure why she was still hanging out with him.

At the turn of the handle, Elion heard a scrabbling of paws from behind on the marble. "Oh, hey girl," he said, happily bending down to rub Watson's back. "Did you miss me?"

She barked as he pulled the door open, and before he knew it, she zipped out the yard and up to his car. He laughed and shook his head.

"Come on now, you can't come with me," Elion chuckled. A quick glance over his shoulder told him Rob had vanished again and he sighed. At least he wasn't awkwardly hovering. "Watson," he called with a whistle.

She ran in a circle a couple of times and howled. He was evidently going to have to go get her.

"Come on sweetie," he called, stepping outside. Of course the door swung shut behind him. That was okay though, in theory Jodi was close enough to let them back in. That, or he'd have to have another awkward conversation with Rob.

Watson sprinted back to him, but before he could try and pick her up, she darted off again. Lucky she was only a medium sized dog as she launched herself at Elion's car door and slammed her paws against the already chipping paint work.

"Watson, no," he snapped. But she didn't seem to care. She just kept wagging her tail and ran around his legs as he walked up the inspect the door. He opened it to check it still swung out okay. As he suspected before, he'd forgotten to lock it. But in the heat of the moment, he could forgive himself.

It opened just fine; she didn't weigh that much after all. So there was no harm done. But she was barking and yowling down the house, jumping into the driver's seat and out again. She head-butted him and ran this way and that, clearly agitated.

Never having had a dog of his own, Elion wasn't sure what to do other than try and get her back inside the house. "Come on, darling," he said. He left the car door open and tried to herd her back towards the house. She was really braying though, jumping on his legs then running away again.

He began to feel worried. Maybe she was sick. As he got closer to the house she raced up and began scratching the door. Jenna would probably hate that, so he jogged the last couple of feet towards the steps.

He had no warning as the blast exploded through the air. The sound of his car squealing apart and the roar of the flames hit just before the heat did. The force knocked him off of his feet as debris rained down around him. He only caught a glimpse of the concrete front step before it rushed to meet his face, and his whole world went black.

28

BLAKE

BLAKE DIDN'T THINK AS HE LAUNCHED HIMSELF AT THE DOOR. His brain only seemed capable of processing actions. The foremost of which was getting to Elion.

Because he couldn't have been in the middle of whatever had just happened. He couldn't. Because they had only just sorted out all their crap and everything was good and-

He yanked open the door to see Elion slumped over the steps, Watson running up and licking his face as blood pooled over the step.

"NO!" He registered the flaming wreck of a car down the drive, but that wasn't his immediate concern. Whether or not Elion was breathing was the only thing that mattered.

He fell down on the front steps and carefully pulled him into his lap. He jammed his two fingers against Elion's throat, pleading to the universe that he'd find a pulse. The little *thrum thrum thrum* made him sob in relief, as did the pitiful moan Elion uttered. He still didn't seem conscious, but he was sure as hell alive.

"HELP!" he screamed, cradling Elion to him. They needed

all the flashing lights right now, and he wasn't moving anywhere until they came. "ANYBODY!"

It felt like it had been minutes, but it could only have been seconds before someone rushed to his side. He felt reassuring hands on his shoulders. Even if it was his dad, after their fight, he was grateful.

"Holy shit, Blake, what happened?"

He didn't recognize that voice. He turned to look behind him to see a guy about his age who he'd never seen before in his life.

"He needs an ambulance," Blake managed to croak out, despite his confusion.

The guy shook his head and moved to the side of them, then took Blake's shoulders in his hands again. "Everything's going to be fine, Blake."

Blake looked between the flaming wreck and down at his beautiful boyfriend's face. "Have you called 911?"

The guy shook his head. "For fuck's sake," he muttered. "Do you even recognize me?"

Blake blinked and looked up as the guy stood. Watson was pawing pitifully at Elion's side, trying in her doggy way to rouse him. What was this guy saying?

Blake was so used to all the various crew hanging around, having strangers in his home didn't seem all that odd to him. But who was this guy? Why did he think Blake should know him?

Fuck, was he one of those psychos who connected with famous people then got pissed when they didn't know them?

"Look, man, I'm so sorry, but right now Elion really needs to get to a hospital." He could hear shouting from inside the house. Reinforcements were coming.

The guy shook his head and pulled out a glass jar with a plastic cap from his hoodie pocket. "Why are you making this so hard?"

Blake frowned and wiped Elion's forehead. He was almost certain it was just a small gash on his temple that was bleeding. He remembered when they were sound-checking on tour once and Raiden had got smacked on the head with a wayward prop. Head wounds gushed like a motherfucker, so he couldn't freak out too much about the blood.

But Elion was still unconscious. Breathing, but not awake.

Watson was growling at the stranger, her tail tucked between her legs and her ears dropped down either side of her head. Blake heard his mother shouting and the door swung open.

"No!" the guy screamed, yanking the cap off the bottle. "No, no, we're finally talking! You have to leave us alone!"

Blake looked between him and his folks. They'd stopped at the threshold, talking in the scene on their front yard. "It's okay," he rasped. "Everything's fine, we just need to call 911."

"Rob?" his dad said.

Blake looked back over. "Rob, is it? I don't know what's happening. Can you help us out?"

The guy, Rob, bared his teeth. "You didn't even remember my *name*, did you?" He laughed, a hollow, grating sound. "And now you want my help?"

He sloshed the bottle in his hand around, disturbing the clear liquid inside. Blake had a sudden, sickening feeling in his gut.

"Yes, I really need your help," he said. Elion was so heavy in his arms. Watson had stopped barking and was now whimpering and licking the bare skin on his arm. "Why don't you tell me what you want?"

His mom made as if to move, but his dad threw his arm out to stop her. He'd spotted the bottle as well.

Rob started laughing so hard it became a sob. "What do I *want?*" he yelled. "I *wanted* you to say hi once in a while. I *wanted* to be in your homecoming court. I *wanted* to be on your show, just for a second. But you're always too good for the little people, aren't you? Mr. Superstar Boy Band!"

He spat on the grass.

Elion's poor car was still blazing on the drive several feet away and it felt like half the street had all come out to look at what was going on. Kala and Seth were there with Marcus, the whole crew fanned out around the property. Half a dozen cameras recording the most terrifying moment of his life.

No one was trying to get near them though, not even his own parents. Blake was thankful; he didn't know what Rob would do if anyone approached. Although he also didn't know how to end this standoff.

Was that sirens wailing in the distance? Or was he merely just so desperate he was imagining things?

This had to be the stalker. He'd brought the letter inside today. But how? Where had he come from? Why had he been able to gain access to Blake's family home?

"What's in the bottle, Rob?" he asked, drawing Elion closer to his body.

Rob snarled. He had tears running down his face and he was trembling. "You're so pretty, so talented. But you're also just like everyone else, you'll see. I'll help you. It's okay, being ordinary. I'll make you normal, like everyone else."

Blake wasn't ashamed to admit he was scared shitless. A teaspoon's worth of the liquid from the bottle had sloshed onto the grass a minute ago, and now it was starting to smoke.

It was acid.

All it would take would be a flick of the wrist, and he could hurt him and Elion beyond imagination. Blake grit his teeth and rolled Elion against his body, protecting his face, getting blood all over his sweatshirt.

"Do you think this will make me like you?" he said. He was probably getting this all wrong, but all he could think of was to keep talking while the sirens drew closer. "You hurt the man I love."

"You don't love him!" Rob screeched.

Blake saw his parents flinch back. He was extremely comforted that they hadn't run back inside to safety.

Rob was close to hyperventilating he was breathing so hard. "You don't know him!" he repeated. "The stupid show put you together, it was an accident! Jodi told me! You didn't know Rodriguez at school either. You just need a chance, I can show you how good we'd be together!"

"Rob," Blake tried.

"You ran off in that band, whoring yourself out," Rob blathered on. He pulled at his hair and swung the bottle wildly again, a couple of droplets landing on the concrete. "You were never a singer, Blake. Why would you do that, why would you leave?"

Blake was aware of all the people around them but they were all so far away. The sirens were so loud now and blue and red lights were flashing against the walls of the house, but they were still no help. All Blake knew was that he had to protect Elion and face off Rob. Even if that meant getting badly hurt.

"I don't remember you," he said, his voice cracking. "I'm guessing we went to school together, but I'm sorry, I just don't know you. That isn't my fault. And it sure as *hell* isn't Elion's. So if you're going to act out some petty revenge fantasy, leave him out of it. I'm here, deal with me. Give *me* all your fucking anger. He had nothing to do with it."

"He was just in the *right* place at the *right* time," Rob yelled.

He snarled at Elion. Blake tucked him in closer, wrapping both his arms firmly around his body and curling his legs up in front of him. He'd die before he let any more harm come to Elion. He knew that with startling clarity.

"I told you to get rid of him, he could have walked away," said Rob. He hiccuped and jabbed his finger towards Blake. *"Heartbeat. Time's stopped,"* he bawled. *"Take heed. My love. Endless looooove, underground! In our truuuuuth, hearts bound!"* He let out a keening noise and stepped closer to Blake and Elion. *"Oh oh oohh!* I know all the words, for fuck's sake!"

Blake was furious and petrified and utterly helpless. He tucked Elion's face into his neck. Whatever this deranged lunatic did, he wasn't going to ruin Elion's beautiful smile.

He felt a tear run down his cheek. "You know those lyrics mean absolutely jack shit?" he spat out, somewhat hysterically. "Literally nothing. The guys were high when they came up with them."

Rob blinked and shook his head. "No, no," he stammered.

From the corner of his eye, Blake saw a shape emerge from around the side of the house. He was too terrified of taking his eyes off Rob to even think about looking properly. Whoever it was, Blake begged to the cosmos they knew what they were doing. If Elion got burned he would never, ever forgive himself.

Watson, damn her, was still there too. She started howling again, scrabbling against Blake and Elion's side, snarling at their attacker. Blake wanted to scream. If she got hurt he'd be responsible for that too, and she was being so damn brave.

The blur behind Rob was moving fast now. Blake's mom flinched.

Rob turned, taking his focus off of Blake and Elion, enabling Blake to scramble backwards a few feet, dragging Elion with him. He looked up just in time to see his sister Jodi raise her softball bat and smack Rob square in the face with it.

He spun away from her, letting the bottle of acid tumble to the grass. His body dropped like a sack of potatoes, an arc of blood spraying from his mouth before he hit the dirt.

"You fucking *asshole!*" Jodi shrieked.

Rob didn't get back up.

Suddenly everything was a frenzy of activity. Blake's mom seized Jodi away from Rob's prone form and hauled her over to collapse by Blake and Elion, steering clear of the acid. His dad started shouting out orders as the emergency services sprinted up the lawn towards them. Firefighters saw to the smoldering wreck of Elion's car while paramedics ran for Elion and the police cautiously marked out the acid spill and approached the unconscious Rob.

Kala led the film crew and they raced around Blake, Elion and his family. Blake hardly registered as the cold, black lenses flew around his face, soaking up the drama of one of the worst moments of his entire life.

He ignored them entirely. He wasn't mad, but he wasn't giving them anything either. His sole focus was on Elion and Elion alone.

Once the authorities were sure Rob was no longer a danger they let a pair of medics tend to him while others swooped in and pried Elion from Blake's grasp. "Be careful," he stuttered.

"We will, son," said the guy as he began his assessment.

Blake's mom was shaking and hysterical, hugging him and Jodi to her as another paramedic draped a foil blanket over her shoulders.

Blake didn't take his eyes off of Elion as the medics did their thing, but he blindly groped for Jodi's hand all the same.

"Thank you," he uttered.

She squeezed his hand back. "Don't mention it."

He laughed. It was totally inappropriate, but he took a

moment to regain his composure. "I'm guessing you got that scholarship, with a swing like that?"

He heard her snicker. "Damn right I did."

They watched as the team rolled over a gurney to Elion. Blake untangled himself from his mom and sister. His dad was still puffing around, trying to make himself look important in front of the neighbors. "I'll ride with him," Blake said.

The paramedics nodded, not questioning his request, and he was eternally grateful.

His sister pulled him into a hug before he could leave, not caring that he was covered in Elion's blood.

"It's going to be okay," she said as Watson wound her way between their feet.

Blake nodded into her neck.

It was going to be okay. He knew it.

29

ELION

ELION FELT LIKE HIS SKULL WAS TWICE AS BIG AS HIS HEAD. HE groaned as consciousness crept over him and light permeated his closed eyelids. His mouth was dry and he felt nauseous.

A warm, strong hand slipped against his and squeezed.

"Baby?"

His heart fluttered. He wanted to reach out for that voice.

"Blake?" he croaked. Or at least he tried. His tongue felt numb and his throat like sandpaper.

"Hang on, wait." Blake sounded panicky. He slipped his hand under Elion's head, tipping his head forward. Cool water touched his lips and trickled into his mouth. He swallowed gratefully.

Slowly, he peeled his eyes open. They were gritty with sleep and stung against the artificial light. Blake face swam into his vision. "Hey," he uttered.

Blake broke into a relieved smile. "Hey yourself. How are you feeling?"

Elion looked around at his surroundings. It was

nighttime. The white walls and beeping equipment quickly told him where he was.

Hospital.

He couldn't afford to be here, what the fuck was happening? He tried to sit up, but Blake quickly put the cup of water down and pinned his shoulder against the bed.

"Hey, not so fast. You've got a concussion," Blake said. His beautiful blue eyes were blazing with concern. "The doctor said you need rest, okay?"

Elion blinked. It was slowly coming back to him now. Something had happened, at the house. "My insurance," he said. "Can't afford..." He wasn't even fully conscious yet, but the burn of his embarrassment tried to pull him almost all the way into waking again.

Blake shook his head and brushed his hair back. "You're covered by the show," he said, warmth saturating every word. "Don't worry about that. You need to rest and recover."

Recover from what exactly? What had happened? At least he didn't have to worry about the money if what Blake was saying was true. Elion found the hand resting on his chest and squeezed it. "Thank you."

Blake sat back down. He was gorgeous as always, but he also looked a wreck. He was covered in blood.

The last of Elion's fogginess was washed away by panic. "You're hurt?"

Blake kissed the hand he was holding again, his lips soft against Elion's fingers. "It's your blood," he said, shakily. He blinked a couple of times, his eyes glassy. "Do you remember what happened?"

All he could recall was Blake's dog going crazy at him. "Is Watson okay?" he asked. "She went nuts, then..." Then he'd hit the door step. No, he'd been pushed. It was loud and hot and...holy fuck. "Was there a *bomb?*" He couldn't believe he was really asking that.

But Blake nodded. "The stalker put a device in your car," he said. Anger simmered in every word. He looked murderous. "The police think it activated when you opened the door. If you'd have sat inside…"

His words trailed off as he furiously clenched his teeth. His grip had become vice-like around Elion's hand. He used his free one to rub Blake's fingers, urging him to ease up.

"Hey, hey," he said. "I didn't. Watson saved me." He realized that was true, and he felt the tears pooling in his eyes. "She wouldn't stop barking and running around. She herded me like a sheepdog back towards the house." He chuckled and wiped some of the wetness from his eyes. "I think I owe her a steak or a bone or whatever she likes best."

"Carrots," said Blake, covering his mouth as he laughed. It was laden with heavy relief. A couple of his own tears escaped and he brushed them off. "Are you serious?" he asked. "She pulled you away? She's going to be the most spoiled dog in the whole damn country. I'm going to buy her a golden kennel."

They chuckled wetly for a few moments before lapsing into silence. Blake couldn't take his eyes off Elion, but that was fine. Elion could stand to be looked at like that forever.

"A bomb?" he said eventually. "From the person writing those letters?"

Blake scowled again. "The guy was seriously deranged," he said.

"A guy?" Elion repeated in surprise.

Blake nodded. "He had all these crazy fixations on me. I think he thought if you were out of the way that we could be together." He took a deep, shuddery breath. "When you were passed out, he threatened both of us with a jar of acid."

If Elion hadn't felt sick before, he was about ready to throw his guts up at that. "What happened?" he managed to ask.

To his surprise, Blake laughed. "You might want to ask Jodi that."

Elion had too many questions. "Okay, but is he still out there, or-?"

"No, no," said Blake. He probably realized Elion was too overwhelmed for him to dance around the subject. "Jodi knocked him out cold and now the cops have him. We're safe."

Elion blinked. Jodi had done what? He'd definitely have to ask her about that. But he had other, more pressing concerns.

"Who was he?" he asked.

"Some guy who said he went to school with me. Us, I guess." Blake told him with a shrug. "My dad called him Rob."

Elion sat up so fast Blake didn't have a chance to stop him. "Rob *Matherson?*" he spluttered.

"Yeah, you remember him?"

"Not from school," Elion admitted. "But I've seen him recently, with Jodi. Is she okay? Is she here?"

Fucking Rob Matherson. He *knew* there was something he hadn't liked about that guy. So much for a harmless celebrity fascination.

Blake rolled his eyes, his face darkening. "Everyone's here. Oh!" he squeezed Elion's hand. "I promised I'd go get your mom as soon as you were awake. She didn't want to leave you but I made her go eat with Jodi. A nurse should probably take a look at you too." He stood up and cradled the back of Elion's head. "Will you be okay for a minute?"

Elion looked around the hospital room again. He could now see all the colorful flowers on the bedside cabinets of his private room and on the window-sill. He was safe here. Everything was okay.

"I'll be fine, baby," he said. "Just, hurry back okay?"

He sounded a bit pathetic, but his nerves were still frayed. Having Blake near him made things better, as usual.

Blake smiled and kissed him gently. "You won't even know I'm gone."

Elion doubted that, but he really wanted his mom, as pathetic as that was for someone his age. Plus, the sooner Blake left, the quicker he'd be back. So Elion nodded and waved him out the door.

He downed another couple of mouthfuls of water, then slumped back against his pillows.

Rob had written those letters. Loser Rob. Elion snorted to himself. He guessed that Advanced Chem wasn't so boring to him after all. Psycho.

They were so similar in so many ways. Both left behind in this small town when the rest of their class had gone off into the world. Elion felt just the smallest bit proud he hadn't turned out like Rob. Bitter and twisted.

He was in love. And he had his whole life before him.

Movement at the door startled him, but it wasn't Blake. Jenna Jackson walked in with two cans of Diet Coke balanced in one hand and a bag of skinny popcorn in the other. At seeing Elion, she stopped short.

"Oh you're awake!" she cried with a smile. Then she leaned back out into the corridor. *"He's awake!"*

Elion winced, wondering what time of night it was and hoping not too many patients were asleep already. Very quickly though, his concerns swung right back around to himself.

Kala and Marcus led half a dozen more crew members into the room. Elion's mouth dropped open as they set up lights, sound and props with their usual clinical efficiency. More flowers and candy and teddy bears were pulled from nowhere and a makeup artist began powdering his nose without even saying so much of a hello.

"Um, Kala?" he said, feeling like he was going to scream. "I was just almost blown up."

Kala stopped talking with one of the P.A.s to dart over and grab his hand. "I know," she said dreamily. "I'm so glad you're okay. Now we're definitely in with a chance for an Emmy." She fussed with his hair fondly. "I told you you were good at this."

Elion wanted to say something to the effect that almost dying was not a *talent*, but as she moved away Jenna walked back in, accompanied by a very unlikely pair.

For once, the neckline on Nessa's top was so high it was almost to her collarbones. It was still sprayed on, but that coupled with the full-length jeans looked like her attempt at demure. Next to her walked Karyn.

Elion looked between the two of them. But they were definitely not pulling each other's hair or even throwing the side-eye. In fact, they looked positively chummy.

"What-" he said faintly as Jenna had a word with Kala.

Nessa and Karyn glanced at each other. "Oh, we're cousins," Nessa said flippantly.

"Yeah," Karyn giggled. "Didn't you know?"

"Hey, who's got our flowers?" Nessa asked.

Elion just watched on mutely as P.A.s gave them both massive bunches as well as wiring him for sound.

"No," said Karyn. "We need to swap. If I have the bigger bunch, you can get jealous."

"Oh, right," agreed Nessa with a nod, handing over her bouquet. "So you need to fangirl, while I flirt. Where's Blake?"

"Getting my mom," said Elion. Of course their rivalry was fake. For fuck's sake – nothing was real on this show. "Look, I know you guys want to make a good episode, but I really do feel lousy right now."

That was putting it mildly. The room was spinning, he

was nauseous and the pain on the side of his head was becoming unbearable. He could feel the cold sweat all over his skin, despite the heat from the lights.

"Oh honey, you've done so well," said Jenna. She stepped over and went to touch him, but tactfully withdrew her hand when she saw how damp he was with perspiration. "Oh, can we, um, get some more powder?"

"Or a nurse?" Elion mumbled.

They were already filming though, and Nessa and Karyn were jostling to put their flowers the closest to him. They took turns fussing over him and the cameras circled.

"Can you believe it," said Karyn sympathetically, taking his hand. Nessa took the other one. Elion looked helplessly between them both.

"Believe what?"

"Rob!" they both said together, then scowled across the bed at each other.

"The P.A.," said Karyn.

"The one who gave Blake the faulty shoes."

"*You* gave him the faulty shoes," Karyn shot back.

"No, Tyler did!" snapped Nessa. "You weren't even there!"

"Hang on," said Elion. Their shouting was making his head worse. "Rob...was a P.A.?"

Nessa and Karyn looked at Kala.

"Uh, yeah, Nessa whispered. "Didn't you see him with Seth? They were practically inseparable."

Elion hadn't seen Seth in weeks. Fuck...were he and Rob in it together?

He was cut off from responding by three more people trying to enter the already overcrowded room. "What the fuck?"

Elion was stunned to realize it was his own mother who had cursed. She *never* swore in English. As if to prove his point, she let out a string of shocking profanities in Spanish as she stormed into the room, Blake and Jodi following behind her.

"No," she shouted. "No, no, *no!* My boy almost *died,* and you're here for your silly little TV show still?"

Elion sagged in relief. Blake and Jodi pushed past Nessa and Karyn to sit by his bed, and his mom squared off with Kala.

"Get out, *now.* Elion needs rest. He is not here for your entertainment!"

Elion liked Kala. He did. But he'd be a fool to think anything came before getting a great show to her. "Mrs. Rodriguez," she said kindly. "I think you'll find that Elion's contract states-"

Music blasted through the room. Despite his terrible headache, Elion snapped around to see Blake holding his phone aloft.

Blake smirked. "Sorry, what was that?" he asked with mock concern. "I couldn't hear you over Taylor Swift and her iron clad copyright laws."

Kala blinked. "Blake..." she said. There was no way she could film anything useable with this song playing and they all knew it.

"No, Kala," he snapped.

They had to shout a bit to be heard, but it was worth it. Elion still felt like he was going to pass out, be he was also bursting with pride.

"You're not filming Elion here," he said. He slipped his hand against Elion's and looked down at him. "This show has put him through hell and I won't take another minute."

"Blake," said Jenna, waving her hands in the air. He held the phone away from her though. "Sweetie, we need this. For the show."

"Screw the show," said Blake. "That's it, I quit." He looked down at Elion. "Unless-"

"I quit," said Elion loudly. Enough so they definitely heard him over Taylor. "Thanks for the hot, awesome boyfriend, but now it's time to go."

"Blake!" shrieked Jenna.

Elion's own mom came and stood behind where Blake was sitting. She threw her arms around his shoulders though and jutted her chin out. "Cameras out, now!"

Blake held the phone up higher as Taylor went for another chorus and Jodi opened the door.

"Off you go," she said sweetly, batting her eyelashes.

Jenna looked between her children and seemed like she was going to put up a fight. But at that moment a tall, middle-aged nurse stormed in with a face like thunder.

"What the-" she said faintly. "Out. Now. All of you!"

"No," whimpered Elion as she pushed her way through to him. "I want some of them here."

She narrowed her eyes and looked around at everyone as the Taylor song started over again. "You can have two."

"I need three," he said.

She sighed.

"Okay everyone except-" she let him point at Blake, Jodi and his mom "-you, you and you. Everyone else, out. If I catch you in here outside of visitor hours again, I'm calling the police."

They all tried to protest, but the tall nurse – Becky, according to her name tag – was formidable. Elion gratefully slumped further into his bed as she made Kala, Nessa and all the rest march out.

Karyn, bless her, swopped in to give him a kiss on the cheek before she went. "I'll visit tomorrow," she said, squeezing his shoulder. Despite her nefarious tactics to get ahead on the show, she was kind of a sweet kid.

The door clicked shut and Blake immediately killed the music and pulled Elion into a hug. "I'm so sorry," he moaned.

Elion laughed. "That was pretty funny," he muttered as Becky checked his vitals. She winked at him and patted his leg.

Blake, Jodi and his mom crowded around him, careful not to get in the nurse's way. "How are you feeling?" Elion's mom asked.

He shook his head. "Wretched," he said shakily, trying to smile. He looked at Becky. "Is there anything I can get for that?"

She huffed. "Of course honey," she said. "You also need to sleep. So you guys get five minutes, okay?"

His visitors nodded as she bustled off to – hopefully – fetch Elion some drugs.

"Did you mean that?" Jodi asked her brother with a smirk. "Did you really just tell Mom to shove it?"

Blake scrubbed his face and his shoulders slumped. "I'm just so tired, you know?" he said.

Elion's mom fussed with his pillows and swept his wet hair back. "They tried to make fools out of all of us," she said with a frown. "But what you boys have…" She bit her lip and reached out to take Blake's hand. "It's real. Isn't it?"

"Very real," said Elion.

"I love him," said Blake over the top of him. Then he blushed and looked at Elion rather than his mom. "So, um, yeah. We can quit."

Jodi drummed her fingers against the metal bed frame. "Okay, hear me out," she said. "But, you guys have a *massive* fan base."

"That's true," said Elion's mom. Naturally she knew more about his social media presence than he did.

"You guys are a little bit gay royalty," Jodi continued. She gave her brother a light punch on the arm and a grin. "So, how about we think of a compromise?"

Elion sighed in relief as the nurse, Becky, came back with

painkillers to add to his I.V. "Elion will need to sleep soon," she warned the room.

He felt the fuzzy, welcome relief almost immediately. "Thank you," he whispered to her as she left.

"What kind of compromise?" Blake asked. Elion suspected he wanted to finish this talk before he passed out.

Jodi shrugged and looked at Elion's mom. "How about; you see out this season. Get through the end of year performance. Then you can renegotiate your involvement. Seems to me like Nessa and Karyn would die to be the stars. You could work with that so you could step down from the show."

That solved one issue, Elion thought. He wanted him and Blake to have some distance from this toxic production and have a chance to flourish as a real couple. But what about their fans? It was beyond amazing to think he was inspiring young queer kids in a way he never saw growing up.

"Could we," he said. He struggled with his words. Sleep was laying thickly over him. "Do like a thing, like on Twitter or Insta or something. Like…have a presence as a couple. That we did ourselves, and the show had nothing to do with?"

"A vlog," said his mom, snapping her fingers.

"A vlog," agreed Jodi.

"A vlog?" asked Blake.

"Video blog, babe," Elion mumbled. "That could work – just a little thing."

Blake stroked his hair as he snuggled into his pillow. "The two of us making a video. About what?"

"Us," said Elion, grinning broadly. "Just, like, being awesome and in love and stuff." He laughed, the drugs seeping into his system. "Show 'em all how it's done."

Blake smiled indulgently at him. "Wouldn't that be boring?" he asked.

Elion blew a raspberry. "I'm delightful," he said as his eyelids drooped. "And…have you met you? You're, like, uh, the most best and wonderful…"

His tongue was fat and heavy against his teeth. Sleep enveloped him.

The last thing he saw was Blake nodding. "Okay, baby," he said, his words swimming around Elion's brain. "Let's do that."

30

BLAKE

THE HOSPITAL KEPT ELION IN A FEW MORE DAYS BEFORE letting him home to his mom. Blake visited every day before or after his classes and brought all the presents from his students and their parents to cheer Elion up. The kids were so sweet, hand making get-well cards and buying him candy with their allowance. It warmed Blake's heart to see how so many of them had accepted him as being Blake's partner.

A few of the parents had pulled their kids from the classes over the whole Rob debacle. Blake couldn't say he blamed them, but included amongst them were some of the outwardly homophobic families, so he'd been thrilled to see them go.

Seth was no longer in the picture. According to the cops, Rob had been encouraged a fair bit in his stalker behavior by Seth, who had no doubt been angling for a dramatic finale to the show.

That was enough for Blake's mom to fire him, but apparently he'd lawyered up and so far hadn't been officially charged with anything. Blake had heard that he was already out in California, getting ready to make a documentary about eighteen-year-olds who got breast implants as a graduation gift.

Kala had taken Jodi's suggestion to ease Blake and Elion away from the limelight pretty well. They were in contract negotiations but it looked like after they got through this season, Blake would be allowed to simply teach and Nessa would take the lead on the drama side of things. She and Karyn had already sent him deliriously happy thank you video messages.

His mom had also come around to the idea of their own separate vlog surprisingly easily. She liked the idea of him being on both, even if he'd just be dancing on Feet of Flames.

With Seth no longer calling the shots, he and Kala had been free to make some changes to the show's cast to fill the spots. Their first stop had been to Mercy's house, the girl who hadn't made the cut despite Blake's loud protests. The look on her face when he told her she was in the class had made him want to cry, especially when she showed him how far she'd come with practicing all her techniques. Kala got to capture it all on film, and everyone was happy.

That morning, Mercy's mom had come over with homemade casserole for Elion when he got out of the hospital. She'd also presented him with a pair of beaded bracelets. Apparently, she crafted them herself as part of her online business.

The jewelry was made from healing crystals and she had tailored each bracelet for him and Elion. The little stones represented different things, like revitalizing energy and protection for Elion, and clarity and strength for Blake.

Blake wasn't sure he really believed in any of it, but they were beautiful. Even better, he loved the idea of Elion and him having something matching to wear. It made his heart sing in a way his voice was never quite able to manage.

He arrived on the Rodriguez's doorstep for the second

time in the past couple of weeks with a camera crew in tow. But Blake had made Kala completely aware that she was only there to film him welcoming Elion back home. Then she and the other guys had to go. Because Blake fully intended to spend the whole night reassuring himself that Elion's body was fine and no lasting damage had been done.

With Lucy's permission to stay the night, of course. He was going to show her what a model son-in-law he could be.

She was the one who greeted them at the door. The affection in the immediate hug she gave Blake brought a lump to his throat.

His own mom seemed to be under the impression that the last few days had been all about her. She'd been wailing to anyone who would listen about how she was going to be in therapy for PTSD the rest of her life.

That had pissed Elion off no end. Primarily because the hospital nurse Becky had pulled him aside and suggested that Elion was going to suffer with exactly that after his ordeal.

He had mentioned that to his mom largely in a bid to get her to stop overreacting and being selfish. She had stunned him though by seriously considering his words. "You boys will probably need counseling even more than me," she'd said, without there even being any cameras around to capture her philanthropy. "If you want to see a specialist together, I'll get your father to pay."

Blake's dad still wasn't speaking to him. After his disgusting outburst on the day of the bomb, he was either too angry, too proud or too embarrassed to apologize. But Blake didn't really care. He meant what he said about not jumping through hoops for him anymore. And if he paid for therapy so Elion could heal and move on the best way possible, then Blake would take that as recompense for all the times he'd made feel Blake less than a man.

He'd never been close to his dad, so he wouldn't miss a relationship with him if he wanted to continue being an ass.

Lucy was thrilled at the casserole and took down Mercy's mom's number to get in touch to say thanks. She was so effortlessly friendly, it was inspiring.

Kala filmed Blake heading down to Elion's bedroom to present him with the gifts from school and a big hug. Then they were done. He watched on as Kala shooed the camera crew out the door, and Lucy loudly announced she was spending the evening with her PFLAG friends and for the boys not to wait up.

Within five minutes, Blake and Elion had the house to themselves. Blake's heart started racing.

Elion looked so much better than he had the first couple of days in the hospital. The color had come back to his cheeks, and once he stopped being so drowsy and the pain wore off, his lovely smile had returned.

"Hello stranger," he said when Blake had successfully chased everyone else away and returned to his bedroom. Elion was dressed in sweatpants and a t-shirt and propped up on about a dozen pillows and snuggled under several blankets, despite the fact it was a gorgeous spring day outside.

Blake wasn't sure he'd seen a cozier, more inviting sight in his life. He kicked off his shoes and crawled under the covers, taking him into his arms and kissing him softly.

"Can I please look after you?" he asked.

It had been torture only being able to hold his hand since the attack. Even the few kisses they'd been able to steal when no one else had been around had done nothing to ease his desperate need to check Elion's body over for himself. He had to make sure it was still perfect, even though he'd only sustained superficial cuts in the blast.

Elion cradled his face and they looked into each other's

eyes for a moment. "You're always the one looking after me," he said.

"Not true," Blake insisted. He thought of all the many ways Elion had cared for him already in their short time together. "But right now, all I need from you is to make sure you know how loved you are, and how fucking thankful I am that you're still in one piece."

Elion bit his lip. "Okay."

Blake took things very slowly so as not to aggravate the concussion Elion was still getting over. For a while they just kissed gently, their bodies sliding down the pillow pile until they were lying down facing one another.

Only when Elion began to whimper for more did Blake give it to him with a chuckle. "Such a brat," he teased.

"I'm the patient," Elion pouted, a playful glint in his eye. "I need treatment. From your cock."

Blake laughed so loud he was immensely grateful they had the whole place to themselves. But he was also feeling turned on and possessive, wanting to claim every inch of Elion's skin as his own.

He started by peeling his t-shirt off and sucking his nipples like Elion had done for him in L.A. He moaned and arched into Blake's mouth while his hands roamed over Elion's sides and along his arms. It was fairly obvious that under his sweatpants Elion wasn't wearing any underwear. All it took was to slip his hand under the waistband to find that gorgeous rod of hot, velvety skin.

Blake's own cock was filling and straining against his jeans. But he ignored it for the time being, enjoying the friction of his arousal against his clothes as he stroked Elion's dick and kissed his mouth.

He murmured nonsense that would probably embarrass him horribly post orgasm, but he didn't care. He told Elion how gorgeous and perfect he was, how badly he needed him, how he would always be there and never let anything bad happen to him. All the while Elion allowed himself to be touched and beautifully turned on by Blake's hands and lips. It was heaven.

Blake disposed of the pants soon enough then hastily divested himself of his own clothes without emerging from under the comforter. He carefully nudged Elion onto his side so they were spooning.

He'd planned to fuck him again, but he got caught up cuddling and kissing the back of his neck. His cock slid naturally between the top of Elion's thighs, rubbing his erection against his taint and balls in the most amazing way. He reached around to stroke Elion's dick again, sucking on his earlobe as he did.

"Is this okay?" he asked.

Elion let out some sort of squeak in response. "Don't stop," he managed to utter.

They could fuck later, Blake decided. This way they didn't have to pause to put on a condom, and he was all in favor of carrying on at this juncture. He could feel his climax building.

They rocked together underneath the comfort of the piled-up bedding. They were overheated and gasping for air, but also cocooned and safe. "I love you," Blake whispered into Elion's hair. "Love you so much, baby."

Elion came all of a sudden over Blake's hand and into the sheets. "Sorry," he said with a nervous laugh once he caught his breath.

Blake kissed his cheek. "Nothing to be sorry for."

Elion quickly used his t-shirt to mop up the mess as best he could. Then he turned to face Blake, rolling him onto his back so he could spoon up to his side.

Despite Blake's insistence that he wanted to look after Elion, Elion was determined to do all the work to ensure he got his orgasm too. He fished some lube out of his bedside drawer to make his fingers nice and slippery while he jerked Blake off, kissing his mouth hungrily and swallowing up his needy groans.

"I love you too, baby," he said. "Want to watch you come. Show me I'm the only one allowed to do this."

Blake was teetering on the very edge, but he still cupped Elion's face with his hand. "The only one, Elion," he said. "I'm all yours. You're mine."

Elion kissed him even harder, speeding up his hand and milking Blake's orgasm from somewhere so deep inside him he felt like his spleen might shoot out his cock as well. He cried out, his vision going white then black as he caught his breath.

Elion chuckled to himself over the mess they'd made. Blake watched sleepily as he insisted on cleaning him up. It felt like such a tender act, even more intimate than the sex they'd just had.

They rearranged themselves on the dry side of the bed. For a while, they simply lay in each other's arms, eyes closed, not quite dozing but resting peacefully.

When Blake was around Elion, he felt whole. Complete. He wanted to ask if Elion felt the same, but the way he wound his limbs possessively around Blake's body told him he probably already knew the answer.

"I'm going to get my own place," he announced suddenly.

Ever since he'd said it to his dad during their argument he knew it was the only way forward. Now he'd renegotiated the terms of the show he just wanted to focus his energy on dancing and teaching. No more drama.

He couldn't do that with his dad breathing down his neck about being too queer and tarnishing the family reputation.

Elion looked up from where his head had been resting on his shoulder and smiled. "That's wonderful, babe."

Nerves flared through Blake's insides, but he'd thought about this enough over the last couple of days. "I was wondering if you wanted to move in somewhere together," he asked.

Elion's eyes widened comically. Well, it would have been funny if Blake wasn't so terrified.

"I know it's fast," he said hastily. "But I don't care. *Carpe Diem.*" He lifted up Elion's wrist and kissed the tattoo of the phrase there. "I almost watched you die." A lump rose in his throat. It was very hard to say that out loud. "I don't want to tiptoe around when we could just be sharing a bed and making breakfast and watching TV and literally have sex whenever we want-"

Elion cut him off by grabbing his face and kissing him. "I'd love to," he said. There were tears in his eyes. "I'd love that so much. If we can work out the finances-"

It was Blake's turn to cut him off. "We'll keep the rent proportions fair, okay. I know you won't want to be kept or anything, but if we don't get a fancy place we can both pay our way. The most important thing is creating a little space that's just ours."

Elion chewed his lip. "Actually," he said heavily. Blake's heart fell. "I was thinking...maybe...of going to community college in the fall. Taking some classes. I don't know how much I'd be able to work."

Blake's hopes leaped like a jack-in-the-box. He tried not to get too excited in case he made Elion skittish, but honestly, he couldn't be happier.

"Babe," he said seriously. "I've got good money from the advertising revenue off of the show, but I also get paid for teaching too, remember? That plus my trust fund from the band means I'm really okay for money. It would mean the absolute world to me if you'd let me support you going back to school. I want you to achieve everything and not be held back."

"You don't need to do that," Elion mumbled, predictably, not meeting Blake's eye.

Blake lightly touched his chin and encouraged him to look back up. "You'd have to work hard," he said, his voice low and commanding. "But I know you'd do that. You're amazing. That's all I'd want. It would be a privilege to help you after the way you helped your mom. You deserve this."

Elion licked his lips, worry clear on his face as he thought it over. "I could pay you back?" he suggested.

Blake shook his head. "You can just pay more rent and bills when you're done studying."

He realized they were talking about years in the future, but that didn't scare him. He had no doubt this was what he wanted. That Elion was the counterpoint to his soul, the melody to his rhythm, and he could picture them spending the rest of their lives together.

"Do you know what you want to study?" he asked, stroking back a lock of black and pink hair.

Elion hesitated. Then he took a deep breath and smiled. "Nursing," he said with conviction. "I first thought about it when Mom was sick, but then I talked about it with the Becky and the other nurses this week. I think that's what I want."

Blake felt fit to burst with pride. Elion was caring and hardworking and smart and already showed promise with his first-aid skills. "I think you'd make an amazing nurse," he said, hugging him close.

They didn't make a definitive decision on getting a place together that night, although Elion promised he'd seriously think it over. They did however make love several more times, satisfying Blake's concerns that Elion's body still worked exactly as it should do still.

When he finally fell asleep in the small hours of the morning he was filled with excitement and hope for the path that lay before them. Building a home was just the start of their adventure together.

He couldn't wait.

EPILOGUE

TWO YEARS LATER

Elion

"Welcome and hello!"

"I'm Blake."

"I'm Elion."

"And you guys are awesome!" they finished together. It was the way they started all their YouTube vlogs.

Elion grinned, glancing at Blake sat beside him.

It was crazy to think that advertisers and sponsors actually *paid* him to sit by his gorgeous boyfriend once a week and just hang out and chat. It was slightly crazier to think that hundreds of thousands of people tuned in to watch them do it.

But they did, and as their intro suggested, they were an extremely awesome bunch.

Knowing that people from all over the globe cared about them was strange but incredible. That they made a difference to people's lives was humbling. They were simply sharing their day to day lives, their highs and lows. But they were doing it as a same-sex couple, and for thousands of viewers, that really helped and inspired them.

All they did was film for ten minutes every Thursday in their spare room. They used Elion's computer he normally did his course assignments on. No matter how his classes were going or what Blake's schedule was doing, they always carved out a few moments to put something together, the two of them.

No producers or crew, nobody fabricating drama. Occasionally Kala still got in touch with Blake. She couldn't seem to help herself. If she got an idea for the direction of an episode based on audience reactions, she always let them know. Elion thought it was sweet in a way.

Other than that, they were left to their own devices. Feet of Flames still filmed at Blake's school, but he was only involved as a teacher, working with his students like he'd always intended. Nessa and Karyn had flourished as the main stars, building up a new cast around them. But the fans that had fallen in love with Blake and Elion as their own love had blossomed on screen were more than happy to follow them to their own show.

Unfortunately, their ship name was still Belion. But their followers had made the word kind of cool with all the effort they put into supporting him and Blake. They drew art and wrote fanfiction and made their own videos and ran Tumblr blogs dedicated to their relationship.

Elion sometimes felt bad for being semifamous for absolutely no reason. But then he remembered how much he would have loved to watch a happy couple of two guys when he was growing up, and it didn't seem so frivolous.

In years to come they'd have a record of how their relationship grew, too. It still tripped Elion up sometimes, thinking about the future in that way. But it was a long time since he'd allowed himself to trust in Blake, to believe that they'd go the distance. So why not daydream about one day showing their kids how their daddies got together?

He hid a smile and focused back on the video. Gone was the fly-by party boy who thought getting breakfast after a one-night stand was flirting dangerously close to commitment. Now his idea of perfection was take-out, Netflix and cuddles with his man. He never would have predicted that.

"Today's a special episode for us," Blake was saying.

"That's right," Elion agreed.

They always worked out roughly what to say beforehand as they shot the videos in one take. Generally, they didn't do them live just in case they massively fucked up. But occasionally, like today, they did.

Live episodes were often so they could get audience participation and read out Tweets and comments as they came through. They had recently done a big fundraiser for charity that had gone on for a whole hour getting people to pledge money until they hit their target. That had been pretty nerve-wracking, but they'd done it, and the sense of achievement had been incredible.

"Today's our hundredth show," Elion carried on, waving jazz hands in excitement. "And, as promised, we've got a big announcement."

Blake leaned in, resting his hand on Elion's knee below where the camera could see. He was always finding little ways to touch him. It made Elion feel loved in a way something like a bunch of flowers could never achieve. Every time they held hands in public, every stolen kiss in the privacy of their own apartment, it all made Elion feel cherished and claimed. He knew he was a lucky guy.

"We're going to announce the news in just a sec," Blake said. "Then we want to talk to you guys and find out what you think. Are you ready?"

Elion felt nerves fluttering in his belly like butterflies. Which was kind of dumb, it wasn't his news after all, not really. Except he felt so proud of Blake for getting on Dancing Dreams he wanted to cry. There was no doubt in his mind that he'd win the contest, but more than that, he was going to get to show the world what an incredible dancer he really was.

The plan was cheesy but simple, and hopefully fun. They'd ask the viewers to close their eyes, then Blake would hold up a sheet of card with the show's logo on it and play the theme song. Blake asked the camera if they were all ready, then for extra effect, asked Elion to close his eyes too.

He acted it up, covering his eyes with his hands and drumming his feet on the floor.

"Really ready?" Blake asked.

"Ready!" Elion cried.

He was supposed to wait to look until the theme song played a few notes and Blake yelled 'Surprise!' Instead, Elion took a second to recognize the track that filled the room.

"You're the light in my dark,
You give me that spark,
But you don't even see it.
You have my heart,
You're a work of art,
But you can't see, it's you I cherish."

It was the Below Zero song that Blake had sung to him in the meadow. He'd confessed several months later that that was the day he'd fallen in love. He just hadn't realized it at the time.

Confused, Elion lowered his hands and blinked. Blake was holding the card up, except it didn't have the Dancing Dreams logo on. And he was also no longer sitting in his chair.

He was down on one knee.

Elion's hands flew back to his face, this time to cover his mouth as tears sprung in his eyes. Even though the sign said it all, Blake still asked the question.

"Elion Rodriguez," he said, his voice shaky. "Being with you is the best thing that's ever happened to me. I can't imagine my life without you. Will-" His voice cracked and he tried to steady himself with a nervous laugh. "Will you marry me?"

Elion launched himself from his chair and tackled Blake to the carpet. He appreciated the viewers would only be able to hear their shrieks, but he didn't care. Just for this second, he wanted it to be just the two of them.

"Yes," he whispered, kissing his lips. "Yes, yes, yes." He grabbed the *'Will you marry me?'* sign and shot it up in the air for the camera to see. "YES!"

Blake pulled them both to their knees so the viewers could see and hugged him like he never wanted to let him go. He was crying and laughing and rocking him back and forth, all to the sound of the song that had stolen Elion's heart years ago.

Eventually, they crawled back into their seats to start answering the hundreds of excited, loving messages they were already receiving. But not before Blake retrieved a ring box from his pocket. The edges of the band were black with pink stones running around the middle. Elion absolutely loved it.

They would announce about the next step in Blake's dance career a week later. The rest of that night was spent sharing their love with fans from all over the world. Celebrating the start of forever.

Together.

ACKNOWLEDGMENTS

The release of this book coincides with me taking the plunge and fulfilling my life-long ambition of becoming a fulltime author. Words are normally my jam, but I don't think I can adequately thank all the people who have supported me on this journey, and will continue to do so. Mum, John, Dan, all the Welches and my dear friends. You are, put simply, the awesomest.

Thank you to my family and beta readers, Mum and John. Your dedication and enthusiasm gives me life. Thank you Dan, for the unyielding support that comes in a million different forms. Most notably, for making me a cat mom. All writers need kitties, everybody knows this.

Thank you to my awe-inspiringly talented author buddies. Alyson Pearce, Amelia Faulkner, Ed Davies, Aubrey Cullens, Lynn Van Dorn, Anna Martin. You guys deserve medals for all the freaks outs you've helped me with haha!

Special thanks to Aria Tan from Resplendent Media for the stunning cover and Meg Cooper for the excellent editing.

Also thank you to you, the reader, for choosing this book

out of so many to take a chance on. I sincerely hope you enjoy.

ABOUT THE AUTHOR

HJ Welch is a contemporary MM romance author living in London with her husband and two balls of fluff that occasionally pretend to be cats. She began writing at an early age, later honing her craft online in the world of fanfiction on sites like Wattpad. Fifteen years and over a million words later, she sought out original MM novels to read. She never thought she would be any good at romance, but once she turned her hand to it she discovered she in fact adored it. By the end of 2016 she had written her first book of her own, and in 2017 she fulfilled her lifelong dream of becoming a fulltime author.

Scorch is the first in her Homecoming Hearts series. She also writes contemporary British MM romance as Helen Juliet.

You can contact HJ Welch via social media:
Newsletter – Subscribe here for news and FREEBIES!
Website – www.helenjuliet.com
Email – hello@helenjuliet.com
Twitter – @helenjwrites
Instagram – @helenjwrites
Tumblr – @helenjwrites
Facebook Page – @HJWelchAuthor
Facebook Group – Helen Juliet Books

THANK YOU

Dear Reader,

Out of all the many books out there, you chose this one to read. Thank you. It means so much to share my tales of love, drama and happy-ever-afters with you all.

If you enjoyed reading Blake and Elion's story, I would very much appreciate it if you would like to share your experience with others online. Reviews, recommendations, fan works and general love is the best way for me to reach new readers.

If you'd like to meet with other Homecoming Hearts fans, why not join our Facebook group? Helen Juliet Books. We're very friendly! You can also subscribe to my newsletter via www.helenjuliet.com for news and extra freebie scenes from the Homecoming Hearts series!

In the meantime, please look ahead to catch a glimpse of the next book, Spark...

Lots of love,
    HJ Welch

SPARK

Joey's dreams are over. Below Zero is dead and gone. He knows he's destined for stardom, but showbiz is tough and he has nowhere to go but the last place on Earth he ever wanted to be: Home, with his homophobic family who spent their lives trying to tear him down. Now all they will do is gloat over his fall from grace.

Gabe loves his town. He thought he had it all: a man he loved, purpose as a volunteer firefighter, and a home to call his own. Except now he's alone, forced to try and rebuild from scratch. But how can he start over when his heart is already broken?

An unexpected road trip brings Joey and Gabe together and the sparks fly between them, but it can't last. Their worlds are too different. But when Joey hits rock bottom, Gabe is the only one who can save him. Protect him. Keep him warm.

Gabe's saved lives before. But can he rescue hearts?

Spark is a steamy, standalone gay romance novel with a HEA and no cliffhanger.

9 781999 706739